Dear Readers,

Many years ago, when I was a kid, my father said to me, "Bill, it doesn't really matter what you do in life. What's important is to be the *best* William Johnstone you can be."

I've never forgotten those words. And now, many years and almost two hundred books laters, I like to think that I am still trying to be the best William Johnstone I can be. Whether it's Ben Raines in the Ashes series, or Frank Morgan, the last gunfighter, or Smoke Jensen, our intrepid mountain man, or John Barrone and his hardworking crew keeping America safe from terrorist lowlifes in the Code Names series, I want to make each new book better than the last and deliver powerful storytelling.

Equally important, I try to create the kinds of believable characters that we can all identify with, real people who face tough challenges. When one of my creations blasts an enemy into the middle of next week, you can be damn sure he had a good reason.

As a storyteller, my job is to entertain you, my readers, and to make sure that you get plenty of enjoyment from my books for your hard-earned money. This is not a job I take lightly. And I greatly appreciate your feedback—you are my gold, and your opinions *do* count. So please keep the letters and e-mails coming.

Respectfully yours,

William W. Johnstone

WILLIAM W. JOHNSTONE

BLOOD BOND

PINNACLE BOOKS
Kensington Publishing Corp.
http://www.kensingtonbooks.com

PINNACLE BOOKS are published by

Kensington Publishing Corp.
850 Third Avenue
New York, NY 10022

All Kensington Titles, Imprints, and Distributed Lines are available at special quantity discounts for bulk purchases for sales promotions, premiums, fund-raising, and educational or institutional use. Special book excerpts or customized printings can also be created to fit specific needs. For details, write or phone the office of the Kensington special sales manager: Kensington Publishing Corp., 850 Third Avenue, New York, NY 10022, attn: Special Sales Department, Phone: 1-800-221-2647.

Pinnacle and the P logo Reg. U.S. Pat. & TM Off.

First Pinnacle Books Printing: January 2006

10 9 8 7 6 5 4 3 2 1

Printed in the United States of America

Every man hath a good and a bad angel attending on him in particular, all his life long.

—Robert Burton

Dedicated to my blood brother, Bob Van Dunk. When you read this one, Bob, read it with the Sioux eye open and the Crow eye closed.

Chapter 1

The body was still warm, and Matt Bodine's eyes did not linger long on the hideously tortured flesh of the man. The man's bare feet were still in the smoldering fire. One look at the expression frozen on his dead face told him that the man had died long and hard.

Bodine stood up and carefully swept his surroundings with his eyes, missing nothing. He watched as a bird flew in and landed on a branch. The bird began preening itself and Bodine relaxed. A squirrel came down the side of a tree and began searching the ground for food. Had there been more people around, the animals would not be so careless.

Bodine walked back to his horse and picked up the reins where he'd ground-reined the big line-back dun stallion and tied the reins to a low branch.

Then the man squatted down and pulled the makings out of his vest pocket and rolled a smoke, licking the tube tight and lighting up. He smoked and pondered the situation, not liking any of it.

This act of torture was supposed to look like the work of Indians. But after only a hasty look-around, Bodine knew it was not. The men who had done this all wore moccasins, but they didn't walk like Indians; they walked like what they were: white men. They had also stepped on a couple of branches, breaking them. No Indian would have done that, unless he was drunk. And there was no smell of whiskey in the air.

Bodine finished his smoke and stood up. A tall, lean young man, with much of his weight in his chest and shoulders and arms. Just a shade over six feet and weighing one-ninety. A good-looking young man, in his mid-twenties. He wore walnut-handled .44 Colts, the handles worn smooth from use. In the boot, a Winchester .44, loaded full up with 17 rounds. Bodine carried a long-bladed bowie knife in a sheath behind the right-hand Colt, sharpened to a fare-thee-well. He shaved with it most of the time.

He wore faded jeans, scuffed boots, and a buckskin shirt made for him by a squaw in his adopted Cheyenne tribe. They adopted him—in a way—when Bodine was just a young boy. He also wore a necklace of three multi-colored rocks around his neck, pierced by a leather thong.

Bodine again looked at the body. He knew what he had to do and he didn't want to do it. With a silent sigh, Bodine ground out his cigarette under the heel of a boot and stood up, walking to the body and pulling the naked man away from the nearly dead fire. He looked around, found the man's clothing, and was just starting to go through them when he heard the horses coming.

That would be the Army patrol he was scouting for. He waited until they came into view and waved them to a halt, walking over to them so they would not trample any sign he might pick up later.

"Damned heathens!" Lieutenant Gerry spat the words. Gerry was new to the West, having been posted in Montana only a few months back. But it hadn't taken him long to hate the Indians.

"It wasn't Indians," Bodine told him. "White men did this."

"What!"

"The scalping is all wrong. It was very carefully done. Indians usually just cut a line and then tear the scalp loose. And those aren't Indian moccasin prints over there." He pointed. 'White men were in those moccasins. I haven't started looking for other signs."

Gerry dismounted and walked to Bodine's side. He glanced over at the tortured man and swallowed a couple of times. "Know him?"

"No. But I know this . . ." Gerry looked at the scout.

"Somebody didn't like him very much."

Gerry looked hard at Bodine to see if the scout was kidding. He couldn't tell. Bodine's face was always impossible to read. Just like a damned Indian. And tanned just about as dark.

Gerry had been briefed about Bodine on his first day at the fort. Colonel Travers had both complimented and cursed Bodine. "Bodine doesn't have to work for us, Lieutenant. Although," he was quick to add, "I'm glad he does. Bodine has money. His father owns probably the largest ranch in Wyoming Territory. Down on the Crazy Woman. Bodine has his own spread and runs his own cattle. His spread is on the Powder and butts into his father's ranch." Travers punched a large wall map with a finger. "Right there. Together, they control thousands and thousands of acres. Not only that, but they own it! They filed on some, proved it up and staked it out. They bought the rest and hold legitimate deeds."

"If he's so wealthy, why does he work for the Army for fifty dollars a month?"

"Best answer I can give you is this: because he wants to. I give Bodine very few orders. I suggest a lot of things to him. But that doesn't mean he's going to do it. My adjutant, Major Dawson, gave Bodine a direct order one time. Bodine told him to stick it in his hat. He refuses to sign a contract with the Army."

"Maybe he can't write?" Gerry suggested.

Travers chuckled. "Bodine's mother was trained as a schoolteacher, Gerry. He's very well educated for a man raised on the frontier. He's also an adopted member of the Cheyenne tribe. A blood brother to Two Wolves, who is the son of Medicine Horse." He smiled at the startled expression on the young lieutenant's face. "Yes, Gerry, *that* Medicine Horse. No one knows this country like Bodine. No one."

"But we're at war with the Cheyenne!"

"We're at war with certain elements within the tribe. We are not at war with Medicine Horse, and I pray to God we never will be. Medicine Horse was educated back east; married a white woman from Vermont. They had one son before she died of fever. Two Wolves. Sam August Webster Two Wolves. His mother died when he was about nine. He can read and write and speak English, although he prefers his father's tongue. He's also a damned trouble-maker."

That prior conversation rolled through Gerry's head as he watched Bodine cast for signs, walking in slow, seemingly aimless circles around the small clearing. He disappeared into the brush and moments later popped back out behind the cavalry, startling Gerry. Man could move like a ghost.

"All their horses were shod. Which doesn't mean a whole lot. Lots of Indians ride shod horses they've stolen."

"Murdering thieves," the lieutenant said, before he thought.

"It's a game to them, Lieutenant," Bodine corrected. "The taking of horses. And before the white man came along, many Indians didn't kill unless forced to it. They counted coups. With a stick or club. And Indians didn't invent scalping. The white man did. Bear that in mind. Toss the dead man across a saddle and come on. His horse is over there."

Bodine was on his mean-eyed stallion and gone before Gerry could mount up. It irked him. Lots of things irked

Gerry about Bodine. *He* was supposed to be giving orders to the scout, not the other way around. Bodine would listen politely and attentively when Gerry outlined what they would do in the field. And then Bodine would do exactly the opposite.

It was irritating! After all, Gerry was a West Point man. Which, he reflected sourly, meant about as much to Bodine as the hole you leave when you stick your finger in a stream.

The trail, which half the time Gerry could not see, led to a small settlement on the still ill-defined Montana/Wyoming border. The town, according to Colonel Travers, was a den of iniquity, populated by ladies best described as soiled doves, gamblers, thieves, foot pads, rustlers, murderers, and the like.

Gerry had never been to the town of Cutter. Tell the truth, he was sort of looking forward to it.

To say that Gerry was naive was understating it.

The small patrol rode down the wide street, all the men conscious of eyes on them, and most of the eyes were anything but friendly.

"We'll lose the trail here," Bodine said. "We might find the horses, we might even find the men. But that won't give us anything that would stand up in any court of law. They'll just say they found the body and came into town to report it. There is no law in Cutter, Gerry. None. So watch yourself."

"I am perfectly capable of taking care of myself, Bodine," the lieutenant answered testily.

"Right."

A woman seated on the second-floor balcony of a saloon called the Kittycat called out to Gerry, suggesting some things she'd like to do with and for him.

Lieutenant Gerry's neck and face turned as red as the sun and Sergeant Tom Simmons, a grizzled veteran of many years on the frontier, had to struggle to keep from laughing out loud.

"See!" a man yelled, pointing to the horse with the body of the tortured man lashed across the saddle. "I told you all what we seen."

"It's that damn murderin' half-breed and his bunch that did this!" another shouted.

"They're talking about Two Wolves?" Gerry asked.

"Yes. And someone at the fort has been talking, as well."

"What do you mean?"

"Whoever set this thing up had to know the area we would be patrolling so we could find the body. Think about it."

"Everybody on the post knew. It might not have been deliberate."

"That's true. I'm just wondering what Two Wolves has done this time to get everybody so stirred up."

They reined up in front of the combination dentist/barber/undertaker's building and dismounted. The same man filled all three jobs. A crowd began to gather, and they were a surly and profane lot.

"Your show, Lieutenant," Bodine said softly.

"Anybody here know this man?" Gerry asked, raising his voice to be heard as Sergeant Simmons lifted the dead man's bloody head with a gloved hand. He couldn't lift him by the hair—he didn't have any.

"I seen him around a time or two," a citizen said. "He drifted in here from Idaho, I think. Called hisself George."

"Any last name?"

"Not that I ever heard."

The undertaker pushed his way through the crowd. "Does he have any coins in his pockets?"

Gerry looked at Bodine. "A few greenbacks."

"That'll do for a simple buryin'. Some of you boys get him into the back."

"You soldier boys come to get Two Wolves?" another asked.

"We don't know that Two Wolves had anything to do with this," Gerry said. "We were on routine patrol when Bodine found the body."

Eyes shifted from the lieutenant to the scout. Not being a terribly talkative man, Bodine could spend several days in a town and leave without anyone knowing his name.

But all knew his reputation. And it was no different in the rip-roaring, wide-open town of Cutter.

Matt Bodine had killed his first man when he was fourteen. The man's brothers came after the boy when he was fifteen. They got lead in Bodine, but when the gunsmoke cleared, Bodine was standing over their bodies. At sixteen, rustlers struck his father's ranch the night before a trail drive was to start. Bodine's guns put two more men in the ground and wounded another two. The drive went on as scheduled. At seventeen, Bodine was a man grown and went off to live with the Cheyenne for a year. He'd been spending forbidden time with them—sometimes weeks at a time—since he was just a boy.

At eighteen he was riding shotgun for gold shipments. Four more men were buried after two unsuccessful attempts to rob the shipments. At nineteen, he began part-time scouting for the Army. That was in '68, when everyone with any sense knew the white men were going to break the treaty with the Sioux. But to be fair, both sides violated the treaty.

Between nineteen and twenty-five, the guns of Matt Bodine became legend in the west. But not just his guns, for Bodine's fists were just as feared. He knew Indian-wrestling, boxing, and plain ol' barroom brawling.

"You Bodine, huh?" a man asked, sticking his unshaven jaw out belligerently.

"That's right."

"My name's Simon Bull."

"Is that supposed to impress me?" Bodine had heard of Bull. He was a fast gun and was just as good as his reputation.

"It might someday." Bull said mysteriously, then turned and stomped up the boardwalk, disappearing into a saloon.

"You always try that hard to make friends?" Gerry asked Bodine.

"See you sometime tomorrow," was Bodine's reply. Before Gerry could lift a hand, Bodine was in the saddle and gone.

"Damn the man!" Gerry said. "His orders were to stay with the patrol."

"Did you hear them orders put like that personal, Lieutenant?" Sergeant Simmons asked.

"Well . . . no."

"Bodine's orders is usually to scout for the patrol. I 'spect that's what he's gone off to do."

"Are we supposed to wait here for him?"

"It don't make no difference, Lieutenant. Bodine will find us."

"How?" Gerry demanded. "He won't know which direction we've gone. Does he possess some sort of mystical powers?" The last was said with no small amount of sarcasm . . . and just a touch of jealousy.

Simmons spat a stream of tobacco juice on the ground. "There's them that would say so, sir."

Chapter 2

Bodine possessed no magic powers. He just used the senses the good Lord gave him, such as looking at something and actually seeing it in its entirety.

And it was logical to Bodine to assume that if the colonel sent a patrol out on a five-day scout, there would be two and a half days out and two and a half days back. It was now the downswing of the third day, which meant the patrol would be going back to the fort. Logical.

An hour before dusk, Bodine came upon a small, down-at-the-heels-looking band of Blood Indians, distant relatives of the Blackfoot. Bodine lifted his hand in greeting and it was returned.

"I am looking for my brother, Two Wolves."

"You are Bodine, who used to be called He-Who-Falls-Down-A-Lot?"

Bodine laughed and the Bloods chuckled with him. Everyone knew that story and how it came to be that Medicine Horse named him that.

"Yes."

The Blood sub-chief pointed toward the mountains.

"There." He looked long and somewhat hard at Bodine. "It is odd that a man who scouts for the blue bellies would be a *tsis tsis tas.*"

"My adopted father, Medicine Horse, proclaimed me to be one of the people, a human being."

"It is good. Medicine Horse is a wise chief." He lifted his hand in farewell and was gone without a glance back at Bodine.

Bodine rode for the mountains and made camp at dark, deliberately building a fire much larger than he normally would, and after eating, rolling up in his blankets by the fire, something else he would not normally do. Usually after eating, he would move several miles farther on before making camp for the night.

Bodine was in his blankets, but he was far from asleep.

His blood brother, Two Wolves, was as much a loner as was Matt Bodine, preferring the solitary beauty of the vast and, for the most part, empty-appearing wilderness to the lodges of his people. And contrary to public belief, Two Wolves did not run with a band of trouble-making, malcontented, renegade young bucks. For Two Wolves was much like his father, Medicine Horse. Two Wolves was not at war with all the whites . . . just a few of them.

He was like several of the big ranchers in this area, who took what they wanted by force and lived without reason or compassion for other people, the land, and its animals. Who, according to Two Wolves's way of thinking, had as much right to exist as the two-legged animals. Perhaps more right. Two Wolves had dealt them some misery: ripping down fences, running off cattle, burning down line-shacks. Two Wolves had killed, but always in self-defense; even his most vocal enemies would admit—although never aloud—that Two Wolves was not a cold-blooded savage.

What he was, mostly, was a pain in the rear end.

But for all his good points—and they far overshadowed

his bad side—that still would not stop many ranchers from hanging him on the spot if they could get their hands on him. Or shooting him.

Bodine lay in his blankets and waited for the arrival of his blood brother. He knew that when it came, it would come as suddenly as a striking rattler, and to unsuspecting eyes, appearing to be just as deadly.

The stallion stopped grazing and lifted his head, ears alert. Bodine tensed under the blanket, one hand gripping the edge of the blanket. A whisper of a moccasin on grass reached him, followed by the faint smell of grease and wood smoke.

Bodine exploded out of his bedroll just as a buckskin-clad shape came hurling out of the night. Bodine flipped the blanket over the shape, grabbed the ends tightly and, using his foot, tripped the man, sending him to the ground.

Two Wolves rolled, freeing himself from the blinding blanket, and leaped at Bodine, his hands reaching for the man's throat. Bodine sidestepped and grabbed a thick wrist, turning as he did and using a hip, and tossed his blood brother to the ground.

Two Wolves came up with a snarl and slapped Bodine, open-handed. The blow stung, smarting Bodine's cheek and wetting his eyes. Bodine promptly returned the slap, twisting Two Wolves around.

The stallion had returned to grazing. He had seen all this foolishness many times before. Had it been a real enemy, the stallion would have joined Bodine in killing the man.

Grabbing Two Wolves around the waist, Bodine lifted him off his feet and threw him to the ground. Two Wolves sat on the cool ground and laughed.

"It was your turn anyway," the half-breed finally said. "I graciously allowed you to win."

"You allowed me nothing, Brother. Come. Sit. The coffee is hot. Have you eaten?"

"I nooned," Two Wolves said, pouring a tin cup full of the cowboy coffee, hot and black as the wages of sin. He slurped the brew and smacked his lips after the first sip, the way of showing approval and thanks. "How did you find me?"

"I saw a small band of Bloods. They said you were in the mountains."

"There are many mountains." Two Wolves broke off a hunk of bread and with his knife speared a piece of bacon from the blackened skillet.

"But only one where we summered that time."

"This is truth."

The two men, although not related by family, could easily pass for physical brothers. They were both the same age, and both possessed the same lean-hipped and heavy musculature. One pair of eyes were black, the other blue. One had raven black hair; Bodine's hair was dark brown and worn shorter.

Both wore the same type of three-stone necklace. "Why did you come to the mountains?"

"To see you."

Two Wolves moved a flattened hand from side to side, telling Bodine that while that was not an outright lie, neither did he believe that was the real reason.

"A man was tortured to death not far from Cutter. Happened early this morning. Some are placing the blame on you."

"You know better. The only person I have ever put through pain was myself."

The coming of manhood. Bodine knew it well. He would carry the scars on his chest until death took him.

"Why are they blaming it on you?"

"They have to do something to create more hate toward me. Why not this?"

"Do you know who might have done it?"

Two Wolves shrugged. "Any one of a hundred people. Five hundred. Everyone knows I am *Onihomahan.*"

Friend of the Wolf.

"No more than I am, Brother."

"This is truth."

Both men revered the wolf and had crawled up into wolf dens many times in their youth. Both had raised wolf cubs as pets.

"So it is solely because of your deep concern for our Brother the Wolf that the white man wants to see you dead?" This was spoken with no small degree of sarcasm.

"But of course." This was said with a twinkle in the dark eyes.

Now it was Bodine's turn to flatten his hand and move it from side to side.

Two Wolves grunted and drank his coffee.

"The wolves kill cattle, Brother."

"So does the rain which produces floods, and the sun which dries the water holes, and the lightning and thunder which causes the cattle to stampede, and the wind which can hold tornadoes. Does the white man stand and shoot at the wind and the drops of rain and the flashing of lightning and the booming of thunder? The white man is a stupid creature. That which he does not understand, and will make no effort to understand, he wishes to destroy."

"This is also truth."

Two Wolves grunted and looked at his blood brother. "Sometimes you do make sense. It is good that you spent time with us and became a human being."

"And you could have had more time at the university back east. Our fathers were disappointed that you came back so soon."

"The young men were pale and silly and afraid. What few girls were there were even paler and sillier and more afraid.

And ugly. It was disgusting. How can one be expected to learn with so much foolish laughter and the stench of fear in his nostrils? The woman who sat opposite me in one class looked like a bear's behind. I kept expecting her to charge."

Bodine lay back on the cool grass and laughed until his sides hurt. His laughter was infectious and soon Two Wolves was rolling on the ground, laughing.

Bodine had learned early that the talk of Indians having no sense of humor was completely false. Many of them just had a different sense of humor. And when around the white man, they had learned to maintain a stoic expression, since many didn't speak the language and didn't know what was going on most of the time. And for good reasons on both sides, neither side really trusted the other.

The young men wiped their eyes and drank more coffee, enjoying the warmth of the now small fire and the closeness of brothers being together.

"Now more truth," Bodine said.

"My father and his small tribe were given the land they now live on, correct? To be theirs forever and ever?"

"That is correct. That was part of the treaty of 1868, the same treaty that closed the Bozeman Road and abandoned Forts Phil Kearny, Reno, and C.F. Smith."

"Uh-huh. And that same treaty created a reservation, guaranteeing that all lands west of the Missouri River to the borders of Montana and Wyoming would be Sioux and Cheyenne, forever and ever, correct?"

Bodine sighed. "This is truth."

"The white man lied—again."

"Sadly, this is also truth."

"Unless of course, the land has shrunk without our knowing it."

"The land has not shrunk. But your father's land has not been bothered."

"Ahh! Not *yet.* Hear me well, my brother. The Northern

and Southern Cheyenne are talking. The *Tsis tsis tas* and the *Suhtai*. The Men. The white man separated us from our friends, the Arapahoe, and stuck us with the hated Crow, those eaters of dung."

"You were at peace with them for a time, I recall Medicine Horse saying."

"Long before we were born, and then for only three years. That is not the point and please stop changing the subject. Now listen to me, Bodine, the *Shi shi ni wi he tan iu* has begun in some areas."

Bodine's eyes narrowed at that news. The Snake Dance, or dance of the snakes. The Comanches—themselves feared fighters—had been driven from their lands by the Cheyennes long years ago. The Cheyenne had given the name *Shi shi ni wi he tan iu* to the Comanche, not intending it to be a compliment, for literally translated, it meant Snake Men. To some Cheyenne, it became a victory dance. And a dance before war.

The Cheyenne were feared by most of the plains Indians, with the exception of the Sioux. While the tribes did fight, there was never the open hatred that existed between the Cheyenne and the Crow, the Dakotas, the Assiniboins, and the Kiowas. The Cheyenne fought with the Pawnees and the Shoshonis until all intertribal wars ceased on the Northern Continent.

The last great battle the Cheyenne fought with the Kiowas, the Comanches, and the Apaches took place in 1838. In 1840, a truce was made that had not been broken to date.

Two Wolves pointed a finger at Bodine. "You know, Bodine, that the Cheyenne are the greatest warriors who ever lived."

Bodine nodded his head. That was a point that few would argue.

"You know," Two Wolves continued, "that when my people met the Assiniboins—the *Ho Hes*—we were defeated because the *Ho Hes* had guns and we did not. It was a relative of mine who rallied the Cheyenne and said, 'The *Ho Hes* have attacked us and killed some of us. Now I say that from this time on, we shall fight with all people we meet and then we shall become great warriors.' "

"I know the story. And it is truth. The Cheyenne are the greatest warriors who ever lived."

"There is war talk, my brother. Even in the lodges in my father's camp there is war talk. If this pompous, strutting rancher, this Tom Thomas, causes my father and his followers to be pushed off land that was given them by the president himself, there will be war."

"You cannot win a war against the whites, Two Wolves." Bodine spoke softly. "They are too many . . ."

Two Wolves noticed that Bodine used "they" instead of "we."

". . . and they are like ants. They just keep coming and coming in an endless march across the plains. It's 1875, Two Wolves."

"And that means? . . ."

"You cannot stop progress. But I will see what I can do about this Tom Thomas. I've heard of him, and he's an arrogant one, all right. Is he hiring gunhands?"

"Yes."

"Simon Bull?"

"He is one of them, so I have been told. And he also has a man from the East, New York City, I am also told, whose name is Whacker Corrigan. He was something called a Shoulder-Striker in the city. Whatever that means."

"That means he was a bully. They're henchmen of crooked politicians hired to keep the people in line and make sure they vote the way they're told to vote."

'What a marvelous thing, this democratic system of the white man."

Bodine was still chuckling as Two Wolves slipped back into the darkness and was gone.

Chapter 3

Bodine caught up with the patrol when they were halfway between Cutter and the small garrison on the Tongue.

"Did you find out anything?" Gerry asked him, irritated that Bodine could find them so easily in such a vast wilderness.

"Two Wolves didn't kill that man."

"And how did you reach that conclusion?"

"Two Wolves told me."

"You *saw* him?"

"Of course. He's my brother."

"Why didn't you bring him in, damnit! You know we want to talk to him."

"I'm paid to scout for the Army, not arrest people."

Lieutenant Gerry ground his teeth together in frustration but managed to keep from vocalizing his feelings. Bodine was impossible! "Bodine, what would you do should the Cheyenne attack this patrol?"

"They won't."

"What would you do if the Sioux attacked this patrol?"

"They won't."

"Damnit, man!" Gerry twisted in the uncomfortable cavalry saddle.

Bodine smiled faintly, knowing what Gerry had on his mind. "If Indians attacked this patrol, Lieutenant, I would fight."

But against whom? Gerry thought bitterly. *Us, or them*? And that was a point he intended to pursue with Colonel Travers.

"You're out of line, Lieutenant," the colonel told him. "Bodine sides with the Indians when he thinks they're in the right, and tells them up front when he thinks they're wrong."

"I don't trust him." Gerry stood his ground. "I won't go over your head, Colonel, but I do wish to exercise my right and lodge a written protest."

Travers smiled thinly, staring at Gerry. *The boy has a good sand and gravel bottom to him, the colonel thought. But if he doesn't learn to bend that stiff New England neck he won't last out here.*

Colonel Travers had been in the Army since the early '50's, a well-thought-of man and a highly capable leader. He was a veteran of four years of fighting during the Civil War and of ten years on the Plains. He had fought Indians and had many friends among the various Indian tribes. He respected the Indian and knew that in many cases—but not as many as the Eastern press allowed—the Indian had been given the short end of the stick in dealings with the white man.

"Write your letter of protest, Lieutenant. I will put it in your file."

"Thank you, sir." Gerry saluted, wheeled about, and left the office, his back as stiff and unbending as his neck.

Travers walked to the door and called for his sergeant. "Get Bodine for me."

Travers waved the scout to a chair and poured them coffee. "Lieutenant Gerry doesn't trust you, Matt."

"I sort of figured that out myself, Colonel. Maybe it's time for me to resign."

Travers sat down behind his desk and stared at the scout. "In a way, yes. But you'll still be on the Army's payroll . . . not that you need the money," he added with a smile.

Bodine arched an eyebrow and waited.

"I'm going to tell you something, Bodine; something that I have no business telling you. But, unlike Lieutenant Gerry, I know you and trust you to do the right thing. General Sheridan has ordered that an examination be made of the Yellowstone River, from its mouth to the junction with the Bighorn."

"You're not serious!" Bodine sat up from his slouch in the straight-back chair.

Travers held up a hand. "Wait, there's more. He's also ordered that several sites be recommended for permanent Army bases, forts from which Indian raids could be controlled. General Forsyth and Colonel Grant are to be in charge. The expedition is to be kept as secret as possible."

"Damnit, Colonel, that area was to be set aside for the Crow and the Cheyenne—a stupid move if ever the government made one, knowing how the Crow and Cheyenne feel about each other. Now this, on top of that fool rancher Tom Thomas . . . Does the government want the lid to blow right off the pot?"

"The tribes will be given land a bit farther south of the original proposal."

"Oh, sure." Bodine's words were caustic. "So Tom Thomas can have the best water and the best graze and to hell with promises made to the Indians."

Travers shrugged his shoulders. "It wasn't my idea, Bodine. I just follow orders. The expedition will leave Fort Buford on May the 26th. Three companies of infantry, three hundred fifty rounds of ammunition per man, a Gatling gun, and one month's rations for the field."

"And you want me to do what?"

"Ride up there and tell your Indian friends to leave the troops alone."

"Oh, is that all?"

Travers ignored the sarcasm and nodded his head.

"Colonel, I don't have that many friends up in that area. That's Crow, Nez Perce, and Gros Ventre country. And you know as well as I do that they are heavily armed and spoiling for a fight with Sitting Bull's warriors and the Cheyenne. The Nez Perce and Gros Ventre I can talk with; the Crows hate me and you know why."

"If you don't want the job, Bodine, just say so."

"You don't have anyone else to send, do you?"

"No, I don't. Not nearly as qualified as you, that is."

Bodine suddenly smiled. "I might take a friend with me.

Travers groaned, knowing full well what friend he was talking about. "Bodine! . . ."

"You want me to take the job or not?"

Travers sighed and held up a hand. "All right, Bodine, all right. Do it your way. You've got a couple of weeks to decide how best to approach it. And here is something else to think about: George Custer is making big talk about how he would deal with the Indian problem."

"Yellow Hair is a pompous jackass!"

"True. But you didn't hear me say that," Travers added with a smile. "Whatever our personal feelings, George is a very capable soldier."

"He's going to get a lot of people killed, Colonel. Mark that down in your book. I don't know where or when, but Yellow Hair is heading for a lot of bad trouble and a hard fall." He stood up. "All right, Colonel. I'll ride for the north. I'll leave in a week. I want to see my folks before I go."

* * *

Bodine headed south, out of Montana and into Wyoming, back into his home range. He followed trails that he had been riding since he was just a boy.

He crossed the Clear and then, twelve miles later, forded the Crazy Woman, riding up to his parents' ranch just in time for supper.

"Good Lord, boy," his mother told him, after kissing his cheek and stepping back to look at him. When's the last time you had a bath!"

Bodine grinned at her. " 'Bout four days ago, I reckon."

She pointed to the house and stamped her foot. "Go!"

"Yes, ma'am," Bodine said, and went, while his father stood and grinned at him.

Sarah Bodine watched her oldest go into the house. His father waved at an old ranchhand and pointed at Bodine's horse. The old man was one of the few who could handle the mean-eyed stallion named Rowdy. And even then, it was an uneasy truce.

"He'll be twenty-five in August, Matthew. Where have the years gone?"

"Good years, mother. They were so good, we didn't even notice they were passing by."

Bodine's younger brother, Carl, was third in command of the ranch, with the foreman being the number two man. His sister, Betty, was seventeen and looking around for a husband. She had her eyes on an unsuspecting young man from a nearby town, only some thirty-five miles away, to the east. Some folks predicted great things for the little village of Gillette.

While Bodine was soaping and scrubbing, bellowing out a slightly bawdy song, Betty stole his clothes and when Bodine stepped out of the wooden tub, he found he was left with only his boots and gunbelt. He wore one holster in front and the other in back while he beat it to his room, cussing under his breath while his family had a good laugh at his expense.

Betty made up with her brother by baking a huge apple pie, sprinkled lavishly with cinnamon and sugar and topped with a big hunk of homemade cheese. Bodine vocally forgave her, but his sister knew from the gleam in her brother's eyes that she'd be wise to inspect her bed very carefully before retiring, because there was most probably going to be a dead fish under the covers, at best; a live grass snake, at the worst.

When Bodine indicated he had things to say after supper, there was no talk of the ladies doing the dishes while the men discussed matters of great importance. This was still the wild frontier, and women shared in everything: the good times, the bad times, the heartbreak, and the danger. The whole family took coffee and sat out on the front porch.

"Seen your blood brother lately, son?" the father asked.

"A few days ago, up north of here. He's fine. Sends his best. He'd like to see you all but conditions being what they are, he knew you'd understand why it was best he stayed away."

"Medicine Horse came by the other night. He's worried."

"He should be. I have to go away for about a month. While I'm gone, I want you to stock up on ammunition. It'd be good if each hand had at least two hundred and fifty rounds. No one rides alone. No Cheyenne is going to bother us. And probably most Sioux aren't. But there are always going to be little renegade bands looking to lift some hair and make a name for themselves."

"Trouble coming, son?"

"Bunches of it. If this country can survive the next year or eighteen months, we'll be sitting home free for the most part."

"Those damn politicians aren't going to try to back out on agreements with the Indians, are they?"

His son's silence gave him his answer.

"Medicine Horse and his people?"

"He'll have to fight, father. He'll have no choice in the matter."

"I thought we'd seen the worst back in '66, with Red Cloud and Crazy Horse and the army fighting over at Reno and Phil Kearny and C.F. Smith."

"Nothing like what is yet to come, I'm guessing," Bodine spoke softly.

Bodine spent the next few days letting Rowdy get a good long rest with all the corn he could eat. He knew that after three days of inactivity, the big stallion would be tearing down the barn and terrorizing the other horses in an effort to get back on the trail.

Bodine chose and packed his supplies carefully, with his dad remarking, "Looks like you're packing for two, there, boy."

"Could be, Dad."

"Two Wolves throws a pretty wide loop, son. He was spotted over on the Clear a couple of months back."

"He swings wide, that's for sure. But I pity the men who ever try to take him."

"It might be you someday, son. You ever think about that?"

Son faced father. "I've thought of it. So far, though, he hasn't done anything worth killing over, to my mind."

"There are those who won't agree with you."

Bodine smiled, and the father struggled to keep from backing away from those cold eyes. "Not to my face, they won't."

Chapter 4

Bodine pulled out under a sky filled with stars, pointing Rowdy's nose north. The huge stallion was ready to go, having had his fill of lollygagging about in a barn. He was a horse meant for the wide-open sky and the trails of the plains and the mountains.

Bodine topped a ridge just at dawn and found himself face to face with a dozen Cheyenne. They were not painted for war, but they were traveling light, and were heavily armed. And they were not of Medicine Horse's lodges. Several of them had bloody scalps tied onto their reins. Crow scalps, from the look of them. Probably scouts the band had ambushed.

"Bo-dine," a young sub-chief said. Bodine noticed there were two fresh scalps tied to the mane of the subchief's horse. "Does Bo-dine ride to help the soldiers who are preparing to invade us to the north?"

So much for the secrecy of the mission. "I ride in search of my brother, Two Wolves. It is my hope that Two Wolves will ride with me to the north, to talk among the tribes, to let the soldiers come and go in peace—as long as the soldiers do not break the peace."

The sub-chief grunted. Bodine could see that he saw the logic in that idea, even though he was opposed to more soldiers.

"You know my name, but I do not know yours."

"I am *Ma it sish o mi o.*"

"I have heard of Pushing Ahead. You are said to be a great warrior. Around the fires, many songs have been sung about you."

The sub-chief straightened on his horse and swelled his chest. "And songs have been sung about Bo-dine. I have sung songs about Bo-dine."

"I am humbled and honored."

"Two Wolves is on the mountain," Pushing Ahead said, pointing north. He turned his pony's head and led his band away from Bodine.

Bodine sat his saddle and watched the Northern Cheyenne until they had faded into the hills, heading east. Bodine swung Rowdy's head and rode straight east for an hour, before once more cutting north.

That the Northern Cheyenne were this far south worried him. It could mean that a gathering had been called for, and that meant trouble.

Bodine thought about the country west of him. If a gathering had been called for, and he was the site-chooser, Bodine would pick the Rosebud Mountain area; maybe even close to the Little Bighorn.

"They know about the expedition, Bodine," Two Wolves said. "When it is over, there will be much dancing and feasting as the scalps dry on the lodge poles."

"No, Two Wolves. That cannot be allowed to happen."

Two Wolves smiled. "Did I say the scalps would be hair from the soldiers? You are reading things into my words that are not there, Bodine."

Bodine put a hand on Two Wolves' forearm. "Brother, there must be no trouble."

The half-breed sighed. "There are three hundred lodges of Crows." He drew in the dirt a winding line that Bodine recognized as the Narrows above the mouth of the Bighorn. "The Crows claim to have thousands of rounds of ammunition for their Sharps. Sitting Bull is here!" He jabbed at another spot on the twisting line. "A day before the blue bellies arrive, the Sioux will strike and the Crows will die." He smiled, and with the smile, a wicked glint sprang into his eyes.

Bodine began to put it together. "The wagons of new uniforms that were taken some months ago and the Gatling gun stolen about the same time. Several months ago, cannons were stolen . . ." He trailed off into silence, broken only by the faint popping of fresh sticks on the small fire against the chill of night in the mountains.

Two Wolves looked confused. "I know nothing of any uniforms or Gatling guns, Bodine."

"It's an ambush, Brother."

"Of course, it's an ambush!" Two Wolves' words held a note of exasperation. "Sitting Bull's warriors will kill the Crow. I just explained that to you, He-Who-Falls-Down-A-Lot. Did you fall off your horse today and land on your head, Bodine?"

"Fifty or sixty men could do it. If they were very careful and knew the terrain, they could pull it off. The Crows would blame the Army and would then stop all assistance. The Sioux would blame the Army and the Crows and then declare war on the whites."

Two Wolves looked at Bodine across the fire. Neither one of them would have normally sat this close to a fire, much less looked across it, thus ruining his night vision. But this was a mountain sacred not only to the Cheyenne but to many other tribes, some of whom no longer existed. Those were called The People Who Came Before. All were safe as long as they remained on the mountain. To the Cheyenne, the mountain was a perfect circle, just like their lodges. The circle kept the family unit intact.

It was when one left the mountain that worries about keeping your hair had best be in the forefront.

"Who would stand to gain by such a move, Bodine?"

"The people who want the land the Indian now occupies. Those who want the Indian rounded up and confined, or killed, preferably. This would be an easy way to get rid of a lot of homesteaders, Two Wolves. My dad told me about this Tom Thomas. He's a very ambitious man and doesn't care how he achieves his goals. A lot of this is prime land along here, Brother. And some still believe gold is there for the taking. You can bet that Tom Thomas is behind this plan."

"Can you prove it?"

"No. And he's too smart a man, cunning might be a better word, to allow himself to get caught. He'll do the planning behind the scenes and allow others to carry them out."

"Have you ever met with Sitting Bull or Crazy Horse, Bodine?"

"No."

"The *Unkpapa* medicine man is very powerful. And he does not trust the white man. And that will probably include you, Bodine. No matter that you are the adopted son of my father. If we get inside the village, you'll be safe. Leaving might present a problem," he added, and then smiled. "For you."

Before dawn, the men were riding. They rode north for a time, and then turned west, toward the Rosebud. The days were blistering hot and the nights cold. They saw no white men for the first two days. At midday of the third day, they saw smoke from a cabin and veered toward it.

As they drew nearer, they could make out three cabins, with about two hundred yards between them; a large barn obviously served all three families.

"Smart," Bodine said. "Strength in numbers. Probably be a town here someday."

"Don't count on it." Two Wolves cautioned. "A gathering has been called."

"I guessed that much."

"Bodine, it has been almost seven years since the Sioux signed the treaty guaranteeing them the land around their sacred Black Hills. Since that time, all the white man has done is lie and break promises, allowing other whites in to dig up the earth for gold."

Bodine offered no reply. Why should he? Every word Two Wolves said was true. Bodine glanced at Two Wolves. Except for his shoulder-length hair, he could pass for a white man. He hoped one of those settlers whose homes they were fast approaching didn't panic and shoot Two Wolves out of the saddle.

Four men suddenly appeared out of the homes, each with a rifle. "State your business!" came the shout.

"Women in the buildings, by the windows," Two Wolves said. "They're armed."

"I see them. I'm Bodine!" he raised his voice. "Army scout. This is Sam Webster with me."

"You! . . ." Two Wolves choked back a profanity.

"You want to be a dead Two Wolves or a live Sam?" Bodine asked.

"A point to be pondered, to be sure."

"Welcome then, Bodine. I've heared of you. A light and sit; the women's got grub on."

Over a noon meal of venison and beans and cornbread,

Bodine tried to keep the talk light, but the men would have none of that.

"Damned Injuns ridin' through the country again," one of the farmers said. "Seen a whole passel of 'em day 'fore yesterday. Headin' west. They didn't bother us none, but that don't make me trust 'em no more than I ever has. Which is none at all."

"They have twin necklaces, momma," one little girl said, pointing to the multi-colored stones around the necks of the men.

"We're blood brothers, ma'am," Bodine explained. "Sam is half Cheyenne."

Eating stopped as the settlers looked at Two Wolves as if he had suddenly grown horns and a tail. Which, Bodine reflected, he certainly would if he could, just to scare the pants off the settlers, and then laugh about it.

"And I am an adopted member of the Cheyenne tribe," Bodine finished it.

"Don't see how you stand it," one man said. "Injuns smell different."

"As you do to us, Two Wolves told him. "This is really excellent venison, ma'am," he complimented the cook. "Almost as good as dog."

The woman dropped her spoon into her plate as her mouth fell open.

Bodine stood up and reached for his hat. "We must be going, folks. Thanks for the meal."

Not a word was spoken as the men swung up into leather and rode away. When they were a safe distance from the house, Two Wolves burst out laughing.

"You ought to be ashamed of yourself, Brother," Bodine said, trying to keep a straight face. "I know damn well you've never eaten a dog in your life."

"Of course not. My mother did change that much about my father's tribe. But did you see the expression on that woman's face!" With a wild whoop, Two Wolves jumped his horse ahead of Bodine's and the race was on. For now, just two young men having fun, with neither of them knowing that the race was leading them toward destiny and the turning point of the Indian wars.

They left their horses and carefully climbed up a ridge overlooking the Crow encampment. "Jesus!" Bodine breathed.

Two Wolves grunted. "Even more lodges than I expected," he admitted. "I would say five hundred in all."

"Does Sitting Bull trust you?"

"Yes."

"Ride. I'll try to convince them to meet with the Sioux. I'll see you in Lost Valley in two days."

They made their way back to their horses, a good mile from the Crow camp.

Two Wolves broke the silence. "Big Face is the chief of this gathering of cowardly coyotes. He is a snake who will strike when your back is turned. Don't trust him."

"Two Wolves," Bodine said, just a note of irritation in his voice. "Do you even know why you hate the Crow?"

"Of course," Two Wolves said with a smile, then he turned his horse and rode off toward the Sioux camp, many miles to the north and west.

"You're just like a damned Injun!" Bodine shouted to his back, grinning as he said it.

Two Wolves laughed and clenched one fist, extending the middle finger in Bodine's direction.

"Now where in the hell did you learn that?"

"At the university. From that girl who looked like a bear's behind!"

Chapter 5

Bodine rode slowly toward the huge Indian encampment. He really was not expecting any trouble from the Crows; they all knew he worked for the Army and most Crows were friendly toward the whites. Nearly all the Army scouts were of the Crow tribe.

Bodine knew that there was almost never any trouble getting into an Indian's camp. While you were there, the Indians would feed you and provide you a place to sleep. Trying to leave alive was the problem.

He rode slowly toward the center of the camp, trying to find the largest and most highly decorated tipi. That one would belong to Big Face.

He saw several Crow that he knew and spoke to them in their language. They politely returned the greeting as they stood and watched. Bodine reined up in front of what appeared to be a sub-chief's lodge and dismounted. The flap was pushed open and a huge Indian stepped out.

"Fat Bear," Bodine said. "I come with news of great importance."

"I admire Bo-dine's courage," the sub-chief said, walking

toward him. "The adopted son of the Cheyenne is either a very brave man or a fool."

"I have ridden far to bring the news. I am hungry."

Fat Bear looked crestfallen. "I am sorry. I have forgotten our ways." He struck himself on the chest as punishment, called for his woman to bring bowls of food, and instructed his children to bring robes for them to sit on.

After a mostly silent meal of venison and Indian pudding—corn, milk, and honey—with eating being serious business with no place for talk, Bodine smacked his lips and rubbed the grease from his hands onto his forearms. "Fat Bear is a great man," Bodine said.

"This is truth," Fat Bear agreed, obviously pleased with the compliment.

"I would want no other than Fat Bear to ask Big Face to meet with me."

"Fat Bear would probably be the only one who could arrange that. Bo-dine was wise to come to me."

Any one of the tribe's sub-chiefs could have approached Big Face, but a little ego-stroking never hurt.

"I will see Big Face. Eat, eat, Bo-dine. Your trail has been long." His eyes glinted and his smile was faint. "You and your brother, Two Wolves, have ridden hard."

Bodine expected that. Keeping his face bland, he said, "My brother has gone to see the Sioux. He carries the same news as I."

Fat Bear grunted. "Why did Two Wolves go to the Sioux and not you?"

"Because I do not know Sitting Bull and Two Wolves does. I know you and Two Wolves does not."

Fat Bear grunted and nodded his head, accepting that as logical. He walked away, disappearing into the village. A moment later he returned and waved Bodine toward him. "Big Face will give you a few minutes. Come."

When Bodine saw that no pipe was present, he knew that he was not trusted and that this was not going to be a terribly friendly meeting. At least not at first. He was going to have to be convincing, and do it quickly.

Big Face had the tribe's medicine man with him, as well as a dozen sub-chiefs. Fat Bear sat down beside Bodine and looked at him. "Speak, Bo-dine."

"I believe that certain white men are going to try to trick the Crow and the Sioux. The Sioux have plans to attack the Crow here in your camp. An attack by the Sioux would not be unexpected, and you and your braves would surely win the battle, killing the Sioux." They probably would not win, but once again, Bodine practiced ego-stroking.

"How are white men going to try and trick us, Bodine?" Big Face asked. "And why? We have been friends with the whites for many years."

"Because of that friendship. And these white men that I speak of want you all—every Indian, everywhere—to be confined to reservations. They do not want you to be allowed to leave the reservations to hunt. They want your lands. And they want you to declare war against the white settlers, to drive them out, so their land can be taken over by greedy men."

"That may be why. Now the how of it."

Bodine explained about the theft of uniforms, cannons, and the Gatling gun. He carefully explained about the Army expedition on the Yellowstone, and that the soldiers were exploring, not hunting war.

Big Face thought for a moment. "It is a good plan," he finally admitted. "Before the real soldiers get here, the fake pony soldiers will attack us, killing many, and we will think the Army has turned on us. It would be their hope that the Crow and the Sioux would become as one against the whites. It is a good plan, but it is also a silly plan. The Crow and the Sioux will never be friends. When we meet, we fight. It has been that way forever; The People Who Came Before Us fought the Sioux."

"This is truth. But I know that Big Face and his warriors are giant people, and they can see the wisdom in putting aside their hatred for a month to make sure this silly plan will fail."

"Oh, of course, *we* would do that. The Crow are not only braver, but much wiser than the Sioux. But would the Unkpapa and the Ogalalla do the same?"

"That is what my brother, Two Wolves, will try to arrange when he gets to the Sioux camp in the morning."

"How do we know we can trust you, Bodine?"

"You don't. But here is what I will do: If an agreement can be made between the Crow and the Sioux not to fight during this period of exploration, I will ride to intercept the Army on the river and tell them of the plan; tell them of the fake soldiers and what they plan to do. Your scouts and the Sioux scouts can find the fake soldiers and the Army can arrest them. I will then return here, and here I will stay, in this camp, until it is over. I can offer you no more than my life."

"And Two Wolves?"

"I walk only in my moccasins. I cannot speak for another man."

"This is truth. Only a fool tries to put words in another's mouth. Leave us, Bodine. We will talk this out. A tipi has been readied for you. Rest. We will call you when we have decided."

"It is a trap!" Lone Dog said, his eyes boring into the eyes of Two Wolves.

"Wait!" Sitting Bull held up a hand. "I think it is not a

trick. Bodine has gone to the camp of the dungeaters, where he is not welcomed and not liked . . ."

"We don't know that!" Lone Dog interrupted the great and respected Unkpapa medicine man.

"You would not be able to speak to me in such a manner if your tongue were removed and then fed to the coyotes," Sitting Bull told him, acid in his words. "Must this come to be?"

Lone Dog shook his head and shut his mouth.

The Ogalalla chief, Crazy Horse, said, "Two Wolves is a man of truth, like his father, Medicine Horse. I believe him. This would be something that Tom Thomas would do. I think that in a very few months, the town of Cutter will be no more."

"It is nothing but a rotten mass of maggots anyway," Two Wolves said. "It will not be missed."

"I shall lead the attack against this Tom Thomas and the den of thieves at Cutter," Lone Dog proclaimed.

"But for now," Crazy Horse put him down with one sentence, "see to the needs of Two Wolves' horse."

All the Sioux sub-chiefs seated around the leaders put their hands to their mouths to hide their laughter. Lone Dog stalked away, his back stiff with anger. The pipe was lit and passed around.

Sitting Bull said, "One good laugh is not enough for a day. Two Wolves, tell us again how He-Who-Falls-Down-A-Lot got his name . . ."

The boy was a good three miles from his folks' small ranch and farm, even though his dad had told him time and again not to stray more than a whoop and holler from the house. But when you're a young boy with a fast pony, it's awful hard to stay tied to mom's apron strings when there was so much country that just about yells at a fellow to come investigate. Besides, hadn't his dad said he wished he had another hand to help with the place?

Matthew might be only ten years old, but he figured he could ride with the best of them, and his little paint pony could fly.

So Matthew set out to practice his roping on some cows. But he found a wild, skinny Indian before he came to the herd.

Well, sort of a wild Indian. But he was skinny-looking.

The Indian's pony had stepped into a prairie dog hole and went head over hocks, breaking its neck when it landed, and pinning the Indian under its body.

At least Matthew thought it was an Indian. The boy trapped beneath the dead horse was brown like an Indian and had dark hair. But there was something about the face that didn't ring true with the other Indians that Matthew had seen. The boy also wore a necklace of three multi-colored stones, pierced with a leather thong. The boy's eyes was open, and they wasn't blinkin' none. But they were dark like an Indian's.

Whatever the tribe, the boy looked dead to Matthew. First dead person he'd ever seen this close up. Except for old man Becket. He'd been gettin' some relief in the outhouse when a cyclone come up. Pa said he reckoned the old man had died of a heart attack. Wasn't a mark on him.

But his dad had said you sometimes couldn't trust an Indian. They'd fake you up close and then jump up and stick a knife in you.

"Hey!" Matthew yelled. "Are you dead?"

The dark eyes shifted, watching him. The Indian boy said nothing.

"All right. So you ain't dead. What's the matter, cat got your tongue?"

The boy spat at Matthew.

"My dad was right. You're all savages!" Matthew yelled at him.

"No! Cheyenne!"

The words came out quickly, with practically no accent. And that startled Matthew. "Indians don't talk American like Americans. But this one did and he sure understood me. That was odd." It was then that Matthew began adding things up, such as, if there was one Indian, it stood to reason that there was more around somewheres.

He stood up in his stirrups and looked all around him. But he could not see anything past the first of the rolling hills. He looked back at the Indian boy. "Is your leg busted?"

The Cheyenne stared at Matthew for a moment. "Broken? No. Trapped."

"You speak good English. All right, so your leg ain't broke, just trapped." Matthew slid off his pony and walked up to the boy. But not close enough for the boy to make a grab at him.

"If I had any sense, I'd hightail back to the house and get my pa."

"No! What's the matter—are you afraid of me?"

"I ain't skirred of nothing."

"Medicine Horse say whites tremble like old women when the Cheyenne come around."

"Medicine Horse? Is that your pa's name?"

"Yes. Great chief."

Matthew turned around and walked back to his horse.

"You leave me?" the Indian boy called.

"No." Matthew took a canteen from the saddle horn and walked back to the trapped boy. He knelt down and held out the canteen. "You want a drink?"

The boy grunted and took the canteen, pulling the plug and drinking deeply. He nodded his head in thanks and handed the canteen to Matthew. Matthew hesitated, then drank without wiping it clean. The Indian watched him closely.

Matthew corked the canteen. "How long you been here?"

"Dawn."

It was about ten o'clock. Long time to be trapped under a dead horse.

"How come it is your folks ain't lookin' for you?"

"They look. No find."

"Why didn't you holler for them?"

The boy's smile was thin. "So white men can find me and kill me? No."

"My dad wouldn't have hurt you!"

"I don't know that." He smiled again. "But I see your pony and come to steal it."

"Steal my horse! But you got a horse. Had a horse."

"Want more."

"It's wrong to steal."

"Not from your enemy."

"I'm not your enemy."

The boy grunted. "Maybe not. We see."

"You got a name?"

"Two Wolves."

"I'm Matthew. Call me Matt. Look here, Two Wolves, I get you out; what you gonna do?"

"Join people."

"But where are they?"

"I know where. I find."

Matthew sat back on his heels and thought for a moment.

"Let me have your knife."

"Why?"

"I gotta dig a trench so's you can pull your leg free! You gotta trust somebody sometime, don't you?"

Two Wolves thought for a long moment, then slowly pulled a long-bladed knife from a beaded sheath and handed it to Matthew. Matthew went to work, being careful not to cut the swollen leg of Two Wolves. So intent was he in his work, he did not hear the horses walk up the hill, the riders to sit their mounts on the crest of the knoll and watch.

But Two Wolves saw them.

Matthew was sweating by the time he finished. "OK," he panted. "Let's give 'er a try, Two Wolves."

Between the two of them, one pushing and the other pulling, Two Wolves pulled his leg free and lay back on the grass, clearly in a great deal of pain. It showed in his eyes; his face was emotionless.

Matthew handed the knife back to Two Wolves, handle first. The Indian boy managed a smile and sheathed the blade.

"How you gonna walk, Two Wolves? Look here, lemme get you on my horse and take you home with me. Ma can take a look at that leg."

"I will not have to walk, Matthew."

'Well, how you gonna get home, fly?"

"Ride with them." Two Wolves pointed.

Matthew whirled around, lost his balance in all the loose dirt, and fell on his butt. He stared in horror at a dozen or more Indians sitting their ponies on the crest of a hill. The Indians were smiling at the antics of the white boy. They slowly walked their ponies down the hill, leaving one brave to watch the house, far in the distance.

The Indians carried old muskets, spears, and bows, with quivers of arrows on their backs.

Matthew almost peed his longhandles. He tried to stand up in the loose dirt, and fell down again.

A handsome brave wearing three feathers in a beaded headband walked his horse up to Matthew and Two Wolves. "He saved your life," the brave spoke in perfect English.

"You would have found me long before I died. So it doesn't count."

"But it does. I have spoken." He looked at Matthew, his obsidian eyes not giving much away. But there was a definite twinkle in those dark eyes. He spoke to Two Wolves in his native tongue.

The boy climbed painfully to his feet. Matthew turned to help and Two Wolves waved him back. He hobbled to the brave and grabbed onto the man's outstretched arm, swinging up behind him.

The man stared long at Matthew. "I am Medicine Horse. Chief of the Cheyenne. A life saved is a life owed." He removed a necklace identical to Two Wolves and tossed it to Matthew.

Matthew fell down catching it.

Medicine Horse laughed and said, "Ride safe among us. I shall call you He-Who-Falls-Down-A-lot."

Chapter 6

It was a meeting that would have gone down in the history books—if any historians had been aware of it. Big Face sent Fat Bear and the Sioux sent Running Man to meet in Lost Valley. Big Face said if he even looked at a Sioux it would be so disgusting a sight, his head would hurt for a week, and Crazy Horse and Sitting Bull both agreed that for men of their position to look upon the ugliness of any Crow except a dead one would be infinitely worse than stepping barefoot into a fresh pile of buffalo dung.

The two sub-chiefs of the Sioux and the Crow sat with their backs to each other and talked.

"I sit this way because I do not want my eyes contaminated by the sight of that bloated pig," Running Man said.

"I sit this way because I do not want my eyes to be forever crossed by gazing—however briefly—on the ugliness of a Sioux pus-face!" Fat Bear said.

"Now that we have most of the pleasantries out of the way," Two Wolves commented dryly, "would anyone care to smoke the pipe?"

Running Man spat on the ground and made a horrible face.

"I would rather kiss a vulture," Fat Bear said.

Bodine shrugged his shoulders. "You both know why we are here. Is it agreed that the Crow and the Sioux will not fight during the time of the Army expedition on the Yellowstone?"

"Big Face has agreed to this."

"Crazy Horse and Sitting Bull have agreed to this."

"I don't suppose you'd like to shake hands on this?" Two Wolves asked.

With their backs to one another, the men stuck their hands out and shook hands with the air. Both men then vigorously wiped their hands on the grass.

"Is this all?" Running Man asked.

"The pact is agreed upon," Bodine told them.

"Good," Fat Bear said. "The smell of that rotting coyote is very offensive to me."

"Likewise, the smell of cowardice is nearly overpowering, Running Man countered.

"You must be sniffing at yourself," Fat Bear told him.

"That's it!" Two Wolves stepped in before the one-minute-old peace could be broken. "This meeting is concluded."

The Crow and the Sioux stood up and walked to their horses and rode away. Not once did they look back at each other.

"Whew!" Bodine said, taking off his hat and wiping his forehead. "I'd a never believed it."

"As soon as the Army leaves the Yellowstone, they'll be back at war."

"Just as long as we can help trap those phony soldiers and perhaps expose Tom Thomas, they can go back to fighting."

"Where will you intercept the Army?"

"They left on May 26th. This is the 29th, unless my reckoning is wrong. I can't be seen in any towns; Thomas may have people looking for anything out of the ordinary. I'll intercept them between the Tongue and the Rosebud."

"Do you have to return to the Crow camp?"

"No. I offered to, but Big Face said it was not necessary. As soon as I tip off the Army, I'll get word to you—somehow—and you can join me."

"You want me to roam around between the camps and make sure the agreement is not violated?"

"I'd appreciate it. Do you think Lone Dog is going to cause any trouble?"

"Yes. Just as soon as the Army leaves the Yellowstone. I'm convinced that Lone Dog will break with Sitting Bull and start attacking the settlers. I don't think we can stop him. And the town of Cutter is going to be wiped from the face of the map, Brother."

"That's firm?"

"As firm as a rock."

Bodine stood up from his squat. "I'm going to be traveling fast. I'll take only a few supplies and leave the rest with you."

"Ride safe, Brother."

Bodine rode the north side of the Yellowstone, heading east for the mouth of the Rosebud. He planned to avoid all the little settlements that had sprung up on the Yellowstone. Rowdy's breaking a shoe changed all that. On foot, leading Rowdy, Bodine walked into a small village and up to the blacksmith shop.

The smithy took one look at Rowdy, looking walleyed at him, and said, "I ain't touching that bastard!"

"I didn't want you to. I'll shoe him."

"If he gets shoed, you will!"

Rowdy showed his teeth to the smithy as Bodine bent to the task.

"Your name wouldn't be Bodine, would it?" the smithy asked.

Bodine looked at him.

"I ain't tryin' to be nosey. It's just they's some hard-cases over to the saloon. My boy was fetchin' me a bucket of beer this noon and heard them talkin'. If your name's Bodine, them gunnies is here to kill you!"

"I'm Bodine."

"Then you better ride, mister. One of them ol' boys is Utah Jack Noyes. And my boy says he heard one of them men say somebody named Thomas has got hired guns all up and down the river huntin' you."

So someone at the fort was in Thomas's pocket. That didn't come as any surprise to Bodine. Thomas was a rich man and didn't mind spreading his wealth around to get what he wanted.

He finished shoeing Rowdy and put him in a stall. After rubbing him down, he gave him some corn and patted the dun on the rump. "Relax, Rowdy. I got some business to take care of."

Bodine wiped the dust from his guns and checked the loads. He usually carried his guns with the hammer over an empty cylinder. He took a moment to fill up the six holes in each Colt and slipped his guns back into leather, the hammer thongs off, and walked out of the barn.

Bodine looked up and down the wide street of the village. A couple of general stores, a saloon, an apothecary shop, and a cafe. That was it. Bodine walked across the street to the cafe and stepped inside.

The menu was simple: beef with potatoes and gravy, and apple pie. Bodine ordered that and a pot of coffee.

He sat with his back to a wall and his eyes on the batwing

doors of the saloon. When his food came, he ate slowly, savoring the taste of food he hadn't had to cook himself. The pie was delicious—although not as good as his sister could make—and Bodine had another cup of coffee with the pie.

A citizen wandered into the cafe, started to sit down, then took a look at Bodine. He left the cafe at a fast walk and crossed the street, entering a general store. A few seconds later the store owner pulled down the shades and locked his store doors.

Bodine put some coins on the table and stood up, settling his hat on his head, conscious of the eyes on him from the kitchen of the cafe.

The little village had become silent. The smithy's hammer no longer sang against the anvil, its metallic sound echoing around the village. The short street was void of life, human or animal. The two horses that had been tied at a hitch rail in front of the saloon had been moved to a safer place, hopefully out of the line of fire.

Bodine stepped off the boardwalk in front of the cafe and walked slowly across the dusty and rutted street, stepping up onto the boardwalk in front of the saloon and pushing open the batwing doors.

Inside, he stood for a moment, allowing his eyes to grow accustomed to the sudden dimness of the beery-smelling barroom. He began spotting and locating the few people in the saloon.

The four men sitting at a table were local cowboys. The slick-looking man dressed in a black suit was a gambler. The one man who sat alone was fat, and with the sour expression on his face, looked like he might be having troubles with his wife.

Utah Jack Noyes stood at the bar, holding a shot glass of whiskey in his left hand. The man was smiling at Bodine. Bodine did not know the two men who stood on either side of the Utah gunfighter.

But that was all right: he hadn't known the names of many of the men he'd killed.

Bodine walked to the bar to stand at the curved end closest to the door, so he could face the three gunslicks, all looking at him.

"What'll it be?" the barkeep asked, a nervous quality in his voice.

"Nothing. Get out of the way."

The bartender complied very quickly, moving from behind the bar to stand amid the tables.

"Place suddenly started stinkin' like an Injun," one of the men said, moving away from Utah and the other man.

"You're probably smelling yourself," Bodine told him. "Way you look, you haven't bathed in six weeks. Is that fleas I see jumpin' around on you?"

Utah Jack laughed at the expression on his friend's face, his eyes quickly returning to Bodine. "I've been wanting to meet you for several years, Bodine. I'm Jack Noyes."

"Better known as Utah," Bodine acknowledged. "I saw you three years ago over at Silver Bow."

"Did you now? Ah, yes! I remember. The Mac Kenny boys."

"That was pretty good shootin'."

"Yes, it was, wasn't it?"

"Considering that you shot one of them in the back as he was leaving the barber shop."

Utah Jack's smile faded. "I seem to recall I shot him from the side."

"His gun was still in leather with the hammer loop in place when I saw him."

"Are we gonna have a de-batin' society here?" the third gunhand asked. "Or are we gonna kill this punk?"

"Relax, Jones," Utah said. "Plenty of time. The impatient one is Jones, Bodine. The other one is Callaway." He jerked his head while his hands remained at his side.

"I'm not impressed." He kept his eyes on Utah. "Why do you want to kill me, Utah?"

"Now there is an interesting question, Bodine. I suppose it should be addressed. A man should know why he is about to die."

Talk was that Utah Jack was the son of a minister and had a good formal education behind him somewhere back east. But he'd raped and then killed a girl and had to go on the run, changing his name to avoid the law. He'd become a very feared gunhand.

"For sure, Utah, one of us is about to die. Maybe all four of us. 'Cause you know damn well I'm not going down easy. I'm gonna get lead in every one of you."

"That is a risk that men of our profession must always consider, isn't it, Bodine?"

"*Your* profession, Utah. I never asked for the name of gunfighter."

"My, how noble of you, Bodine." The sarcasm dripped like scum from his mouth.

"Tom Thomas paying you boys to kill me?" Bodine dropped the question in fast and very unexpectedly.

And it shook Utah; shook him hard, just as it did the other men. But the Utah gunfighter recovered quickly. Bodine then knew that Thomas was not as slick as he thought he was. He had slipped up this time. And if he had done so this time, chances were good that he'd left a backtrail of trouble behind him a time or two before.

"I never heard of the man," Utah said

"Your a damn liar!" Bodine said, and both grabbed iron. Bodine's slug took the tall gunfighter in the belly, doubling him over and slamming him to his knees on the freshly saw-dusted floor.

Bodine's draw had been so smooth and so fast, it had caught them all off-guard.

As soon as he had shot Utah Jack, Bodine dropped behind the edge of the bar and crawled behind the bar, as Utah moaned on the floor.

"Where the hell did he go?" Jones shouted.

Bodine holstered his Colt and grabbed the sawed-off shotgun that western barkeeps always kept behind the bar. He reared back the hammers and fired through the bar, knowing he was just about even with where the three men had been standing.

A hoarse and horrible scream confirmed that his location was true as the buckshot struck Jones in the side and hip and knocked the man sprawling into a table.

Bodine rolled to the far end of the bar and came up with both hands full of .44s just as Callaway turned, a wild look in his eyes.

Bodine let the lead fly as he cocked and fired as fast as he could pull the trigger, each round striking the man in the chest or belly. Callaway's shirtfront became stained with blood and the man slowly sank to his knees, the .45s slipping from suddenly numb fingers.

Bodine quickly reloaded one Colt and stepped out from the edge of the bar. The saloon was filled with eye-smarting gunsmoke.

Quickly, Bodine reviewed the situation. Jones was unconscious and dying, his right side and hip horribly mangled from the double charge of buckshot. Callaway was dead, on his knees, with his head pressed against the footrailing.

"Damn your eyes, Bodine!" Utah Jack cursed him, blood leaking from his mouth. He tried to lift his right-hand Colt but the strength was leaving him as the pounding hooves of the Reaper's horse silently galloped closer.

Bodine reloaded his other Colt and held it in his left hand. He didn't think Utah was quite through—not just yet. Over the years, the gunfighter had proved to be a tough man to kill. And sneaky.

Bodine watched as Utah, on his knees on the floor,

slipped his left hand toward his belt buckle. Probably carrying a derringer, Bodine thought.

"Who sent you, Utah?"

"You had it pegged right, Bodine." Utah didn't have long and the man knew it. The blood from his mouth was tinged with pink, indicating he was not only gut-shot, but lung-shot.

"Tom Thomas?"

"Yeah." The word was more a painful moan pushed past bloody lips.

"You want me to give him any messages before I kill him?"

"Yeah. I suppose so."

Bodine waited for the man to gather enough strength to talk. His left hand had reached the belt buckle and the fingers were fumbling.

"You can give him a message when you both get to hell, Bodine!" Utah Jack Noyes grabbed for the two-shot .44 derringer and Bodine shot him between the eyes.

The son of a preacher died with an oath on his lips, a startled look on his face, and a blue hole in his forehead.

Bodine replaced the spent brass and holstered his Colt, walking toward the batwing doors and some fresh air, his spurs jingling softly.

"What you want us to do with the bodies?" the barkeep called.

Without stopping, Bodine said, "Do what you usually do with bodies—bury them!"

Chapter 7

Bodine didn't look back as he rode out of the little settlement on the Yellowstone. But he knew his reputation had taken another giant step, and it was a renown he had never sought. He was a man who had been born with the natural ability of perfect eye and hand coordination; a gun was merely an extension of either arm.

He made camp for the evening, eating a can of beans and some bread he'd bought the day before from a farmer's wife who looked like she could use the dime.

Bodine was rolled in his blankets and sound asleep as darkness spread over the land.

On the second day of his wait beside the Yellowstone, Bodine's vigilance paid off as the *Josephine* steamed into view. The steamer was commanded by Captain Marsh Grant, had a capacity of three-hundred tons and a crew of twelve officers and thirty-one men. And Captain Grant didn't like the idea of tying up just because one man was waving at them from the shore.

"That's Bodine, General," one of the civilian scouts aboard said. "If he wants to talk, it's important."

"Tie it up," Grant instructed.

The general was stunned when he heard Bodine's news. "Man, you can't be serious!"

"I got the Crow and Sioux to agree not to fight until this expedition is over, General. On the stipulation that these phony soldiers are arrested. Sitting Bull and Big Face sent representatives to meet with Two Wolves and me in Lost Valley. Fat Bear and Running Man agreed to the plan." He then told the officers about his gunfight in the village.

"You killed all three of them?" Captain Grant exclaimed.

"Yeah. They were too confident and too damn slow. Utah Jack Noyes confirmed that it was Tom Thomas who hired them to stop me."

"We'll be able to stop this so-called army, Bodine," the general said. "But we'll never be able to get a conviction against Tom Thomas."

"Why?"

"He's a big man, Bodine. Lots of friends back in Washington, including a lot of pull within the War Department. There are certain members of Congress who would not be opposed to a plan such as the one you just described; no matter what the cost in human life. And, I'll be willing to admit, some Army officers as well."

"Then they're fools," Bodine said flatly. "The Indians have been pushed just about as far as they're going to be pushed. You're no Johnny-come-lately out here, General. So when I tell you that a gathering has been called, I don't have to tell you what that means."

"Do you know where it's been called?"

"If I had to take a guess, I'd say somewhere in the Rosebuds, somewhere between the Bighorn and the Little Bighorn. But that doesn't make any difference; it isn't going to be a mass gathering, just the chiefs and sub-chiefs. If they don't want to be found, they won't be.

"Now then, listen to me. Big Face has agreed to abandon

his camp, leaving the lodges in place and intact, with a few braves behind to keep the fires burning. They'll slip out just before dawn on the morning of the attack. Two Wolves will let them know when Thomas's men get into position on the ridges around the camp."

"We'll be about a mile behind them," the general said grimly. "In force. I've got three companies of battle-tested men with me. Where do you want us to tie up?"

Bodine pointed to a spot along the river. "Right there. I checked it out coming up here. Even if Thomas has spotters along the river, they won't be alarmed by your docking there. It's a natural spot, with good cover. You're going to have to force-march your men to here!" He jammed a finger against the map.

"If we have to engage in a fight with any men along the river, it'll be a dead giveaway," the general said.

"You won't have to," Bodine told him. "Because there won't be any of Thomas's men there."

"How can you be so sure?"

"Because I'll be there first," Bodine said with a tight smile.

On the way back to where he would rendezvous with the Army along the Yellowstone, Bodine came upon a small hunting party of Sioux.

He drew a map on a piece of paper. "Ride to Two Wolves," he told them. "Give him this. Then tell Sitting Bull and Crazy Horse the Army will be docking and marching inland to arrest the men dressed up like soldiers. Go like the wind."

Bodine left the banks of the river and rode inland for several miles before once more turning west. He knew that Thomas had men spotted along the river, and he wanted them to see the *Josephine* as she steamed along. He didn't want Thomas's men to see him.

When he reached the area adjacent to the proposed landing site, Bodine turned south. He found a natural three-sided corral for Rowdy, with water and graze for several days, and covered the entrance with brush and small limbs, leaving it so Rowdy could break out easily enough if Bodine did not return before the water ran out. He left his boots and slipped on moccasins. Bodine put together a small packet of food, slung his canteen, and picked up his Winchester.

"I'll be back," he said to Rowdy.

The big stallion showed him his teeth and returned to grazing.

Bodine took his time working his way toward the river; he wanted to get there just about at midday. And then, he would begin his deadly work.

To the south and west of Bodine's position, Two Wolves was keeping a wary eye on Lone Dog and the band of young braves who looked to him for leadership. Two Wolves didn't trust Lone Dog, and with good reason: Sitting Bull and Crazy Horse didn't trust him either.

"He should have been named Mad Dog," Running Man told Two Wolves. He put a finger to his temple and made a slow circle. "He envisions himself to be a great war chief. He is not. He is simple. But out of that simpleness, or because of it, he is fearless in battle. That is why so many young braves follow him."

Two Wolves was torn. But that was not an unnatural emotion within the man. He had always been torn between his white side and his Indian side. His sympathies lay ripped on both sides of the invisible line. And there were so many lies told about him, over and over again until a great many people believed them.

Two Wolves had never led any band of Indians against any settler. He had never killed except when he was attacked—and even then, Two Wolves would try to make a run for it rather than fight. It was not done from cowardice, but rather from an unwillingness to kill needlessly. As he had said many times, he did not hate all whites; just some of them. He hated the broken promises and the greed. He hated what they were doing to the land, but understood that when whites came, most came to stay, so the land was carved up and cut up and planted and fenced. It was the spoilers whom he despised.

Men like Tom Thomas.

Word had drifted back to Two Wolves about Bodine's fight in the village. A drifting cowboy had told a friendly band of Gros Ventres and the Indians had brought Two Wolves the news. Two Wolves had heard of the gunfighter Utah Jack; he could have told Utah that bracing Bodine was pure poison. Bodine was like those Vikings that Two Wolves had read about. Only death stopped them, and that type of man was very hard to kill.

"Be careful, brother," Two Wolves muttered. "Your enemies are many."

Bodine spotted the first lookout easily. The man was busy rolling a cigarette. Bodine let him roll it, lick it, and take a draw. Then he cut his throat, lowering the body silently to the ground along the Elk River, the true name for the Yellowstone, so named by the Crow Indians long ago.

In the Crow language, the words "yellow" and "elk" sound much alike, and the first French fur traders didn't understand Crow very well and got the words mixed up, naming the river La Roche Jaune—River of the Yellow Rock.

Jim Bridger, known by everyone as a skillful weaver of very tall tales, told of a river that straddled the Continental Divide. For once, he told the truth when describing the north-flowing Yellowstone, as it ripped its way out of the wild Absaroka Range north to the plains of Montana.

Bodine took the second man out as silently as he did the first and then waited in the cottonwoods for the fun to start.

"Hey, Sonny!" the last man called. "You got any tobacco? I'm plumb out."

Sonny was in no shape to reply. He lay draped over a log, his head nearly severed by the big razor-sharp blade of Bodine's knife.

"Boy, you better answer me!"

Silence.

"Tim! You better go check on Sonny. I think he's done gone to sleep."

Forever.

The man's words echoed back to him over the rush of water. Bodine waited, as silent as death. His knife had been cleaned and sheathed. He wanted this one alive.

He heard the man coming, making no effort to be quiet in his approach, stomping and cussing his way through the brush. As he passed Bodine's position, Bodine stood up and hit him in the back of the head with a rifle butt. The man dropped to the damp ground, out cold.

When the man woke up, he had a terrific headache and found his world was all upside down. His hands were tied behind his back and he was strung up by his heels, hanging from a tree limb.

When he saw what Bodine was doing, just beneath his head, he started sweating. "Hey, partner! What you fixin' to do?"

"Build a fire"

"I can see that! But you're settin' it up right under my head!"

"That's right."

"You're Bodine, ain't you?"

"That's right."

" 'Bout half raised by them damn no-count Injuns."

"That's half right."

"What you gonna cook on that there fire?"

"Your head."

"Aw, man! I ain't done nothing to you. 'Sides, you cain't do that to me—I'm a white man."

"So was the man I found over near Cutter."

The upside-down man had nothing to say about that.

"What's your name?"

"Ford."

"Well, Ford, you feel like talking to me?"

"I'm talkin', I'm talkin'!" Ford knew Bodine's reputation, and knew that if Bodine said he was gonna cook your head, that was exactly what he was gonna do. In many ways, Bodine was more Injun than that damn no-good Two Wolves.

"Who tortured George to death?"

"I don't know."

Bodine walked to the rope and slowly lowered Ford until his head was about a foot from the unlit fire. Bodine squatted down and struck a match.

"Wait a damn minute!" Ford hollered. "I remember. It was Clint Peters, Stan Martin, and two guys name of Bradley and Fergus."

"Who do they work for?"

"Tom Thomas, I reckon. We all do. But mostly we're hired by Whacker Corrigan."

"Who works for Thomas."

"Sure."

"Everything right on schedule for the attack on the Crow village by Thomas's fake soldiers?"

Ford moaned; almost a cry of anguish. "I knowed it wouldn't work. I just knowed it."

"You tell me what you know, Ford. And when the Army gets here, you're going to tell them, aren't you?"

"Whatever you say, Bodine. You got the matches."

Chapter 8

Bodine kept Ford tied securely all the rest of that day, that night, and part of the next day, until he heard the *Josephine* making its way down the river. He then strung the man back on the limb, head down over the still-unlit fire.

"Oh, I say now, Bodine!" The general protested the sight. "This is barbaric!"

"So is the killing of innocent women and children. Talk to him, Ford."

"I ain't got nothing to say. Bodine made me say all them things he's a-gonna tell you, General. I . . ."

Bodine thumbed a match into a flame and dropped it into the tinder-dry twigs and small sticks.

Ford started squalling as the heat reached his head, even though he was still several feet above the small flames. "I'll tell you! It was all Thomas's idee. I'll tell you everything, General. Just get me down and away from this goddamn heathen!"

Some of the soldiers started to move forward. The general waved them back. "Tell your story, man," he ordered.

When Ford had finished, and it was a quick telling, the

general waved an aide forward. "Take this . . . person on board and get his story on paper. Have him sign it, have it witnessed, and then chain him, hand and foot, and lock him down." He looked back at Bodine and sniffed a couple of times, a frown on his face. "What is that disgusting odor, Bodine?"

"Dead bodies. I had to cut a couple of throats."

"You really love them damn stinking redskins, don't you, Bodine?" a grizzled sergeant asked, hatred in his voice.

Before Bodine could reply, the general had whirled on the man. "Sergeant Whitehall, I have lost a great many personal friends on the western frontier. But I do not hate all Indians for that. Many of their ways not only seem savage to us, they are savage. But we are taking a way of life from them. You can hardly expect them to welcome us with tea and cookies. You joined the Union Army fresh out of Texas and fresh out of the Confederate Army. How did you feel when the Yankee reconstructionists invaded Texas and took control of everything?"

"I hated ever' damn one of them and still do!"

"Bear that in mind before you start cursing Indians. Now get my horse and let's start moving. We've got a way to travel."

They made a cold camp that night, the meal consisting of hardtack and water, and were ready to move out long before dawn the next morning. Two Wolves had slipped into camp and was sleeping beside Bodine when he awakened. Chuckling, Bodine took his blood brother to meet the general.

"How in the name of Billy Hell did he get into camp?" the general exploded.

"Walked in, General," Two Wolves told him. "Your guards were very alert, never fear. But being alert to a white man is a much different thing than to an Indian. It is as Bodine pointed out to me before we undertook this quest: the fake soldiers would never have slipped up on the camp of Big Face. The braves of Big Face would have killed them all long before they got into position. But even I agreed it was better handled this way."

"Then you believe this will show the Indians that we are to be trusted to do the right thing."

Two Wolves smiled in the pre-dawn darkness. "No, General. It will not. The Indian is going to be pushed and shoved and herded and killed regardless of what happens here. When you take the Cheyenne away from their round tipis and put them into square houses, that will be the end of the family as we believe."

"But that's nonsense, Two Wolves. You're an educated man. You know that is foolish!"

Two Wolves shrugged. "The red side of me knows it is not foolish; the white side knows it is. But we will do our Ghost Dancing many times before you finally win, General. And I assure you, General, the Arrow-Keeper has been very busy of late."

"The Arrow-Keeper?"

"Ma huts," Bodine explained. "They were once four arrows of great quality and workmanship. They are kept in the Arrow-Keeper's lodge, wrapped in a piece of coyote fur. To see the arrows, one must bring gifts and have a valid reason to see them. Such as war."

"I see," the general muttered. "*Were* four arrows?"

"War is coming, General," Two Wolves predicted. "You see, we lost two of the sacred arrows to the Pawnees many years ago. That is why such misfortune has fallen on us. Already some of the Cheyenne women are packing. On the trek to war, the entire camp moves. And the women have been praying to the Sacred Hat—*Is si wun.* If many more promises are broken, war is sure to come."

"And which side will you be on, Two Wolves?"

"I don't know, General. I just don't know."

* * *

General Forsyth held his troops back while the fake soldiers destroyed the Crow village with cannon fire and heavy raking from the Gatling guns. The sixty-odd men, all dressed up like the Army, then mounted up and went charging into the burning and smoky village.

They found nothing.

"We been had," the commander of the fake soldiers muttered.

"No," one of his men said, looking at the ridges around the village. "We been captured!"

"What the hell do you mean, Josh?"

Josh pointed and the commander's eyes followed his finger.

The ridges were lined with troops from General Forsyth's command.

Their predicament was summed up very profanely. The commander then dropped his rifle to the ground and put his hands into the air. He was still cussing as the regular Army made their way into the burning camp.

General Forsyth ordered the fake soldiers to be bound together, with their hands tied behind their backs, and special hand-picked men—Sergeant Whitehall not among them—to escort the prisoners, riding the prisoners' horses, back to the river to await transportation to Fort Buford to be tried in a court of law.

"We'll never be tried in no court, General," one of the fake soldiers said with a grin. "And you know it."

"Perhaps not," the general conceded. "But you're going to be damned uncomfortable for several days. I can assure you of that. Now empty your pockets. I want all your cash on the ground."

"What!"

"You heard me. And when we're through with the horses, they'll be given to this Crow village as partial reparation for the damage you thugs have done. Now do it!" he barked the orders.

Bodine and Two Wolves stood in the background, smiling. They both knew it was a small victory, one that the historians would never know of; and even though the odds of anything ever legally happening to the captured men in the employ of Tom Thomas were slight, it was still counted as a victory.

"Know him?" Two Wolves asked Bodine, looking at the man who had commanded the fake army.

"His name is Walker. He's a gunhand from down Texas way, so I hear. Rode with Bloody Bill Anderson's bunch for a time. He's pure scum."

"He keeps staring at you."

"He knows me. Right now he's thinking how much he wants to kill me."

"You keep on making enemies, you're soon going to pass me in that department."

"I'm sure getting there. Let's get out of here, Brother. Our job is done."

"Speaking of jobs? . . ."

"I guess I'm out of one. That should make Lieutenant Gerry happy. How about you?"

"I'm a no-count Indian, Bodine. I'll just go back to the mountain and see what happens."

"How long has it been since you've seen your father?"

Two Wolves' face tightened. "My father and I don't see eye to eye on most things, Bodine. But when the whites try to take the land that was given him by the President, he will have no choice but to fight."

"Those are the words of Medicine Horse?"

"No. They are my words!"

* * *

The Army's Yellowstone expedition of 1875 continued on without further trouble. The Bighorn River, 127 miles above the Tongue, was reached on June second. The expedition stopped at Pompey's Pillar, and conditions along the river worsened from that point on. On June seventh, the attempt to navigate farther was halted and the order was given to turn back. When the Army passed the position of the destroyed village, they could see where the Crows had rebuilt their camp along the banks of the Yellowstone—and the camp had grown.

General Forsyth made the recommendation that the mouth of the Tongue would be an excellent spot for a fort—right in the middle of Indian country and easily accessible by boat. The general further stated that a good wagon road through the Yellowstone Valley was necessary.

By the time Forsyth got back to Fort Buford, Walker and his men had been released. No charges were to be brought. That the men had been wearing Army uniforms was unfortunate, but not against the law, since all insignia had been removed, and there was no law against a civilian militia acting on their own against hostiles. Indeed, it was written in the Constitution of the United States that a militia was allowed. Their only mistake was in mistaking the Crow village for that of the Sioux. Apologies would be made and monies given to the Crow for the destruction of their village.

Walker's Militia was therefore legal and could be allowed to stand ready to repel hostiles.

"Damn!" Bodine told his father upon hearing the news.

"We're alone in our anger, son. Just like we have always been. But think about this, boy: No Indians have bothered us in fifteen years. Many others have not been so fortunate. We can't blame the whites for the way they feel, and really, no one should blame the Indians for their actions."

"Dad, I'm not placing blame. I just think this whole country is about to explode. For sure, the town of Cutter is going to be wiped from the map."

"That would be no great loss," the rancher said, considerable heat in his voice. He had lost several hands in gunfights in that haven for thugs and gamblers and assorted other scum of the West.

"I agree, Dad. But it won't stop there. A Sioux victory against Cutter would only fan the flames for braves like Lone Dog."

"Is the gathering over in the Rosebuds?"

"I doubt it. I'm going to find Two Wolves. We'll ride over there for a look-see."

The father arched an eyebrow but offered no other comment, vocal or otherwise. If his son was going to ride into the jaws of danger, the elder Bodine knew he could not stop him. Matt Bodine had been riding into the snarling mouth of danger since he was ten years old—usually with Two Wolves at his side.

That his son was hated by many whites was not news to the elder Bodine. And it didn't seem to bother his son one whit. Others might talk behind his back, but they were damn cautious about what they said to his face.

"Tom Thomas has made the statement that he's going to nail your hide to the barn door, boy."

"He's got it to do. Do you know him, Dad?"

"Not really. I've spoken to him and seen him on several occasions. There is something about him that makes any decent person want to back up. It's like when you look into the eyes of a rattlesnake."

"There's an answer for that, too."

"What?"

"Shoot the snake in the head!"

Chapter 9

"We won't be welcomed there, Brother," Two Wolves said. "They won't be disrespectful to us, but they will let us know that the gathering is none of our business."

"I'm aware of that," Bodine said, tightening the cinch on Rowdy. The stallion had puffed up the first time, as he did nearly every time Bodine threw a saddle on him. It was almost as if the horse thought it would be funny to see Bodine fall out of the saddle. And maybe he would. "I just want to see how many tribes are there."

"I can tell you that now. Sioux, Cheyenne, and a few Pawnee and Arapahoe. Contrary Belly is there. Black Wolf and Last Bull. White Shield. Wolf That Has No Sense. Lone Dog. Chief Comes in Sight. Many more."

Bodine smiled at him. "We'll just mosey over like we didn't know it was going on. We'll act real surprised to see them."

"I'm sure we'll convince them of that."

They rode off the mountain and headed for the Rosebud Mountains, to a spot Bodine remembered, not far from the banks of the Little Bighorn.

"Are we going to visit Cutter?" Two Wolves asked, a smile on his face.

"Maybe on the trip back. Why? Are you looking for a five-dollar woman, Brother?"

Two Wolves gave him a dirty look and muttered some decidedly choice words about Bodine's character, among other things.

"Why did you ask about Cutter, Brother?"

"I thought it might be nice to see it one more time before Lone Dog destroys it."

"You know something I need to know?"

"Lone Dog has left the hunting grounds of the Sioux. With about a hundred or so young braves—not all of them Sioux."

"Some Cheyenne?"

"Regrettably, yes. Twenty-five or so."

"Do you know where they are?"

Two Wolves shook his head. "No. And I made it a point not to try and find out. I'm walking a narrow enough line as it is."

"You're going to have to step to one side sooner or later."

"I try not to think about that. Hold up. I smell dust in the air."

They were traveling west, and the winds were blowing from the west. It brought with the breeze the smell of dust.

Bodine and Two Wolves headed deeper into the timber and dismounted, standing by their horses, holding their heads to keep them from whinnying when they caught the smell of other horses.

"Field glasses in my saddlebags, Two Wolves. Right side. See what you can find out. I'll hold the horses."

Two Wolves ran down to the thinning timber line. He was back in a moment and stuffed the field glasses back into the saddlebags. "Too late. They're on us. Some of Walker's Militia."

"How many."

"Ten. Heavily armed and looking like they're hunting trouble."

"You want to try to run for it, Brother?"

"Not this time, Brother. Not this time."

They stepped away from their horses, two tall young men who looked enough alike to have sprung from the same loins. Two Wolves carried a Colt .44, holstered, and Bodine knew he was very, very good with it. He held a Winchester in his hands, the hammer eared back.

"There they are!" came the shout. "I told you I seen that damn trouble-makin' Injun."

Bodine and Two Wolves separated, putting more distance between them.

The horsemen faced them in the thin timber, all spread out in a line. Two Wolves had recognized them by the dark brown shirts they had taken to wearing.

"So we meet again," Bodine said. His hands were by his sides, very close to the butts of his .44s.

"We ain't got no truck with you, Bodine. Not unless you just wanna buy in. But we're takin' that damn Injun in for questionin'."

"I doubt that very much," Two Wolves bluntly made his own intentions clear. "Be that as it may, why should you want to question me?"

"He talks right pretty, don't he?" A man grinned the words.

"Answer my brother's question," Bodine said. The tone of his voice told the militia he had bought into the hand. So bet or fold.

"Two settler families was killed early yesterday morning. The redskins moved west and slaughtered two more families early this morning."

"What does that have to do with Two Wolves?"

"We figured it might be his bunch."

Two Wolves spat on the ground in disgust. "You idiot! I do not now nor have I ever had any band of followers."

"Don't you call me no idiot, you goddamn heathen savage!"

"All right!" Bodine shouted. "Two Wolves has been with me for the last two and a half days. You men are way out of line."

"Now we aim to hang that damn Injun, Bodine. Anyways, hell, you'd lie for him and ever'body knows it." Another man stuck his lip into it. "You ain't nothing but an Injun-lovin' son of a . . ."

Bodine blew him out of the saddle before the last profanity had cleared his mouth. Shifting his Colt, Bodine cleared another saddle just as the militiamen jerked iron and Two Wolves' Winchester began barking and spitting lead and flame.

The horses of the militiamen were rearing and screaming in fright; one rider was tossed to the ground, striking his head on a rock and knocking him unconscious.

Bodine shot another one out of the saddle and jerked yet another to the ground, clubbing him unconscious with his Colt.

Not fifteen seconds had passed and the militiamen had six out of their original ten on the ground, about half of them hard hit.

Bodine and Two Wolves jumped as one being, both of them shrieking out a Cheyenne war cry.

"Jesus God!" a militiaman yelled, fighting to stay in the saddle and to stay alive.

The leap of Bodine and Two Wolves took two militiamen out of their saddles. They landed hard on the rocky ground, one of them breaking his arm and the other one having the wind knocked out of him.

The riderless horses, eyes walled in fear, collided with the horses of the two militiamen still in their saddles. The dust was thick and choking from the churning hooves. Two Wolves clubbed one of the riders on the back of the head with his rifle butt, knocking him to the ground just as Bodine and the last militiaman shot it out.

The militiaman lost as Bodine's slug struck him in the shoulder, numbing his arm. With a curse, he held up his one good hand in surrender.

"I ain't believin' this," the man still in the saddle said. "I seen it, but I don't believe it."

"Our medicine was good," Bodine told him. "Now step down and let me patch that shoulder before you bleed to death. We got a long ride ahead of us."

"Where we goin'?" the man asked, dismounting with a grimace of pain.

Two Wolves looked at Bodine and both men started laughing.

"To Cutter!" Bodine said.

They rode into the whore-town of Cutter just as the late afternoon's sun was sinking, blood-red and bubbling as it reluctantly surrendered the light of day. Three of the militiamen were tied across their saddles. Two more were tied in their saddles to prevent them from falling out. They were unconscious, or nearly so. The rest had their hands tied behind their backs, the horses roped together in a line.

"Tom Thomas," Two Wolves told Bodine.

"Yeah. And he looks mad enough to eat an anvil. Well, you wanted to see Cutter."

"We all make mistakes."

"By God!" the well-dressed man in a dark suit yelled at Bodine. "I'll see you men hang for this . . . this outrage!"

"Big sucker, isn't he?" Bodine said. "And younger than I thought."

"Damn both of you!" Thomas shook his fist at the bloody parade.

They reined up in front of Thomas.

"Tell him," Bodine said to the last man wounded in the bloody gunfight.

"We started it, boss," the man groaned. "It was fair right down the line."

"Where are the others?" Thomas demanded.

"What others?"

"The men with Bodine and this damn Injun who mauled you people, you fool!"

"There ain't no others," the man admitted reluctantly. "Just these two."

Tom Thomas was so angry he looked like he might explode any second. But there was a different light in his furious eyes as he looked from Two Wolves to Bodine. Any two men who could take out ten of his best and come out of it unscathed . . . He shook that thought out of his head and turned away from the disgusting sight, stomping back into the saloon, almost tearing the batwing doors down with his entrance.

"I'm hungry," Two Wolves said. "How about you?"

"I could eat." Bodine turned Rowdy's head and walked him over to a stable.

After seeing to the needs of their horses, Bodine and Two Wolves walked across the street to a cafe and pushed open the door. The place became awfully quiet when the two men entered and sat down at a table.

"We don't serve no stinking Injuns in here!" a red-faced, pus-gutted man standing behind the counter informed them loudly.

"Then place the food on my left side," Two Wolves told him. "That's my white side."

The waitress laughed at the expression on the owner's face.

"Aw, hell, Harry," she said. "There ain't no point in kickin' up a fuss about it." She picked up a menu and walked to the table, handing the menu to Two Wolves, who took it with a smile and with his left hand.

The waitress laughed and the owner cursed and walked back into the kitchen.

"What'll it be, boys?"

"Is he going to cook it?" Bodine asked, jerking his thumb toward the kitchen.

"Naw. We got a Chink cook. He's pretty good. I'd try the stew and apple pie. Got a fresh pot of coffee, too."

"Sounds good to me," Two Wolves said, his eyes on a huge man who had appeared on the boardwalk across the street.

The waitress followed his eyes. "Stay away from that one, boys," she cautioned them. "He's pure poison. That's Whacker Corrigan. Came out here about six months ago from New York City. Call him Whacker 'cause he likes to whack people."

"Sounds like a charming fellow," Two Wolves said dryly.

"Strong as a grizzly. And just about as mean, too." She walked to the kitchen. "Dish 'em up, Loo Boo," she said.

The Chinese cook muttered under his breath.

"I know it ain't your name. I can't say your name. And my name ain't Wucy, it's Lucy. So it all evens out, don't it?"

Bodine and Two Wolves ate the good stew, both of them keeping an eye on the man sitting on a barrel on the boardwalk across the street. Whacker had not taken his eyes off the cafe.

"If it comes down to it," Bodine said, "don't try to fight him with your fists up close. That'd be suicide. Pick up a club and bust him across the teeth."

"You're reading my mind again."

With the meal finished and the table cleared, the men lingered over coffee.

"We're in this den of crooks," Two Wolves said. "Now what?"

"Feel like pushing your luck?"

"That's what we've been doing all day. Why change it now?"

"Your medicine still good?"

Two Wolves laughed softly. "Sometimes I wonder who is more Indian—you or me?"

"Let's go look into the lion's mouth, shall we?"

The men left the cafe just as night was covering the land. They walked across the street to the Kittycat saloon. Whacker Corrigan stood up and blocked the batwings, a smile on his face.

Chapter 10

"Get out of the way, lard-butt," Bodine told the huge man.

Whacker looked startled for a moment, and then burst out laughing. But he didn't step out of the way. He looked down at Bodine and said, "You feel up to moving me, lad?"

"If I have to."

"By the Lord, I think you'd try it!" Whacker looked at the pair and then shrugged. "All right, lads. I admire courage." He stepped to one side.

Bodine and Two Wolves pushed open the batwings and walked into the saloon. Bodine's spurs jingled as he walked across the freshly sawdusted floor. Two Wolves' moccasins whispered across the floor. Whacker Corrigan entered after them and sat down in a chair. He watched with a smile on his lips.

Tom Thomas stood by the bar, watching the pair with open contempt and disgust in his eyes. He picked up his shot glass and took a tiny sip of whiskey. That move did not escape the eyes of Bodine and Two Wolves. Tom Thomas was a man who was going to be always in control, not allowing alcohol to cloud his reasoning.

Bodine ordered beer and Two Wolves asked for a glass of water. That brought a round of laughter from the assorted scum and trash and gunslingers seated in the big room.

One of them called out, "Why don't you give the savage some whiskey, barkeep? Maybe then he could do a war dance for us."

Two Wolves did not change expression; but his dark eyes suddenly held a very dangerous glint. It did not go unnoticed by Bodine.

"Stinks in here," another man piped up. "Smells like a dirty tipi to me."

"Yeah," his partner said. "You reckon he ever takes a bath?"

"Shore don't smell like it to me."

Bodine turned to face the pair, his right hand held close to the butt of his .44.

The men shut their mouths.

"You always fight that damn Injun's battles for him, Bodine?" Tom Thomas asked.

Bodine cut his eyes. "I never fight his battles for him, Thomas. I can assure you, Two Wolves is man enough to fight his own battles. Which is a lot more than I can say for you."

That stung Thomas, bringing a flush of red from his neck up to his face. Out of the corner of his eye, Bodine could see that the comment amused Whacker Corrigan. And he wondered about that.

Tom Thomas slammed the shot glass down on the bar, the whiskey spilling out, wetting his big, ham-like hand. "Just what the hell do you mean by that, Bodine?"

"It means," Bodine spoke calmly, "that neither Two Wolves nor I have to have our fighting done for us. We've courage enough to do our own fighting."

Two Wolves smiled. He was putting together just what Bodine was up to. And he hoped it would not backfire on them both.

"Say it plain out what's on your mind, Bodine!" Thomas demanded. "Stop dancin' around the issue."

"It means, Thomas, that you don't have the guts to fight your own battles. You've got to hide behind a dozen or more two-bit gunhawks. It means, Thomas, that you're yellow. That you're a coward. That you hide in dark places and wait to strike at someone's back. Is that plain enough for you, Coyote Butt?"

Two Wolves threw back his head and laughed. Cutting his eyes, Bodine could see Whacker Corrigan duck his head to hide his widening smile, brought on by the slur against his employer.

Thomas appeared to be gathering enough steam to drive a locomotive up a steep grade. Then, with a visible effort, he began calming himself. After a moment, a very tightly controlled smile cut his lips.

A lean, hawk-faced man, wearing two guns belted low and tied down pushed back his chair and stood up. "Let me take this pup, boss."

"Sit down and shut up!" Thomas barked the orders. The gunhand sat down quickly. Tom Thomas looked square at Bodine. Bodine could almost feel the heat from the gaze. "All right, you've insulted me in front of my men. You know what I have to do. And I'm admitting that I look forward to it."

"With help from your wild dogs, of course." Bodine stuck the needle in the man again.

"Now you're accusing me of having no honor."

"Honor?" Bodine laughed the word. "A rattlesnake has more honor than you, Thomas. You don't know the meaning of the word."

Thomas took the slur without changing expression.

"Honor?" Bodine kept it up. "You're a two-bit operator who managed to hit it big out here by terrorizing small ranchers and forcing homesteaders off their legally gotten land. How in the hell you managed to get so much pull in Washington is beyond me. I guess that to people who don't know how deadly a rattlesnake is, it might seem pretty and harmless. But I know better. You've been run out of every place you ever tried to alight, or left just before the authorities ran you out."

That hit home. And Bodine made a mental note of it. He doubted that Tom Thomas was the man's real name; he had dropped his birth name years back. He'd used no telling how many aliases in no telling how many places.

"You're a damn stinking liar, Bodine!" Thomas yelled at him.

"And just before I begin to stomp your guts out, Thomas, your men will interfere."

"No, they won't." Whacker spoke the words softly, but loud enough so that all in the Kittycat could hear. "I've bullied my share of men, and whipped every one of them. But I've taken no part, ever, in a gang-up on one man. I shall stand by the Indian and make sure that there is no interference—from either side. If need be, I shall fight shoulder to shoulder beside the Indian. Is that clear, Mister Thomas?" He looked dead at his boss.

Thomas's smile was thin. "A side of you I was not aware of, Whacker. Very well. Of course, there will be no interference. Those are my orders. Are they understood, men?"

The gunslingers in the room nodded their heads.

Whacker Corrigan motioned for Two Wolves to join him at the table. "And bring your water. I have no objection to a man who doesn't drink hard liquor."

Two Wolves looked at the former New York City shoulder-striker and smiled. He picked up his glass of water and joined the man at his table.

Bodine took off his gunbelt, rolled it up, and laid it on the table before Two Wolves.

Tom Thomas removed his suit coat and rolled up his

sleeves. Bodine watched him closely. Thomas was a big man, no doubt about that. And in his prime. He outweighed Bodine by a good thirty pounds, and he appeared to be in excellent physical shape.

Simon Bull sat in the back of the room. He had never seen his boss fight a man with his fists, but he knew that Bodine was tough as an anvil. And tricky as an Indian. This fight promised to be a good one.

But Simon was curious about Whacker's intervention. It showed a side of the man that was not to Simon's liking. Not at all.

Time would tell, he reckoned.

"I'm going to enjoy this," Thomas said, doing a couple of deep knee bends and flapping his arms to loosen up. "I'm going to kill you, Bodine. With my hands. I'm going to beat you to death."

"Maybe, or else put me to sleep with your big fat flapping mouth," Bodine countered. "That's about the only way you're going to whip me, you lard-butted windbag."

Even the gunslingers in Thomas's employ all smiled at that. Bodine had guts, that was a matter of proven fact. Whether he had a chance against the bulk of Thomas was quite another matter.

"You ready, Bodine?" Thomas asked.

"Hell, Thomas, I *been* ready! I'm just waitin' on you to work up enough courage to swing the first fist, that's all."

Thomas stepped away from the bar and held up his fists in the classic boxer's stance. Left and right held up high, far away from his face.

Bodine laughed at the man, his fists held close to his body, just under his jaw, close to his barrel chest.

"You find your impending death amusing, cowboy?" Thomas asked, shuffling his feet in the sawdust.

"No. I find you amusing, you ape! You look like you're about ready to start beating your chest and swinging by your tail at any moment. Who'd your mother breed with, a monkey?"

That did it. Howling his outrage, Tom Thomas charged Bodine. And that was what Bodine had hoped for. He sidestepped and tripped the bigger man, clubbing him on the side of the head as he went down to the floor. Bodine kicked him twice in the side while he was down and then stepped back, allowing the man to get to his boots.

"Foul! Foul!" cried Thomas after the kicks.

"Horse-crap!" Corrigan said. "This isn't the ring. This is bare-knuckle strike and gouge. There are no rules here."

Thomas suddenly lunged at Bodine, the force of his charge knocking the smaller man down. Bodine rolled quickly, avoiding Thomas's boots, and sprang to his feet, smiling at the man.

"Come on, ape-face," Bodine taunted the man. "Is this the best you can do? You fight like a dandy!"

Thomas cursed Bodine and stepped in, swinging. Bodine went under the punches and landed two hard body shots to Thomas's stomach, then stepped back.

Thomas looked at Bodine, sudden doubt in his eyes at the shockingly powerful body-blows he'd just received. Then he hit Bodine with a left that knocked the man backward, the bar stopping him.

Thomas rushed him and landed two more blows, to the face and the stomach, that hurt. Bodine twisted away and managed to land a right that jerked Thomas's head back.

The men circled each other warily. Thomas had given up his boxer's stance and now held his elbows in tight to his ribs and his fists up, to protect his face.

Bodine hit him a combination in the belly that knocked the wind from him momentarily and followed that with a kick to the knee that staggered the big man. Thomas cursed and backed up, limping for a moment on his bum leg.

Bodine stalked him, flipping hard, fast fists at the man,

worrying him more than hurting him, for Thomas blocked most of them with his massive arms.

The spectators in the barroom were strangely silent as they watched the fight, for at this point, Bodine was clearly the man who had taken charge.

Bodine jumped at Thomas, the move startling the man. Then Bodine really got his attention by spreading his nose all over the man's face as a left got through that brought blood splattering. Thomas shook his head and backed up.

Bodine was relentless in his pursuit. He followed the bigger man, throwing punch after punch, bruising the arms of Thomas, hurting him, and occasionally getting a fist through to smash into Thomas's face. Thomas's lips were pulpy with blood and his breathing was ragged through his shattered nose.

But the man was far from being out. Thomas lashed out with a right that rocked Bodine's head back and followed that with a left to the gut that very nearly doubled Bodine over. Bodine backed up, shaking his head and catching his breath. He could taste blood in his mouth.

Grinning through the gore, Thomas's confidence returned and he bulled toward Bodine. Bodine sidestepped, picked up a half-full whiskey bottle and hit Thomas right in the center of the forehead with it, splitting the skin wide open.

With the whiskey stinging his eyes, half blind from the blood, Thomas had to retreat, his hands pawing at his face. Bodine went to work.

Bodine smashed hammer blows at Thomas, each work-hardened fist taking its toll when it landed, head and body. Thomas's face was now a bloody mask, for Bodine had slipped on leather work gloves just before the fight, while Thomas was shadow-boxing, and with the gloves could hit harder, and with each punch, he would twist his fist, further maiming the man.

Gathering all his will, Thomas managed his second wind

and the two men stood toe to toe, hammering at one another. But Thomas's punches had lost their sting and moment by moment, Bodine was pushing him back.

Two Wolves heard Whacker mutter, "Fall man, fall. You're whipped."

But Thomas would not fall.

Bodine finally stepped back. "It's over, Thomas. I don't want to beat you to death. So it's over."

"Fight, you yellow pup!" Thomas snarled at him, then lunged and hit Bodine with a crashing right to the jaw.

Bodine backed up, clearing his head and then getting set. He hit Thomas flush on the teeth with a solid straight right. Pearlies flew from the man's mouth as he staggered back. Bodine followed that with a left that exploded against the man's jaw, nearly crossing Thomas's eyes. Bodine crossed that with another right that connected on the side of the man's jaw.

Thomas's eyes began glazing over.

Bodine set his boots and hit Thomas in the center of his stomach, doubling the man over. He came up from the floor with a right to the jaw and Thomas's boots flew out from under him. He landed on a table, crushing it. He rolled on the sawdust, over on his back, and lay still.

The saloon was silent except for Bodine's hard breathing until Corrigan said, "I'll say this, Bodine. I believe I can take you, but I damn sure am not looking forward to the day!"

Chapter 11

Dawn found Two Wolves and Bodine camped by a little creek, a dozen miles from Cutter. Two Wolves had heated water and had Bodine soak his hands in the hot water while he prowled for herbs to mix, to take the swelling and the stiffness out of his brother's hands.

"It was a magnificent sight to see, Bodine; but rather silly, you will have to admit."

"Why?"

"You humiliated the man. In front of his own men. Now he will have to kill you to save face."

"He'll try," Bodine said grimly. Then he grinned. "But it was worth it just to see that big ape fall!"

Two Wolves did not return the smile. "What's the matter, Brother?"

"I read the wind last night, Bodine. I tasted death and defeat and dishonor."

Bodine did not argue the point. He had personally witnessed too many mysticisms among the various tribes to doubt that Two Wolves actually believed what he was saying. And in many cases, they proved accurate.

"Tell me what else, Two Wolves."

"I saw a line of hills over a little river. In the valley, hundreds of tipis, thousands of Indians, more than have ever gathered before. I saw a great battle and then a great victory unfolding before me." He sighed heavily. "I was witnessing the beginning of the end for my people. My *Red* people."

"Who were the Indians fighting, Brother?"

"The Army. Yellow Hair and his troops."

"Custer is over four-hundred miles away, Two Wolves. The last I heard he was up at Fort Abraham Lincoln, up the Dakota territory. He could be over in Nebraska."

"I know. I am only telling you what I read on the wind."

"I believe you. Why the fight?"

"Lies. Broken promises. On both sides."

"I believe that, too. What is this leading up to, Brother?"

"My destiny. I am going home to my father. To my people. Where my father goes, I will go."

"Did the wind tell you this?"

"My heart tells me this, Bodine. For a time, I wish to be left alone, and please don't take that the wrong way."

"I won't. But I'm still going to the gathering."

"You will find nothing there. It is over."

Bodine didn't question that. It probably was over. "When will I see you again?"

"I don't know, Bodine. I hope it is not on the field of battle."

"Medicine Horse will not fight the Army, Two Wolves. He will take his people and leave."

"If that is the case, I shall be with him. But I doubt that the great war chief Medicine Horse will turn tail and run."

"I hope he does, Brother. For your sake, for his sake, and for my sake."

Two Wolves walked to his horse and swung into the saddle. He looked back at Bodine. "Do not attempt to see me before the leaves turn, Brother. I am asking this of you."

"I will comply with your wishes."

Two Wolves nodded his head, lifted his hand in farewell, and rode away.

Bodine felt a sadness take him for a time. The west was changing and with that change, lives of thousands had to change with it. Especially the Indian way of life. Bodine knew that it was inevitable: the Indians would be rounded up and stuck on reservations; and that was not necessarily all the fault of the white man. Most Indians were not farmers, not tillers of the land, and showed no inclination to adopt that way of life, even though many had tried to convince them if they didn't accept it, they were doomed. The Indians were nomadic warriors and hunters and trappers. But they were vastly outnumbered, a hundred times more with each passing day. While progress was passing them by. Sealing their fate. As it had passed by thousands of people over the long centuries. One either changed with it, accepting it, rolling with the flow, or one became enslaved or imprisoned, or entire peoples just vanished, like the Ones Who Came Before.

Bodine stayed in camp that day, soaking his hands, applying the poultices to his hands, and doing a lot of thinking while Rowdy grazed around him.

Bodine knew that major Indian wars were still ahead. The Sioux and Cheyenne were not going to lie down and let the whites walk all over them without a fight. And if Two Wolves was right—and Bodine had no reason to doubt him—the wars were shaping up to be bad ones.

And, Bodine mused, what part would he play in them?

As far as he knew, he was still employed by the Army; but he didn't know in what capacity. In the morning, he'd amble on over toward the Rosebuds and see about the gathering, then he'd head for the fort and check in with Colonel Travers.

* * *

Bodine wandered around the Rosebuds for two days before coming to where the chiefs and sub-chiefs had held their gathering. He let Rowdy graze while he prowled around the area on foot, finding evidence of several tribes who had attended the gathering. Cheyenne, Blackfeet, and tribes of the Sioux, including Ogalalla, Brule, Sans Arcs, Hunkpapa, and Miniconjou.

Bodine felt a myriad of emotions as he stood in the grassy valley. The whites were going to clear the west of hostiles. But who were the hostiles? Was it the Indians, or the white men. And just exactly whose land was it, anyway? It was at times like these that Bodine's Indian teachings came to the surface to haunt him.

He knew the Indian way of life could not continue; that its time was very nearly over. But he still could not help but feel some sorrow at that. Whether that sorrow—if that's what it was—was misplaced, he didn't know.

What he did know was that education and civilization and progress were all intertwined; all jumbled up, and you could not have one without the other— not and make all three fair and equal for everybody. If that was ever really possible.

With a sigh he walked back to Rowdy and swung into the saddle. Tell the truth, he was glad to be leaving the area along the banks of the Little Bighorn. Place was eerie.

He rode into the small fort two days later. He had taken his time, following the tracks of Indian ponies until they split up, heading for their various camps. Lieutenant Gerry gave him a dirty look as he rode in. Bodine ignored the man. He asked for and was received immediately by Colonel Travers.

"Bodine." Travers shook his hand. "You've played hell, man. Certain people in very high places were not at all happy about you and Two Wolves shooting up Walker's patrol."

"They opened the dance, Colonel. One of them called me a son of a bitch."

"I'd have called him out for that," the colonel said. "That slur was not told to me." He waved his hand. "All right. It's over. It can't be undone." He smiled. "How are your hands, Bodine?"

"They're all right. I'm assuming you heard about the fight?"

"Oh, yes. You whipped Tom Thomas to a fare-thee-well, so I'm told. And for that, you've made a bitter enemy, Bodine."

Bodine shrugged that off as unimportant.

"Do you know who is responsible for the attacks on the settlers?"

"I'm sure it's Lone Dog and his bunch. He's gone renegade on us. About seventy-five young Sioux and twenty-five or so young Cheyenne."

"How does Two Wolves feel about them and what they're doing?"

"Saddened. As does, I suspect, Medicine Horse."

"You've been roaming about amid the hostiles, Bodine. Bring me up to date."

"Big gathering over in the Rosebud Mountains. Sioux and Cheyenne and Blackfeet, mostly. War is looking this country in the face, Colonel. And it's going to be a bad one."

"And it will erupt . . . ?" He tailed that off with a hopeful note that Bodine could supply the answer.

"There is absolutely no way of knowing, Colonel. It all might blow up in our faces this afternoon. But I doubt it."

"Why?"

"They've got to talk first. And that's going to take a long time. Probably well into fall. But let me tell you something, Colonel: We're talking about more Indians in memory than have ever gathered together. Thousands."

"Nonsense!" Travers brushed that off.

Bodine shrugged. "As you wish, Colonel." He pointed a

finger at the colonel. "Now you hear me well, Colonel. We've got two options, and just two. It's coming to a showdown—a final one—and we don't have much time for a lot of red tape. The options are these: the government can either place the Sioux and their allies, namely the Cheyenne, on reservations and keep them there by armed force, or the United States government can make a real, honest effort to obey the Indian treaties, namely by staying off the Sioux and Cheyenne hunting grounds and stopping the prospecting of gold on their reservations.

"Sitting Bull has announced his intention to hold by force all the country west of the Missouri to the Rocky Mountains. And he's going to do it, Colonel. And the Northern Pacific railroad really ruffled his feathers. And you know it."

"Damnit, Bodine. Sitting Bull is wrong about the railroad. Red Cloud and the other chiefs agreed back in '68 not to oppose the building of those rails. Sitting Bull and Crazy Horse are clearly in the wrong and they must be dealt with." Travers slammed his hand down on his desk. "Bodine, what side are you on?"

"I'm on the side of justice, Colonel."

"Well . . . you're right about one thing, Bodine. It's going to blow up in our faces."

"Why?"

Travers stared at him.

"Come on, Colonel. What's the government up to this time?"

Travers sighed. "I probably should not tell you this, Bodine. But . . . all right. Another expedition is being mounted to go into the Black Hills. They're going to make a geological survey to determine the extent of the mineral resources in that area."

"Goddamnit!" Bodine jumped to his boots to stand glaring at the army officer. "Do that, and the Sioux will declare war!"

Travers rose to his feet, facing Bodine across the desk. "They're already at war, Bodine!" he shouted. "Declared, or not!"

"Oh, now I get it," Bodine said sarcastically. "Sure. The government wants to pour more settlers in the Black Hills under the guise of prospectors."

"You said it, Bodine, not I. Besides, I think you're wrong in that assumption."

"When this expedition goes in, Colonel, the Ogalalla and the Hunk papa will go to war."

"I am of the belief that the government will offer to buy the Black Hills and the area around it."

"It's sacred land, Travers. They're not going to sell it. Our noble government so graciously *gave* the Sioux land that was theirs to begin with. Now we're going to offer to buy it back?"

"That is correct."

"And if they refuse, which they certainly will?"

"That will be up to the War Department," he replied rather stiffly.

Bodine sat down and shook his head. "You can just bet that the chiefs know of this, Travers. That was probably the main reason for the gathering."

"How would they have learned of it, Bodine?"

"Probably read it on the wind or saw it in a vision."

"Nonsense!"

Bodine stared at the man. "You've been out here a long time, Colonel. But you still don't understand Indians."

"I don't believe in hobgoblins and the like, if that's what you mean."

"I don't understand all that I know about the Indians, Colonel. But I've seen too much to doubt many of their visions."

"Nonsense! All that is a lot of claptrap and barbaric hooey."

Bodine stared at the man and made up his mind. "May I borrow paper and pen and ink, Colonel?"

"Certainly."

Bodine dipped and wrote for about a minute. He signed the paper, blew his signature dry, and handed the paper to Travers.

Travers looked at it, his face tight. "This is firm, Bodine?"

"Oh, yes."

"Very well. I accept your resignation. This will go into your file. But I must warn you, from this moment on, you are *persona non grata* on this post."

"That's fine with me, Colonel."

"Where is Two Wolves, Bodine?"

"That, Colonel, is none of your damn business."

"I see. Very well. You have fifteen minutes to clear this post, Bodine."

"I'll be gone in five, Colonel." He rose and headed for the door.

"Bodine!"

Bodine turned around. Colonel Travers rose from behind his desk and walked toward him, holding out his hand. Bodine took it.

"Forget the hard words, Matt. You're welcome back here at any time. You've done a lot of good work for us, and thanks for that."

Bodine nodded his head and dropped his hand. "You can retire right now, can't you, Colonel?"

"Why . . . yes. But I don't plan on it. Why?"

"Pity. I'd hate to see your scalp tied onto the mane of a war pony."

Chapter 12

Bodine worked on his ranch that summer of 1875, seldom leaving the spread except to go into a small town located on the Clear River for supplies every now and then. He saw no sign of Two Wolves; but Lone Dog and his bunch were burning and scalping in both Montana and Wyoming. The Army was chasing them all over the countryside, to no avail, and Walker's militia was running around like a bunch of nitwits, shooting every stray Indian they could find, regardless of tribe.

As the summer began to wane and the leaves began to turn, it became apparent that open warfare between the settlers and the Indians was about to come to a bloody head. By this time, the government expedition into the Black Hills had ended, and Colonel Dodge, the commander of the expedition, had located and lined out wagon roads and sites for military posts.

The treaty had clearly been broken and the settlers and prospectors were pouring into the sacred grounds. This move so angered Sitting Bull and Crazy Horse, they began buying arms and ammunition from whomever they could and wherever they could—and if that didn't work, they would just kill the traders and take what they needed.

By September of '75, Crazy Horse and Sitting Bull and their followers were engaged in open warfare with any settlers found in the forbidden region. The government made an offer to buy the region. A gathering was called, and the chiefs voted unanimously to refuse the sale of their land simply because greedy white men wanted the yellow gold.

When Bodine learned of this, he rode to his father's ranch.

"Stock up on ammunition, Dad," he told his father. "All hell is about to break loose."

"But Sitting Bull and Crazy Horse are both over in Dakota Territory!"

"They won't be there long," Bodine predicted. "As soon as the Army starts a campaign against them, they'll move west and link up with the Cheyenne and the Arapahoe. Bet your boots on it, Dad." The image of that area around the Little Bighorn once more entered Bodine's mind. For some reason, he hadn't been able to shake it loose. "Close to home," he muttered.

"What's that, boy?"

Not wanting to spread false rumors, and as far as he was concerned, it was just his mind working overtime, Bodine shook his head. "Oh, nothing, Dad. Just talking to myself."

"You seen Two Wolves?"

"No. He asked that I not bother him until the leaves turn."

"It's about that time, boy."

"I know. 'Bout another week of work at the ranch and I'll go see him." Bodine leaned against the railing at the corral and looked out over his father's spread. "Sure looks good, Pa."

"You helped make it what it is, Matt. Your brother, Carl,

come along just a tad too late to remember much about those bad ol' years your ma and me and you went through. We had some lean times and some hard scrapes."

Bodine remembered. He remembered the blizzards that howled around the tiny cabin, long since gone, to be replaced by one of the finest homes in all of northern Wyoming. Bodine remembered when he was a boy, the sudden and wild and frightening Indian attacks, until he met Two Wolves and Medicine Horse; after that the attacks stopped. Against them. But not against all whites in the area. And that had caused quite a bit of hard feelings, some of it still lingering.

Bodine sighed and brought himself back to the present. "Slim Man came by the ranch last week. Took a chance doing it, too."

"Slim Man? Do I know him?"

"I doubt it. He's like Two Wolves in that he's a half breed. Sometimes he stays on the reservation and sometimes he just wanders. Slim Man told me that he heard the Army is chomping at the bit for war with the Indians, especially the Sioux and the Cheyenne. He said the official attitude toward the upcoming hostilities was one of enthusiasm. He said that the Army had suffered enough humiliation at the hands of the Indians—without really being allowed to strike back in force—and this time it was to be a fight to the finish. They were really looking forward to it."

"Medicine Horse and his followers have been good to us, boy. There was that winter that I hurt my back, and had it not been for the game Medicine Horse supplied us, none of us would have made it."

"I know. I remember only too well."

"You was just a boy, but you did a man's work all that winter."

"Carl did too, Pa."

"Not like you, Matt. You was in your eleventh year and you had to become a man. Far too young, boy."

Bodine laughed. "Then there was that time that grizzly raked your behind and you had to ride sidesaddle all the way home!"

The father shared in the laugh. "I'll damn sure never forget that, you can bet. I skinned that bear out and scraped the hide clean and gave it to Medicine Horse. He kept it for years."

The men rolled cigarettes and smoked in silence for a time.

"You be careful riding out in the wilderness, boy. I think that Lone Dog is crazy."

"Yes, he is." Bodine touched the three-stone necklace that was never removed from his neck. "But this frightens him. He doesn't want any trouble with Medicine Horse. Don't you worry. I'll be careful, Pa."

"Bo-dine is a fool!" Lone Dog spat the words at him. It was the second day out and Bodine had watched Rowdy's ears as they came up, and he had felt the horse tense under him. He had been expecting Lone Dog to find him. Then Lone Dog and some twenty of his warriors had come out of the ravine in a screaming rush, to surround him.

Bodine sat his horse and looked at Lone Dog. The Indian was painted for war and his horse's mane had several scalps tied to it. One of them was very fresh.

When Rowdy's ears had peaked, Bodine had slipped the hammer thong from his right-hand Colt. He held the reins in his left hand. If it came down to it, Bodine felt he could kill three or four—or at least get lead in them—before they dropped him. But he did not think it would come to that.

One could always hope.

"Why does Lone Dog insult me so?"

Lone Dog spat on the ground as the hate shone out of his dark eyes. "Bo-dine will not live long in his fine house once we have reclaimed the land that is ours. The silly charm around your neck will not protect you then."

"You will not reclaim the land, Lone Dog. All you will do is die on it."

Lone Dog went into a screaming rage, and Bodine knew then the man was crazy.

"Stop your silly behavior!" Bodine told him in his own language.

The braves with Lone Dog hissed and some drew back, not knowing what might happen next. Lone Dog had proclaimed himself a chief and one just did not speak to a chief in this manner. And the Cheyenne riding with Lone Dog resented the man's referring to Medicine Horse's amulet as a silly charm. Medicine Horse was powerful, and his medicine was not to be taken lightly.

"You call me . . . silly!" Lone Dog screamed the words, spittle spraying from his mouth.

"If you behave as a fool then you surely must be a fool." Bodine's words were calmly spoken. "Now listen to me. If you continue on the path of war, killing women and children, you only toss water on the fires of peace. And only with peace do any of you have a future."

"Bo-dine has had a vision through pain?" a Cheyenne asked.

Bodine opened his shirt, showing them all the scars on his chest, the pain he had endured as he entered manhood, hooked to the medicine pole. "I have had many visions since becoming a human being. The pins could not be torn free from my flesh. The older man, who was wise in the ways of the spirits who ruled the earth, so decreed. I slept on the hilltop and held many conversations with the Wolf. Two Wolves was on the next hill and did the same as I. For five days and nights!"

Even Lone Dog drew back at this. One day of the self-torture and visions was considered enough to enter a young man into full manhood and be considered a warrior. But five days and nights?

Bodine took a small pouch from his pocket and opened it, showing them all the Wolf hair in the medicine bundle. "The Wolf gave this to me."

Actually, Bodine did not know how in the hell the wolf hair came to be in his medicine bundle. It was not there when he started his vision-quest, but it was there when he'd finished. But he did remember talking with a Great Gray Wolf. Thereafter Bodine did not question the unknown.

"Bo-dine's medicine is good." Lone Dog verbally backed away. "Bo-dine is truly a human being. But because of what you are does not mean I must follow your words. I am a warrior and in my visions, I saw myself driving the whites from our lands. Each of us must pursue our own visions, Bodine."

Bodine did not question that, for that was truth, and one did not argue the truth. Bodine nodded his head in agreement.

Bo-dine is Brother to the Wolf," a young Cheyenne spoke up. *"Ilyi!"* he cried, fear springing into his eyes as he pointed behind Bodine.

Bodine did not turn his head or cut his eyes. He knew he had to play this hand out with his cards close to his vest. Whatever the warrior was looking at had touched his heart. Bodine hoped only that it wasn't a grizzly about to slap him out of the saddle or a puma about to leap.

The Sioux and Cheyenne warriors cried out and turned their horses, leaving Bodine in a cloud of dust. Only when they had gone did Bodine twist in the saddle and look behind him.

A Gray Wolf stood on a hilltop, looking at Bodine.

"Brother," Bodine said.

The Wolf snarled his agreement and then was gone in a distance-consuming lope that could carry him a hundred miles during a day.

"My son," Medicine Horse said, putting both hands on Bodine's shoulders. "It has been so long. Now I have both my sons to share my lodge."

"It is good to see my father," Bodine said. "I have thought of you much over the months."

Medicine Horse was still a tall and powerful and handsome man. But his smile slowly faded as he looked at his adopted son. "There is trouble on the land, son. *Wo iv sto is* has had a vision, and it was not a good one.

Wo iv sto is, or He Who Mounts The Clouds, son of Alights On The Clouds, was a very important man in the tribe, and his words were always listened to closely.

Medicine Horse forced a smile back on his face and took Bodine's arm. "I must be getting old. I am forgetting my manners. Come. We will eat and you can rest and then we will talk."

Bodine ate the stew of buffalo and wild onions and Indian potatoes and then rested for a time in the lodge of his adopted father. He opened his eyes as the flap was pulled back.

"Brother," the brave said.

"Brother." Bodine greeted Two Wolves, as he sat up on the robe and smiled. He was shocked at Two Wolves' appearance but managed to keep his expression bland. Two Wolves had lost weight and Bodine was sure he had been fasting, seeking a vision to give him direction.

"You are rested?"

"I feel fine."

"Come. We must talk."

As they walked through the large camp, Two Wolves said, "My father and I shared the same vision, Bodine. There can be no war. Medicine Horse has spoken. And he has ordered that I return to the white side of me. You know that my mother left me a large sum of money. My father has no use for money; what she left him, he has given to me. Medicine

Horse has said that when I leave this village, I should not wear the Indian clothing, but instead the clothing of the white man. He is my father, and I must obey. However reluctantly."

Bodine was glad, but he hid that joy, for he sensed that Two Wolves was filled with sorrow.

"There is more, Bodine. My father has met with government representatives, and he has agreed to the reservation life. The tribe, his followers, will be settled—for the time being—at the Standing Rock Reservation in the Dakotas. Colonel Travers has suggested that you lead them there. Our father would be honored if you would accept."

"You know I will, Two Wolves. But with both happiness and sadness in my heart."

"I understand the feeling, Brother. My own heart is filled with the heaviness of pain. My father has also said that the others will fight, but it is a fight they cannot win."

"When do we leave?"

"We shall begin packing in the morning. It will be a long trek. Without joy."

"But our father's people will be alive, Two Wolves."

"In a manner of speaking."

Chapter 13

The trek of Medicine Horse's people was to begin in five days. They would follow the Yellowstone up about a hundred and fifty miles and then turn straight east into the Dakotas. When they came to the Cannonball, they would turn south until they reached the reservation. They had agreed that the Army could escort them, only if Bodine led the trek.

Colonel Travers jumped at that, silencing Lieutenant Gerry with a hard look. Lieutenant Gerry would lead the Army patrol escorting the Cheyenne to their new home.

And Bodine was not looking forward to several weeks on the trail with Gerry.

All in all, it promised to be a very interesting trip.

What made it even more interesting was that Lone Dog's following had strengthened during this summer of discontent. His band now numbered close to three hundred braves, all well-armed and all cocked and primed for war. Lone Dog and his braves had been making life miserable for many and ending it for a few.

And Lone Dog had made it clear that he considered Medicine Horse a coward for agreeing to a return to reservation life. Lone Dog just might try to attack the column before they got too far along the Yellowstone.

Bodine approached Two Wolves with this theory.

"He would be a fool to do so. The Cheyenne would eat him alive. What he will probably do, if he does anything at all, will be to wait until we return with the Army patrol and attack us then."

Bodine thought about that and agreed with his brother. "These are not green troops, Two Wolves; with the exception of Lieutenant Gerry. They will stand firm."

Two Wolves nodded and turned away. They were almost ready to go. The following dawn.

Medicine Horse stood in the spreading sunlight and looked back at the land the government had promised would be his forever and ever.

"Forever and ever," he muttered. "Strange that with the coming of the white man, how forever is such a short time." He lifted his arms toward the rising sun and spread them as the sun touched his face. "My people shall look no more on this valley. I have spoken and it is so." He turned to face Bodine. "It is time." Medicine Horse walked to his pony and swung onto its back. He rode slowly to his position near the head of the long column and waited, Two Wolves at his side. Two Wolves had cut his long hair and wore jeans and boots and a leather jacket.

Bodine stepped into the saddle and walked Rowdy past his adopted father and his blood brother, past a line of mounted soldiers. He paused at Lieutenant Gerry's side. "All hail the conquering heroes, Lieutenant." Bodine's voice was filled with sarcasm, and it wasn't lost on Lieutenant Gerry "And all that crap. We kill those who fight us and punish those who have been our friends. Let's go!"

For once, Gerry felt some of the emotion of the moment.

"I didn't ask for this assignment, Bodine. And I don't like it. I am aware of the peacefulness of this band of Cheyenne. If it makes any difference to you, I think this is wrong."

Bodine nodded his understanding. "I didn't mean to lash out at you, Lieutenant. We have a job to do, let's do it."

Gerry turned to a sergeant. "Move them out, Sergeant." A few minutes later, as the long column began to stretch out and settle into the march, Bodine said, "I have an uneasy feeling about this, Gerry. I think this is just the beginning of Medicine Horse and his people getting the short end of the stick handed them."

Surprisingly, Gerry said, "I agree with you, Bodine. I think this move to the Dakotas is only a temporary one. I think the government is deliberately separating the Cheyenne. It was my understanding that the permanent reservation for the Northern Cheyenne was to be in Montana, next to the Crow reservation. The borders of the Cheyenne reservation were to be the Tongue to the west and the Rosebud to the East."

"That was my understanding."

"And it could be that the government is trying to separate the Cheyenne for Medicine Horse's own good. To keep his peaceful tribe away from the warring tribe. Have you thought about that?"

"I have to keep that thought in my mind, Gerry. To keep from getting angrier than I am."

"I . . . sort of understand how you feel, Bodine. I think."

The long trek of Medicine Horse and his people from Montana to the Dakotas was made without incident. On the day before they were to be met by the Indian agent at the northernmost tip of the reservation, Medicine Horse came to Bodine.

"We shall say our goodbyes here, my son. You will not look again on my face."

"Medicine Horse, I . . ."

"No! Hear my words. I have placed myself in disgrace to save my little band of Cheyenne. But that is fitting and just. That is the way of a chief. A chief must take both the glory and the humiliation when one or the other is deserved. What I say to you now, hold in your heart and your head and do not let the words leave your tongue. I am entrusting the fate of Two Wolves into your hands. Keep him safe and out of the valley of the Rosebuds. I have had a vision; a vision that will be shared by many chiefs over the coming months. You will learn of the vision when it is time, and not before. After the snow flies this winter, stay away from the river that runs through the Rosebuds." He smiled at his adopted son. "You have been a good son. And I am glad in my heart that you have stopped falling down a lot."

Bodine laughed with the man, then sobered. "Do you know Custer, Medicine Horse?"

"Yellow Hair? Yes. He is a great warrior. Why do you ask that at this time?"

"I had a dream the other night, while we were camped beside the Cannonball. It was . . . disturbing."

"Tell me of this vision."

"It was June, father. The month of the Moon Of Making Fat. I'm sure of that. I saw many soldiers falling upside down into an Indian camp. Yellow Hair was among them. It was a great battle, my father. It was also the beginning of the end."

"For whom?"

"For you."

Medicine Horse smiled and nodded. "We have shared the same vision, my son. That is good and that is bad. It is good that you are truly a human being. It is bad that you must continue the struggle within your heart. Just as your brother, Two Wolves, must always struggle. We have spoken for the last time, my son. This is goodbye. Remember my words."

Medicine Horse walked away into the night. He did not look back at Bodine.

"Heads up," Lieutenant Gerry cautioned his troops just before they pulled out for the return trip. "Lone Dog is probably going to hit us. Bodine thinks it will be when we're only a couple of days from the garrison. We'll be thinking of a warm bed and hot food and a bath and won't be worrying about an Indian attack. I agree with him. But between here and the fort, we've got several thousand other Sioux and Cheyenne to worry about. Not to mention Pawnee and Arapahoe. So ride alert, men."

"Boring," Lieutenant Gerry said on the evening of the second day out. He stretched his legs out and relaxed after a long day in the saddle. "Just damn boring."

"Pray that it stays that way," Two Wolves said. "My father's power will no longer protect us from the renegades, Brother. Especially Lone Dog . . ." Two Wolves stopped speaking and held up a hand. "Silence. Someone comes."

The fire was quickly doused and the men took their positions around the camp. The troopers were armed with six-shooters and single-shot Springfield 1873 carbines. Most of the Indians, with Winchester or Henry repeating rifles, were better armed than the soldiers they fought. The Army just would not—for whatever reason, probably due to some lard-butted armchair general back in Washington—properly arm its men in the western field of operation.

"Oh, please God, help me!" the female voice came out of the darkness.

"Easy," Bodine cautioned. "It could be a ruse to pull us out there. Just stay quiet for a minute."

"Please!" the voice pleaded. "I saw your fire and know

you're soldiers. I've been watching you since you camped. My name is Terri Kelly. The Sioux hit us yesterday morning, down on the Little Missouri. Killed my uncle and aunt and took several prisoners. I'm hungry and cold and scared. Please help me!" she screamed.

"Stand up and walk toward the sound of my voice," Bodine instructed. "If Indians are forcing you to do this, you're going to be caught in a crossfire."

"If I never see another of those murdering savages again it will be fine with me," the woman's words were bitterly offered.

Two Wolves stirred beside Bodine but said nothing. "All right, I see you," Bodine called. "Come on."

"Sharp eyes, boys," Gerry called.

The woman stepped into the protected area of the soldiers' camp. She wore a dress that was no more than rags. It was torn at the bodice and she held that torn strip with one hand, in an effort to cover her breasts. She was only partially successful.

She sank to her knees in the center of the camp and in a weary voice said, "Dear God! Safe at last." Then she collapsed in a dead faint.

"Double the guards," Lieutenant Gerry ordered, as Bodine got his canteen and moved to the woman's side.

He brushed the honey-blond hair back from her forehead and wetted his kerchief, wiping the grime from the woman's face. He noted that she was quite a beauty. Blue eyes, he would bet, and when they opened, he saw that he was right.

She came awake with a start and a small cry.

"Easy now," Bodine cautioned. "You're safe." His eyes drifted to her full breasts and then back to her face.

"Are you sure?" she asked, noting the direction his eyes had taken.

Bodine smiled at her. "I'm sure. The men are rigging some blankets so you can wash up and change clothes. Have you ever worn men's britches? It's the best we can do, I'm afraid."

"Heavens, no!" Then she managed a smile. "Proper young ladies from Chicago don't wear men's britches. But there's a first time for everything."

Then she started to cry uncontrollably.

Bodine was no hand when it came to weeping women. He took off his jacket and rolled it up, putting it under her head, then covering her with a blanket handed him by a soldier. He sat back in a squat, watching her for a time.

Two Wolves brought some coffee and food and placed it beside Bodine. The woman chose that time to wipe her eyes and look at Two Wolves. Although dressed in white man's clothing, there was no mistaking his Indian side. The woman hissed and drew back in fright.

"Relax," Bodine told her. "This is my brother, Sam August Webster Two Wolves. His father, Medicine Horse, was the first Cheyenne to make peace with the whites and that peace is still good. You have nothing to fear here."

"I'll have to take your word for that." She sipped at the hot, strong cowboy coffee as her eyes drifted back and forth between the two men. "There is a slight resemblance, I suppose."

"We're blood brothers, miss," Two Wolves told her. "Bodine saved my life when we both were just boys. My father adopted him into the Cheyenne tribe."

Her eyes touched upon the identical necklaces both men wore. "Bodine . . . the gunfighter?"

"I can use a gun, miss. When I have to. I'm a rancher down in Wyoming and sometimes scout for the Army. What is your name again?"

"Terri. Terri Kelly. I came out here to teach school at a small settlement on the Little Missouri." Her face hardened. "That settlement is no more."

She paused as Lieutenant Gerry squatted down and began taking notes on a small pad.

"Feel like telling us what happened?" the lieutenant asked.

"Can I wash up first?"

"Of course you can." Bodine held out his hand and she took it, very conscious of the strength in that outstretched arm.

On her feet, Bodine noted that she was no shrinking violet. Terri Kelly was a good five-six or five-seven. And her figure was truly magnificent. It was no wonder the braves were after her; she would have been worth a dozen horses in a trade, once she was beaten into submission.

"I'm afraid you'll have to bathe in cold water, Miss Kelly," Gerry told her. And I don't know what we're going to do about footwear for you. Your shoes are just about gone."

"I can fix her some moccasins," Two Wolves said. "It won't take long."

"You don't have a trace of an accent," Terri said, looking at him.

"I was educated back east, Miss Kelly. As was my father. My mother came from a very old New England family. Connections with the *Mayflower,* and all that."

Her suddenly cool eyes told him what she thought of any woman who would marry a red savage. She turned away and walked toward the strung-up blankets.

"Should be an interesting trip back to the fort," Lieutenant Gerry said.

"For some of us," Two Wolves added.

Chapter 14

Bodine did his best to rig up a saddle for the woman to ride sidesaddle, but finally gave it up in frustration. She would just have to ride astride.

Terri was appalled and the men were embarrassed, looking ever'-which-away except at her, but she gamely swung into the saddle just after dawn.

"We've got a long and dangerous way to go, Miss Kelly," Gerry told her. "Right through hostile country. So be prepared for anything."

"After the other night," she said grimly, "I assure you that I am."

"Colonel Travers will want to hear your story when we reach the garrison," Gerry reminded her. "As will I. We only skimmed it last evening."

She put cool blue eyes on the man. "My niece was drawing water when they came. She was thirteen. They ran a lance through her. Her mother, my aunt, ran to her and the savages killed Aunt Helena. My uncle hid me in the cellar just before they overwhelmed him. I lay amid the potatoes and the canned goods listening while they tortured him to death. But they couldn't make him scream." She cut her eyes to Bodine.

"He died well. They will sing songs about him around the fires."

"Barbaric filth!" She spat the words.

"Different cultures, miss," Bodine told her. "I must tell you sometime about American cavalrymen who impaled tiny Indian babies on their swords and then cut off their heads as trophies. I'll tell you about unarmed old Indian men and women who were lined up and shot down for the fun of it. Ten-year-old Indian girls who were literally raped to death. Little Indian boys who were run down and trampled to death under the hooves of the cavalrymen's horses. Savages, Miss Kelly? We have them on both sides. Believe me. I've witnessed it firsthand."

She opened her mouth to speak and Bodine wheeled his horse and rode to the head of the column.

"That insufferable! . . ." She bit back the last.

"He was raised, sort of, by the Cheyenne, Miss Kelly," Lieutenant Gerry told her. "I could not abide the man when I first met him. If you will pardon my language, I thought him to be an arrogant ass. But I've grown to both like him and to respect his judgment. As for what he said about savages on both sides, well, I have to agree with him. I've both seen and heard of some rather ghastly events about the cruelty of whites toward the Indians. And," he was quick to add, "some equally horrible stories about the Indians and their methods of torture."

Terri sighed. "I suppose I have much to learn about the wild frontier. I only got here in June."

"Yes, Miss Kelly," the lieutenant agreed, remembering his own prejudices and misconceptions as he arrived on the frontier. "You have much to learn."

* * *

"What are we going to do with her, Bodine?" Gerry asked over the noon meal.

"That's Colonel Travers' worry, Gerry. How'd she get out of the root cellar, anyway?"

"They burned the house down over her. She breathed through a tiny hole in the foundation. She waited for several hours after they'd left before making a break for it. The entire tiny settlement was gone; burned bodies everywhere. The men horribly mutilated. Said she just ran in blind fear. Then she came to her senses and began following what she thought was the Little Missouri. That's when she found us."

"She's a lucky woman. If a brave had seen her, they would have taken her and traded her for a dozen horses . . . after a time."

"That is disgusting, Bodine!"

"That's the way it is, Gerry. You're from Maryland, aren't you?"

"Yes."

"Did your family hold slaves before the civil war?" The lieutenant sighed. "Yes, they did."

"Beat them, trade them, sell them?"

"Yes, Bodine! So I am told. I do not remember it. All that was stopped in our family long before the Civil War."

"Right," Bodine said dryly.

Gerry shook his head. "This is a confusing war, Bodine. I thought, before I came out here, that the issues were all clear-cut. I . . . find that is not the way it is. But I am a soldier, Bodine. I will do my duty and obey orders."

"Right," Bodine said.

Terri slowly began to warm toward Bodine as the trek back to the fort continued. Two Wolves did not stay with the column, choosing instead to range out far on either side, or in front. Bodine knew he was deliberately staying away from the woman.

"You've been out here long?" she asked him.

"I was born out here. My father and mother came out years back. The first whites in the valley. Carved a place to live out of a wilderness. Fought Indians and blizzards and droughts and outlaws."

The only sound for a time was the clop of their horses' hooves. Bodine was very conscious of the woman's eyes on him.

"Do you have a wife and children, Bodine? Is that your first name?"

Bodine smiled. "No, to both your questions. And my name is Matt, but everyone calls me Bodine."

"I expected a much older man. Your reputation would certainly suggest it."

"I never asked for that reputation, Terri. But I don't push worth a damn. A lot of men have died because they don't understand what it means to strap on a gun out here. They don't—or didn't—understand that when a boy straps on a gun out here, that boy becomes a man. And the man is expected to use the gun if called out. Out here, Terri, a man's word is his bond. That is why in the West, calling a man a liar can be a killing offense. Nobody trusts a liar. There is no law, or very little of it. From my ranch, I don't even know where the nearest law is. There is a saying, I suppose it sprang from the lips of someone out here, that in the West, a man kills his own snakes and saddles his own horse."

"I will admit I have a lot to learn, but I still find it all very barbaric."

"It is barbaric, Terri. I've read where you have lots of police in Chicago to fight your battles for you. To control the thugs and hooligans and others of that stripe. It isn't that way out here. We usually hang a rustler on the spot. And we hang horse thieves when we catch them. You've been on foot out here; what do you think would have happened to you if you had not stumbled upon us."

"I . . . imagine I would have died, on foot."

"That's why we hang horse thieves."

"Your blood brother seems to be deliberately avoiding me."

"I'm sure he is. He's trying to keep down any confrontation, knowing how you feel about Indians." Bodine cut his eyes. "And speaking of Two Wolves," he said, watching his brother race his horse toward the column, and that was something he would not do unless there was trouble on his heels.

"Gerry!" Bodine shouted. "Head for that creek over there. I think we've got troubles!"

Two Wolves slid his horse to a stop. "Lone Dog and his bunch about a half mile away, Brother. And his following has grown."

"Get Terri to those cottonwoods over there by the creek. At least we'll have water and banks for some cover. Go, Brother." Bodine whacked Terri's horse on the rump and then gave Rowdy his head, racing toward Gerry.

Far in the distance, even over the pounding of hooves, the war cries could be heard, coming closer behind them.

Lieutenant Gerry's command was getting into position along the banks of the creek. In a wider and deeper part of the creek, sheltered by high banks and cottonwoods, the horses were being held.

Bodine, Winchester in hand, leaped from the saddle and got into position on the protected side of the cool and mossy bank.

Lone Dog and his braves circled about three hundred yards out, riding low against the necks of their ponies, offering little target for the short-barreled, single-shot carbines of the soldiers.

"Two Wolves!" Lone Dog called, his voice just reaching those on the banks of the creek. "You would dare to fire at me?"

"You would dare to attack me?" Two Wolves countered with a yell. "The son of Medicine Horse, the greatest Cheyenne warrior who ever lived?"

Lone Dog met with several of his sub-chiefs for a moment, then yelled, "Then ride out and live, Two Wolves. And take Bodine with you. We want the woman."

"Go to hell!" Two Wolves shouted.

Terri looked at the half breed, with a new understanding of him in her eyes.

"Your blood will stain the waters of the creek just like the soldiers, Two Wolves!" Lone Dog shouted. "We want the woman."

Bodine looked at Gerry, who was beside Terri on the bank. "If they overrun us, save one bullet for Miss Kelly, Gerry."

The lieutenant nodded his head, a grim expression on his face.

Terri's face was very pale.

"Get ready," Two Wolves told them all, the hammer reared back on his Winchester. "They're just about ready to charge us."

"The Cheyenne with Lone Dog are pulling back," Bodine observed. "They don't want to fight the son of Medicine Horse."

"Or Bodine," Two Wolves added.

About forty of the braves with Lone Dog had withdrawn, to sit their ponies on the crest of a hill, watching and waiting.

With a cry that seemed to come from a single throat, the braves of Lone Dog charged the creek from both sides. Bodine and Two Wolves knocked half a dozen sprawling, commencing firing with their long barreled Winchesters a few seconds before the troopers. A half dozen more ponies were soon riderless as the seasoned cavalrymen opened fire.

Lone Dog waved his braves back. A dozen dead and wounded was just no good. The Indians had long ago learned that to stand and die was stupid. Better to ride off and fight another day.

They rode off, but they did not go far.

"What are they doing?" Terri asked.

"Determining their medicine is bad for this day," Two Wolves told her, overhearing the question asked of Gerry. "Lone Dog has lost a dozen or more men in less than a minute. That is not good. You see the flankers, Bodine?"

"I see them."

"What flankers?" Gerry asked, looking all around him. He could see nothing.

"Coming toward us through the grass," Two Wolves told him. "Crawling on their bellies. See that bush just to the right of that lightning-blazed tree?"

"Yes."

"It won't be there a minute from now. The bush, not the tree," he added with a wry smile.

Gerry glanced at him, giving him a jaundiced look that even under these circumstances brought a smile to Terri's lips. When the lieutenant again looked over the terrain, the bush had moved several yards.

Bodine lifted his rifle and sighted in the bush. He took up slack on the trigger and fired. A brave screamed and leaped up, his chest smeared with blood. Bodine shot him again and the brave fell over on his back and did not move.

"Here they are!" a trooper yelled, just as the Indians leaped up and closed with the troopers. Some of the Sioux had crept to within a few yards of the creek, as silent as death.

"Every other man, eyes to the front!" Gerry yelled, as a brave leaped at him and Lone Dog's braves charged on their ponies.

The lieutenant lifted his pistol and fired pointblank into the Indian's chest, the slug turning the warrior around in mid-air and twisting his painted face into a pain-filled mask of hate and fury. Gerry lifted his six-shooter and shot the brave in the face, ending it.

Two Wolves shot a brave in the head just as Bodine clubbed another with his rifle butt, kicked him between the legs with a boot and smashed his throat with the butt of his Winchester. Lifting the rifle, he shot another one in the belly and again in the chest.

A hoarse choking cry ended the brief battle. Bodine looked toward Terri. A brave had leaped at her and she had picked up the guidon carrying the colors. The brave had impaled himself on the pole, the end of it going directly in and through the belly. He lay writhing and coughing. Two Wolves walked over and shot the warrior in the head, ending his death-struggles.

Two Wolves stared at the brave for a moment. *"Wohk pe nu numu,"* he said.

Terri looked at Bodine.

"Painted Thunder," Bodine told her. "The son of Gray Thunder, a sub-chief of the Sioux." He glanced at Gerry. "This is not good for us."

"Hell, man! They attacked us!"

Bodine shrugged his shoulders. "We're on their lands."

"Did you see the Arapahoes and the Ho He among them, Brother?" Two Wolves asked.

"Yes. And some Blackfeet and Cree. They're coming together, and that's even worse."

"Let's get out of here." Gerry started to rise.

Two Wolves pushed him back down to the moss. "Not unless you have a death wish, man. Lone Dog is crazy, but he's not stupid. They're just over the rise, waiting for us to do something like that."

"Then we'll stay here," the lieutenant said. "We have ample water and plenty of rations. We'll be safe tonight," he assured Terri with a glance.

"How do you figure that?" Bodine asked.

"Indians don't fight at night," Gerry said smugly.

Both Bodine and Two Wolves smiled. "Many Apaches don't fight at night," Two Wolves told him. "Depending on the tribe, many others don't either; their fear is that if they are killed at night, their spirits will forever wander. But don't take any bets on this bunch not fighting at night. It all depends on their medicine."

The sounds of chanting drifted to them. "What are they doing?" Terri asked.

Both Bodine and Two Wolves listened carefully, then glanced at one another. "They're questioning their medicine for this day," Two Wolves said. "I think it's over. If they start the chant for the dead warriors, we'll know it's over."

After a time, the chanting changed, then stopped. A silence crept over the land, broken only by a horse stamping its foot in the muddy, churned-up creek bottom.

Bodine stood up. "It's over for this day, I'm thinking. We'll wait a few minutes, then get out of here. We'll ride like hell for a time, eat, then ride some more before we make a cold camp for the night. With any kind of luck, we can stay ahead of them. They'll have to take some time to find and to gather up their dead, then carry them off to prepare the warriors for prayers and burial. That'll give us about an hour or so."

"We'll drag some of the bodies off and hide them best we can," Two Wolves suggested. "That will slow them up even more."

"That's grotesque!" Gerry said.

"Beats the hell out of being dead," Bodine said.

"I agree," Terri said. She looked around her. "We've got

some wounded. I know something about nursing. Let's get to work."

She'll do, Bodine thought. She's got the stuff to last out here. But there is something about her I just don't trust. He cut his eyes to Two Wolves, who was also watching the woman.

Two Wolves met his glance and yet another challenge rose up between the two blood brothers. But this time, Bodine was not about to pick up the gauntlet.

Chapter 15

They rode hard for several hours, stopped and hurriedly fixed a meal; then it was back in the saddle again, putting more miles between them and Lone Dog's rampaging war party. When they finally made a cold camp for the night, it was carefully chosen for defense.

They were up and moving as the first beams of silver creased the eastern sky. They rode for an hour, with scouts out in four directions, then stopped and fixed coffee and bacon and bread.

"Sam is really a very striking-looking man," Terri said to Bodine.

"Who?" Bodine looked up from his battered tin coffee cup.

"Your brother!"

"Oh! Two Wolves. Yeah . . . I guess so." Then he smiled. "A couple of days ago you wouldn't have spit on him if he was on fire. What changed your mind?"

"The way he told that Lone Dog to go to hell back at the creek." She inched closer to him. "Both of you could have ridden out, couldn't you? Safely, I mean."

"Yes," Bodine admitted. "We could have." All his defenses suddenly went up and he found himself liking the woman less and less. He had almost made up his mind to ask her to come spend some time at his father and mother's ranch. Now he just wished this journey were over and he were rid of her. That something about her that he just did not trust reared up again. And Bodine paid attention to his hunches.

Brother of mine, Bodine thought, if you want this woman, you can sure have her. But be careful. She's a lot tougher than she first appeared to be the other night, and she's got more twists and turns than a mountain trail. And I think I'd rather bed down with a snake.

"You have a big ranch, Matt?"

"Not too big. 'Bout a hundred thousand acres, I reckon."

Her mouth dropped open. But before she could speak, he added, "My dad's spread is about four times that big."

"Four-hundred *thousand* acres?"

"Yeah. And since Two Wolves is half white, and can own land, his father, Medicine Horse, had my father file on land for him. Two Wolves owns a pretty respectable spread, stretching from where our two ranches butt together all the way to the Montana line. There's a cabin on it, too. Snug little place built on a flat, overlooking a little creek." And I hope that you and Two Wolves will be very happy there, Terri. And do come to visit. About once a year will be plenty.

Bodine felt guilty about those thoughts; felt like a traitor to his brother. But he just didn't like this woman. She had a staying quality to her—he wouldn't deny that—but he didn't think she had fifteen cents worth of loyalty in her. Earlier, Bodine had seen her batting her eyes at Lieutenant Gerry.

The woman was making sure all bets were covered, for a fact.

"Mount up!" Gerry gave the orders. "We'll make the Yellowstone by late afternoon."

Two Wolves joined Bodine later that afternoon. He wore

a smile that could not have been removed with a tomahawk. "What a delightful woman, Brother!"

Bodine sighed and looked at him. "I assume you are speaking of Miss Kelly?"

"Bodine, she is the only woman with us, is she not?"

Bodine grunted.

"What's the matter with you, Brother? The way your mouth is all poked out you look like you have a toothache."

"I do not have a toothache and my mouth is not all poked out."

"Of course not. That must be why you look like a chipmunk with a mouth full of acorns."

Bodine opened his mouth to warn Two Wolves about Terri. Then he closed it. What proof did he have? None. Except a gut feeling, and that might have been brought on by something he ate.

"You were about to say? . . ." Two Wolves urged.

"Not a thing, Brother." You're a big boy, you figure it out."

"Didn't you tell me that the valley needed a schoolteacher?"

Oh, boy! "Yes, I did. We have a school but no teacher. You have someone in mind?"

"Very funny, Brother. As a matter of fact, I mentioned it to Terri. She's interested."

Oh, so it's Terri now, is it? "That's nice."

"She's highly qualified."

"I'm sure she is."

"So?"

"So what, Brother? Why don't you speak to my mother and father about it? They'll get together with the other farmers and ranchers and decide."

"But you won't give her your endorsement?"

"I didn't say that."

Two Wolves looked at him for a moment. "You didn't have to." He turned his horse and rode back to Terri.

Lieutenant Gerry rode up. "What a delightful young lady!"

Bodine rolled his eyes. Here we go again.

"So well-educated. She's the type of person we need out here on the frontier."

"Right."

"It'll be a lucky man who wins her hand."

Lucky if she leaves you with your shirt and boots.

"Right," he said.

"I don't mean to babble on, Bodine. But I am quite impressed with her. To have such spirit after her terrible ordeal escaping from the savages."

It would serve Lone Dog right if he had taken her, Bodine thought. He'd have probably given someone a dozen horses to take her off his hands. "She's had a rough time of it, all right." But why didn't she kick up a fuss and demand that we chase after the Indians and rescue the prisoners they supposedly took? She said she had family and friends among them. Odd, very odd.

Gerry stood up in his stirrups and pointed, a smile on his face. "The Yellowstone, Bodine." He sat back in his saddle and rode forward, to take the point.

Bodine looked back. Terri was riding beside Two Wolves, and jabbering like an excited squirrel. From the expression on his face, Two Wolves was taking the bait—hook, line, and bobber.

"Damn!" Bodine said, glancing back again.

"She's a looker, all right," Sergeant McGuire said, catching the glance as he walked his horse up to Bodine's side. "Both the lieutenant and Two Wolves seem to be quite taken by her."

"And you, Sergeant?"

"Not me, lad. I'm too old a dog; I've sniffed too many trails to be taken in by the likes of her." He was silent for a moment. "And I hope I'm not stepping too far out of bounds by saying that to you."

"You're not. I don't trust her either."

"You're wise beyond your years, then."

"I'm just not a trusting man, Sergeant."

"With Miss Kelly about, that would be wise. Every time she looks at me I feel like I'm naked and shivering in the cold."

The column followed the Yellowstone down to a little town that would soon be named Miles City. There they stopped long enough for Miss Kelly to take a proper bath and to purchase new clothing—with money she borrowed from Lieutenant Gerry and Two Wolves. Bodine had no intention of giving her a nickel. He had judiciously avoided her the past few days on the trail, assuming the role of scout just to stay away from the column.

The column cut south and slightly west, following the Tongue as it wound its way to the garrison, still some one hundred miles farther on.

And as Bodine knew he would, Two Wolves came to his side just before Bodine pulled out for the day's scouting.

"You don't like her, do you, Bodine?"

Bodine faced his blood brother. "No, I don't, Two Wolves."

"She told me you didn't. She's terribly hurt by your attitude toward her."

"I imagine she'll get over it, Brother."

"She's really a very nice person."

"Did I say she wasn't?"

"I need your endorsement to get her on as teacher in the valley, Bodine. You know how many of the people feel about me."

"That attitude will change as the story spreads about you facing Lone Dog and his braves by the creek. As soon as you get settled in at your place the people will gradually begin to accept you. You know that."

"They will not forget the cut fences and the sprung traps."

"In time, Brother. In time."

"You're avoiding the issue, Bodine."

"I'll make a deal with you, Two Wolves. I won't say a word for her or against her. I'll deliberately head for my place as soon as we get close enough, and that will give you a free hand to speak to my parents in her behalf." He looked over his saddle at his brother. "And that is the best I can do."

"I am interested in her as a woman, Bodine, and she is interested in me as a man."

"I gathered as much. Good luck." Bodine swung into the saddle.

"You're jealous, aren't you?" Two Wolves looked up at Bodine.

"You have to be crazy to ask that! I couldn't sleep at night knowing that damn woman was in the same house with me."

Two Wolves stepped back, a hard glint in the dark eyes. "That will be the only time I shall allow you to speak about her in such a manner."

Bodine's smile was very thin. "Don't crowd me, Sam. We've play-fought all our lives. But you back me into a corner, and I'll hurt you. Now you want that woman, you can sure have her. Just keep her away from me."

Two Wolves' eyes darkened further. "It seems this journey has done more than mark the beginning of the end for my father and his people, Bodine."

"Only if you let it, Brother."

Two Wolves dropped his hand from Rowdy's mane and stepped back. "You're judging her without knowing anything about her. That's not like you."

"Study the black widow spider, Sam. Especially the male. Watch what happens to him when the female is finished. Watch very carefully, and make certain you don't end up the same way. Whether you believe it or not, you are still my brother, and I care for you."

Two Wolves touched the necklace he wore. "In words only, Bodine. Nothing else. Not anymore." He turned and walked away, his back stiff with anger.

Bodine did not try to stop him. He looked over at Terri and met her eyes. She was smiling at him; a victorious smile.

Bodine had seen that smile before. On a rattlesnake.

Chapter 16

Bodine left the column long before it reached the fort, despite Lieutenant Gerry's protests that it was not safe for Bodine to be riding off alone.

Bodine rode off alone.

He cut straight south through the heavily-timbered wilderness. At a trading post on the Pumpkin, he stopped for supplies and to listen to any gossip there might be from the men gathered around the plank bar, the heavy plank set up on two empty barrels.

The West of the 1870's was a vast and lonely place, but with few settlers, so nearly everybody either knew or knew of nearly everyone else within a given area. The men drinking at the bar knew Bodine, but that did not stop them from talking.

"Tom Thomas done bought all the land around Cutter," one bewhiskered old man said, nursing his beer. "All them men of his'n done each filed on a quarter-section and proved it up, then Thomas bought it from them. He owns land farther than the eye can see all around that town. He's gonna be a big man soon, I'm thinkin'."

"He was already a big man," another said. "Once he got over that puttin' down Bodine give him."

Bodine caught the sly look given him by the men lined up at the bar. He chose to ignore the comment and just quietly sipped his beer.

Bodine heard the slow clop of horses' hooves on the road outside the trading post. He did not have to slip the thongs from the hammers of his guns. He had done that the instant his boots left the stirrups and touched ground. That was instinct with Bodine.

"They tell me that Tom Thomas done put up a thousand dollars for any man who brings in Bodine across a saddle." The words reached Bodine's ears. "All sorts of gunslicks driftin' in the country. Word is that the money is due to go up most any time."

"Where'd you hear this?" Bodine asked.

"At the Kittycat in Cutter," a man said. "Come from the bartender's mouth hisself."

"A couple weeks ago," another added. "So odds is the ante on you has done gone up, Bodine."

Bodine thought that was a reasonable assumption. He listened to the creak of saddle leather as several men dismounted and stretched muscles after hours in the saddle. He hoped it was just a couple of cowboys; but he doubted his luck would be that good.

Without turning around, he said, "Who's coming in, barkeep?"

"Gunnies, Bodine. Three of them. One of 'em is Stutterin' Smith. I don't know them other two. But they look mean."

Boots thudded on the rough boards and spurs jingled as the batwings to the bar part of the trading post were pushed open. Bodine did not turn around. It was dim in the near-windowless room, and he doubted that the men would recognize him until their eyes adjusted from the bright sunlight of the outside.

"B . . . b . . . b . . . Bring a b . . . b . . . bottle over here, Fats," Stutterin' stuttered at the barkeep. "And b . . . be damn quick ab . . . ab . . . about it."

Stutterin' Smith might have difficulty speaking. but he was hell on wheels with a six-gun, and Bodine knew he would soon be facing a topnotch gunslick. He didn't know the other two, but if they were riding with Stutterin', they were good.

Bodine signaled the bartender over. He came, but he didn't like being this close to what he figured would soon be the line of fire.

"You sure those boys work for Thomas?" Bodine said in a low voice.

"Yes, sir. I'm sure. Now can I please get out of the way?"

"Move."

Bodine drained his beer and held the mug in his left hand. He walked across the rough boards to the table where the three men were sitting.

"Somethang on your m . . . m . . . mind?" Stutterin' looked up at Bodine.

"Staying alive would be first and foremost," Bodine replied with a smile. "There's lot of bad hombres roaming about the countryside. Most of them scum that work for Tom Thomas."

The barroom became very quiet as those words settled in.

One of the men seated around the table cursed, lifting his eyes to Bodine. "You best watch your smart mouth, mister. 'Fore someone takes them guns of yourn and slaps you silly with 'em."

'You feel like you're a big enough man to do that?" Bodine laid down the challenge.

The man started to rise.

Stutterin' pushed him back into the chair. He looked up at Bodine. "W . . . w . . . what's your interest in all this, m . . . m . . . mister?"

"Very personal. My name's Bodine."

Stutterin's face hardened as the two with him uttered low curses. Stutterin' did some fast figuring. He knew that this close, everyone involved was going to get lead in them. And he had heard too many stories about the young man called Bodine to dismiss him as a lightweight. If Matt Bodine was all mouth, as Thomas used to enjoy saying, Thomas wouldn't have gotten the snot whipped out of him.

One man started to rise, his hands lowering to his guns. Bodine swung the heavy beer mug, catching the man in the forehead. The mug shattered, but not before cutting a deep gash in the man's head and knocking him to the floor, out of it for a few minutes. Bodine kept his right hand close to the butt of his Colt.

Bodine faced the second man across the rickety table. Stutterin' kept his seat warm and his mouth shut. He was too old a dog to buy into this game. He'd wait and see just how good Bodine was.

"I'm gonna be a rich man when I collect all that reward money that's on your head, Bodine," the gunny snarled.

"No," Bodine told him. "You're just going to be a dead man."

The gunslick grabbed for the butt of his gun.

Bodine shot him in the guts before the barrel could clear leather. The two-bit gunhand staggered backward, losing his six-shooter. He made a grab for his second gun. A heavy pounding struck him in the chest and the light around him began to fade. He stood for a moment, staring at the tall young man in front of him. He just couldn't believe it. Bodine had drawn his right-hand Colt and fired so fast the motion wasn't even a discernible blur. The gunhand dropped to his knees on the dirty floor and toppled over.

Bodine holstered both Colts and looked at Stutterin'. "You feel lucky, Stutterin'?"

"C . . . c . . . cain't say that I do, B . . . B . . . Bodine."

The man with the bleeding forehead lurched to his feet

with a curse and grabbed for a gun. Bodine hit him with a hard fist and knocked the man through the dirty front window of the trading post. He rolled off the porch and flopped on the ground. The man staggered to his feet and then made the mistake of trying to shove Rowdy out of the way. The horse bit him on the arm, bringing more blood and a scream of pain. Rowdy jerked the reins loose from the hitch rail and tried to stomp the man. The two-bit gunhand hurriedly staggered back into the trading post, blood pouring from his badly bitten arm.

"I think my wing's busted," he gasped. "Somebody ought to kill that damned horse."

Rowdy came through the batwings like a horse out of hell and knocked the man sprawling to the floor. Rowdy then proceeded to use his steel-shod hooves to make a mess out of the man's chest and belly before several of those around the bar could drag the now unconscious gunny away. He left a trail of blood across the sawdust.

Rowdy stuck his big head across the bar, his furious eyes on the barkeep and his big teeth bared.

"Jesus Christ!" the man yelled. "What does he want from me?"

"Give him a bucket of beer," Bodine told the badly frightened man. "That'll calm him down."

Rowdy stuck his head into the bucket of beer and drank noisily while Stutterin' Smith sat at the table and shook his head in disbelief.

"You and Rowdy finish your drinks, Stutterin'," Bodine told the Montana gunhand. "And then me and Rowdy will go our way and you can take these two-bit friends of yours back to Cutter and give them to Tom Thomas. With my compliments."

Stutterin' sighed. "I reckon I can do t . . . t . . . that."

"I reckon you better do that."

Rowdy belched and used his nose to shove the empty

bucket off the bar. The barkeep jumped as the bucket clattered to the floor.

"Git that big ugly son of a bitch outta here!" he hollered.

Rowdy turned his back to the man and broke wind.

True to his word, Bodine did not stop at his parents' ranch. He rode straight to his spread and began helping his few hands get ready for what was seemingly going to be a bad winter along the Powder. For a week he did nothing except move cattle from the higher graze and chop firewood, stacking it alongside the cabin.

At the beginning of his second week back home, as the winds were beginning to hold a sharp edge to them, his father rode down from his place on the Crazy Woman, accompanied by several of his hands. For with the Indian situation as it was, it was not safe to ride alone.

Over coffee, Bodine's father asked, "You and Two Wolves ridin' on opposite sides of the creek, boy?"

"That's one way of putting it."

"I took one look at that woman he brought over to be the new schoolteacher and voted against her at the meetin'."

"And? . . ."

"The others liked her. She's the new teacher at the school."

Bodine shook his head in disgust. "Something about that woman raises my hackles, Dad. I just don't trust her."

"Your ma said the same thing. But there's nothing we can do about it. She was chosen."

"And Two Wolves is in love." It was not a question.

"Head over hocks. And I don't think that woman gives two hoots in hell for him. She's playin' a game with him, son. Battin' her eyes at that lieutenant while Two Wolves does all the work around her little place over by the school. And one of my men seen Tom Thomas come courtin' her."

"Does Two Wolves know that?"

"No. I don't think so. Enough about that, boy. What's this about a bounty on your head and this gunfight you was in over at the trading post?"

Bodine brought him up to date.

His father listened and then slowly nodded his head. "Well, you and me are alone in our thinking about Tom Thomas, son. The other ranchers like him; think he hung the moon and stars. And they don't like it 'cause you whipped him."

Bodine shrugged his indifference and then smiled at the irony of it. "You mean, Dad, the ranchers and farmers are now accepting Two Wolves as a neighbor, but rejecting me?" Bodine laughed out loud. "Well, at least something good came of it."

His father was less than amused. "Tom Thomas is sayin' that Two Wolves came to his senses and accepted his white side while you seem to be leanin' toward the Indians. That ain't good, boy."

"They'll either get over it, or they won't, Dad. Hell, Dad, Two Wolves and Lieutenant Gerry and Miss Kelly can verify that I killed Indians during that fight at the creek. What's the matter with these people around here?"

"Many of them are jealous, boy. You and me, we've got the biggest spreads in North Wyoming. Together, we control over half a million acres, near as I can figure. That makes a certain type of person edgy. There's a lot of minerals on our range, Matt. We got good water and good graze. I figure that when the Indian trouble is over, we're gonna have to fight some of our neighbors, son."

Bodine's gaze was hard and bleak. "The Cheyenne have a saying that might fit those neighbors, Dad."

"Oh?"

"It's a good day to die."

Chapter 17

Before the snows came and the icy winds would blow, Bodine saddled Rowdy early one morning and leading two pack horses, he set out for the settlement that was only a couple of years away from being officially named Sheridan.

As he rode, Bodine mused over why this land was and had been in so much conflict; why were the Indians and the whites killing each other over land that really not many on either side wanted to live in? This particular part of Wyoming did not contain enough agricultural land to support a great many settlers. And the buffalo were rapidly being killed off, so it was not such a desirable place for large numbers of red or white.

On his way to the settlement, Bodine would pass the ghosts that wandered the long silent battlefields of the Wagon Box fight, and the Fetterman slaughter, where back in '66 Crazy Horse and Red Cloud trapped and killed Captain Fetterman and his entire command of 79 officers and enlisted men and two civilian scouts. One third of Fort Phil Kearney's garrison.

No, Bodine knew the current wars were not over control

of territory—the Indians really didn't want it. Wyoming just happened to be where the disputes between the red and the white person's way of life were being settled. And settled they would be—Bodine knew that. There was no way the Indians could win the overall war. They would win some battles, but lose the war.

And perhaps that was as it was meant to be by the Creator of all things. Far be it for Bodine to attempt to second-guess God.

Bodine crossed the Crazy Woman just as it stopped its almost direct southerly flow and began a gentle curve toward the southern tip of the Bighorns. As Bodine rode through the ash and box-elders and toward the rolling hills that, come spring, would have grass clear up to the stirrups, he tensed as Rowdy's ears came to attention. Rowdy suddenly whinnied and Bodine threw himself out of the saddle, taking his Winchester with him as he hit the ground arid rolled just as a bullet sang over the now empty saddle.

Bodine grabbed the reins and pulled Rowdy and the packhorses back toward the banks of the Crazy Woman. He slid down the bank and the horses followed. Bodine quickly built himself a little fort out of old, fallen logs and scooped up dirt. He had water, he had food, he had plenty of ammunition, and the horses were safe. Now all he had to do was wait.

Was it Indians or some of Tom Thomas's men? He'd bet on the latter. He settled down to wait them out.

Two Wolves had left Terri the night before—after a heated argument about Bodine—left in a rage before he lost complete control and belted the woman. He had been raised a Cheyenne, and Cheyenne men were none too gentle in keeping a woman in her place. But all that was behind him now, and he had to keep it behind him.

Two Wolves, or Sam, as Terri and the other whites in the

area had taken to calling him, had ridden long into the night until coming to the Crazy Woman. There, he had made his camp. He had lingered long over coffee and jerky for breakfast and then just saddled up and started wandering, following the Crazy Woman south.

His thoughts were many and jumbled. He felt he truly loved the schoolteacher; had fallen head over boots in love with a woman for the first time in his life. He also felt, with a sour sense of Bodine's saying: I told you so, that Terri was using him. He knew Terri was playing Lieutenant Gerry for the fool, and rumors had reached his ears that Tom Thomas was slipping through her back door late at night, enjoying her perfumed favors.

The ruthlessness of his thoughts upon hearing those rumors jarred Two Wolves right down to his toenails, and he realized that he truly was only a few steps away from what many claimed him to be: a savage.

But was it not normal among men—red or white or yellow or whatever—to behave possessively and sometimes irrationally when affairs of the heart are concerned?

Two Wolves thought so.

But what sort of game was Terri playing? How did she hope to gain by it?

Damn! but he missed Bodine. Missed the close comradeship they had shared over the years. How long had it been since they'd sat and talked? Weeks. But they both had stiff necks, Two Wolves reluctantly admitted, and neither man was given to apologizing.

Two Wolves rode slowly, following the Crazy Woman south.

Bodine had located the positions of two of his ambushers, confirming in his mind that they were not Indians. He would not have been able to spot them so quickly had they been warriors.

Bodine shifted positions and reared the hammer back on his Winchester, laying some .44s around the area where he'd spotted one man. He smiled as he heard the yell; but it wasn't a yell of pain, more like a man very much surprised. He ducked down behind the river bank as the lead was returned. The rifle fire hit nothing, but it did confirm the number of men Bodine was facing. He figured six of them, and they had him in a pretty tight hole. At least for now. Come dark he could slip out easily. But he would have to be very alert and watch behind him. If they boxed him in, that could mean his death.

Bodine waited and watched from behind his hastily built fort.

Two Wolves thought he heard gunfire, but he couldn't be sure. He sat his horse for a moment and listened. Nothing. Just as he was about to swing west, away from the river, the gunfire came again, very faint, but very real. One rifle would bark, then a half dozen or more would reply.

Somebody was in trouble. A fight with Indians? Maybe. But somehow Two Wolves doubted it. Indians would not waste that much ammunition. Two Wolves urged his horse on, but very slowly.

A bullet had tossed sand and pebbles into Bodine's face, not doing any damage except to anger the man. They were getting his range now, and he could expect conditions to worsen from this point on. He guessed the rumors to be true about Thomas upping the ante on his head. He had heard amounts ranging from five thousand dollars to ten thousand. The man sure knew how to hate.

Bodine decided to take the offensive. The horses had water and enough graze to keep them happy for a time. What he didn't want was for some stray or deliberate bullet to kill one of them, especially Rowdy. If that happened, Bodine knew how to make dying a terribly hard and long process for the man or men responsible.

And he was not above doing it.

Bodine left his makeshift fort and started up-river, hugging the bank as he worked his way toward a stand of trees that would enable him to leave the river and get into the thin timber where the gunmen were hiding, tossing lead at him.

Two Wolves had crossed the Crazy Woman twice, trying to determine which side of the river the gunfire was coming from. He finally decided the gunfire was coming from the north side of the river, just about where the Crazy Woman curved toward the west. He moved away from the river to stay in the rolling hills. That move, he hoped, would put him above the heavier gunfire that was coming from those half dozen or so who had the lone man pinned down. Then he would decide whether to help or not.

Bodine had made the thin timber and had spotted two of his ambushers just as Two Wolves, on foot now, and above the attackers, had caught a glimpse of Rowdy. Two Wolves smiled thinly and squatted down, trying to determine how best he could help his ornery blood brother.

Bodine sighted a man in, took up the slack on the trigger, and let the rifle bang. The slug struck the man in the belly and his scream reverberated around the rolling hills as his numbed fingers lost their grip on the rifle and the man pitched forward, beginning what was to be a hard death under the hard, thin sunlight of the Wyoming fall.

Two Wolves leveled his Winchester and shot an ambusher through the neck, the heavy slug almost taking the man's head off. The slug cut the spinal cord and the man slumped bonelessly to the ground.

Two Wolves cupped one hand to the side of his mouth

and called a meadow lark's lilt. Bodine smiled and returned the call.

One of the attackers, sensing the battle was going sour, tried to make it to his horse. Two slugs, one from below and one from above, cut him down, the .44s taking the man in the back and the side.

Another tried to snake his way to the horses. Two Wolves nailed him before he'd gone ten yards, the bullet breaking the man's leg. He lay on the cold ground and yowled his pain.

"We yield!" The call came from the hills. "I'm layin' down my rifle and standin' up."

"Me, too!" the last man yelled.

Both men stood up, weaponless, their hands held in the air.

Bodine and Two Wolves gathered up all the weapons while the prisoners, both of them sullen-faced and silent, sat on the cold ground, their hands behind their heads, watching as Bodine and Two Wolves stripped the bodies of the dead and the man with the broken leg and then they were tied into and over the saddles. Then they watched as the two remaining horses were stripped of their saddles.

"Now you two stand up and peel down to your wherewith-alls," Bodine told them.

"Do what?"

"Strip!" Bodine told the man. "Buck-assed naked and do it quick!"

"I ain't a gonna do it!" one of the men said.

Bodine hit him in the mouth with the butt of his Winchester, smashing the man's lips and knocking out teeth.

"Now what do you have to say?" Bodine asked.

"Awright, awright!" the man spoke through bloody lips.

The two men slowly began to peel until they stood naked and shivering in the cold winds.

"Ain't you even gonna let us have no boots?"

"Nope. Now get on your horses and ride."

"Bareback and with us nekked?" the second man squalled. "Man, that ain't decent!"

"Neither are you," Bodine told him. "Now get on your horses and ride out."

"Man, they's Injuns out there! They find us like this and we're in for a bad time of it."

"That is my hope." Bodine smiled at him. "We'll probably hear the story of you boys riding in when we get to the settlement. Now get out of here."

Cursing, the men rode out, leading the horses carrying the dead and wounded behind them. Bodine and Two Wolves walked back to the river's edge.

Bodine turned to face Two Wolves.

Two Wolves lifted his chin and said, with a very haughty tone, "I have saved your life, and a life saved is a life owed. Now we are even."

"You didn't save jack-crap, Sam. So get off your throne, King."

"Bah! They would have killed you had I not arrived in time to rescue you."

"Why . . . you pompous jackass! If I wasn't in a hurry to get to the settlement, I've a good notion to whip your butt and knock some sense into your head."

"Not on your best day, Bodine."

Bodine unbuckled his gunbelt and laid it on a log. Two Wolves did the same. As he was straightening up, Bodine hit him in the mouth with an uppercut that stood Two Wolves up on his toes. Bodine followed that with a hard, straight left to the belly.

Two Wolves hit the ground and rolled, coming up fast and with a fistful of sand, which he tossed in Bodine's eyes. With Bodine momentarily blinded by the sand, Two Wolves busted him in the mouth with a hard fist and then brought a left around that landed solidly against Bodine's jaw.

Bodine went down and grabbed Two Wolves' ankles, spilling him to the sand. The men wrestled for position, and with neither able to get the upper hand, the men fought on their knees in the damp sand until Two Wolves connected with a hard right to Bodine's jaw, knocking him back.

Two Wolves jumped at him and Bodine put up a boot, catching Two Wolves in the chest and propelling him on over his head, Two Wolves landing on his belly in the sand.

Bodine scrambled to his boots just as Two Wolves was getting up on his hands and knees and jumped on Two Wolves' back, riding him back down to the sand, his brother's head in a hammerlock.

Two Wolves bit down on Bodine's finger and Bodine yelled in pain, loosening his grip on Two Wolves' head. Two Wolves broke free and grabbed Bodine, throwing him to the ground. Bodine kicked his brother on the knee and Two Wolves staggered back as Bodine lurched to his feet.

Then the two went at it, standing toe to toe and slugging it out.

On a hill above the river, a band of Sioux sat their ponies and watched the men fight. They had been out hunting for food and the hunt had been good, and they were pleased, so they had let the naked gunhands ride on, thinking it a funny sight.

"What a terrible sight to see," Fat Bear said. "Brothers fighting like mortal enemies."

Wolf Going Away shook his head in disgust. "What do you suppose they are fighting about?"

"I think Two Wolves has gone crazy since Medicine Horse ordered him to adopt the white man's ways. They are a very strange people, you know."

"You son of a bitch!" Bodine's yell drifted up to the Indians.

Standing Alone shook his head and clucked his tongue in displeasure at the oath.

"Jealous bastard!" Two Wolves yelled at Bodine just a split second before he knocked Bodine on his butt in the sand.

Bull Bear looked at the others in the band. "Jealous?" he questioned. "Of what? What does one brother have that the other wants?"

Bodine got up and knocked Two Wolves down, then stepped back, catching his breath.

Standing Alone observed, "They are not fighting to really hurt the other. That is my belief."

"This is sad, seeing two brothers fight like this," Fat Bear said. "I wish for us to end it." He heeled his horse forward, the others following.

Bodine and Two Wolves were flailing away at each other when the hunting party rode up and into them, the horses' shoulders knocking the two young men sprawling.

"Stop this!" Fat Bear shouted. "I will have no more of this."

"Well, he started it!" Two Wolves said.

"Silence!" Fat Bear roared at him. "Your father's brother took my sister for a wife, so you will obey me. Silly young men. Is there not enough blood being spilled over this land without you two adding to it?"

Bodine pointed a finger at Two Wolves. "He is a liar!"

"Be quiet!" Fat Bear spoke to him as he had to Two Wolves, in Sioux. "You have shared my lodge and my fire and eaten my food. My woman has fixed your shirt when it was torn. Now I ask only that you respect my right to speak without interruption."

Bodine and Two Wolves sat on the wet sand and glared at each other while Fat Bear, a sub-chief, gave them what for, tracing them back to when they were both children and implying that their minds had not grown with their bodies.

Then he dismounted, picked up a stick, and beat both of them on the back, showing them his contempt for their childish behavior.

The stick broke and Fat Bear tossed it to the ground. "Bah!" he said. And with that, jumped back on his horse and rode off, the others following him. As they passed, they refused to look at Bodine or Two Wolves, a sign of contempt.

Bodine got to his boots and felt his stinging back. "That old man still swings a pretty mean stick."

"You deserved it," Two Wolves told him.

Bodine looked at him, smiled, and then flattened him with a right to the mouth.

Chapter 18

They had fought all over the bank, churning up the sand, fought out in the river and back, each one doing their best to try to drown the other, and were on the bank, still flailing weakly away at each other when an army patrol, led by Sergeant McGuire, rode up.

"All right, men, break them up," the sergeant ordered.

Bodine and Two Wolves chose that time to collapse from exhaustion on the sands. Both of them were so tired, so arm-weary, they couldn't move.

McGuire squatted down beside them. "I don't suppose one of you would like to tell me what this is all about?"

"It's personal," Bodine groaned.

"I thought it might be," the sergeant said dryly. "Do you intend to lie here by the river the rest of the day?"

"The sun does feel nice," Two Wolves admitted.

Sergeant McGuire looked at the welts on their backs and shook his head. "How the hell did you get those marks on your backs, boys?"

"Fat Bear came by and was disgusted with us. He beat us for our disgraceful behavior," Bodine said.

"A Sioux war chief came by and he . . . beat you both?" McGuire sighed and stood up. "Are you two going to start fighting when we leave?"

"No," Two Wolves groaned.

"Bodine?" McGuire asked.

"No more fighting this morning."

"It's afternoon, man!"

"Whatever."

"Drag them over there by their horses, boys," McGuire ordered. "Lone Dog's up in Montana. So they'll be all right. Let's go. We've got to make the fork of the Clear and the Crazy Woman before dark." He looked at the two bloody and battered and exhausted young men. "Fat Bear came by and beat you! I'd have given a bottle of whiskey to see that." He walked away, laughing.

The men lay in the shade in silence until the Army patrol was gone. Two Wolves was the first to speak. "Personally, I did not find the hiding from Fat Bear to be all that amusing."

"Nor did I. But you were certainly deserving of yours."

Two Wolves stirred, and then laughed. But that hurt his bruised and swollen mouth so the laughter was brief.

Bodine chuckled, also very briefly.

"All in all," Two Wolves said, "it was a superb fight, was it not?"

"Oh, yes. Even though I kept pulling my punches so I wouldn't hurt you too bad."

"*You* kept pulling *your* punches? I could have knocked you out at the first, but I was feeling charitable and decided to let you save face."

The men lay on the sand and traded insults for a few minutes, both of them knowing the truth in the other's initial statement.

Finally, Bodine said, "If we lie here, we're going to stiffen up."

"I'm afraid if I move I will shatter like glass."

"Those bare-butt jaybirds just might run into some friends and come back here, Brother."

That did it.

Two Wolves stirred and sat up with a groan. "I am forced to admit that I am in no shape for another fight."

"Nor am I." Bodine pulled himself up to a sitting position and reached up, grabbed hold of a tree limb, and hauled himself to his boots. He held out his hand for Two Wolves.

On their feet, the men looked at each other and laughed. Their faces were swollen and bruised and cut; their eyes about half closed. Their hands were puffy from the blows of the long fight and both of them had difficulty straightening up.

"I know a place about five miles from here," Bodine said. "By a little creek that's full of trout. Good cover all the way around."

"Let's go."

They managed to get into the saddle, and had anybody else been watching it would have been a comedy. Bodine pointed Rowdy's nose toward the northwest and led the way, dozing in the saddle as the afternoon warmed slightly.

At the creek, they heated water and cleaned up, then caught some fish and fried them in a battered, old blackened frying pan. They stretched out on their bedrolls and were sound asleep before the sun went down. They didn't wake up until full dawn the next morning.

Two Wolves caught several more trout while Bodine boiled water for coffee. They looked worse this day than they had the day before, the bruises now a sickly yellow-green. Bodine watered the horses and then moved them to a new graze and picketed them.

"So how have you been?" Bodine broke the silence.

"Lousy. You?"

"So, so. I kept busy at the ranch."

"I have neglected my spread. I have wasted my time

courting a woman who, it appears, has been having fun with my affections." He glanced at Bodine. "Aren't you going to say I told you so?"

"No." Bodine speared a piece of fish and munched on it.

"Thank you for that. Since you have had more experience with women than I, how do I end this charade?"

"You just don't go back, Sam. You know she's been seeing Tom Thomas?"

"So the rumors go."

"But do you believe it?"

Two Wolves sighed. "Yes," he admitted. "We had a terrible quarrel the other night, Brother. About you. That is why I was out riding alone."

Bodine did not look at him. "Just about me?"

"No. Terri wanted me to meet with Tom Thomas."

"What about?"

"Probably to turn against you. We never reached that point in the conversation. I was sorely tempted to find a stick and beat her."

Bodine laughed. "That's all in your past, Sam. Although I doubt that you've ever struck a woman in your life."

"True. But with Terri . . . I was very nearly to that point."

"You have any pressing business you have to attend to?"

"No. Nothing. Why?"

"We'll lie around here for a couple of days, get the stiffness out and let the bruises fade, then you can ride with me to the settlement. You probably need to stock up on supplies, too."

"I have no pack horse."

"We'll get you a couple at the livery. Don't argue. I don't feel up to thrashing you again."

Two Wolves lay back on the ground and laughed until his sides hurt.

* * *

On the fourth day after the fight at the Crazy Woman, Bodine and Two Wolves broke camp at dawn. They crossed the Clear, and began angling more north than west, taking their time and keeping a wary eye out for trouble, from both white and Indian.

The bruises had faded and more importantly, their hands had lost the stiffness, for both knew they were more than likely riding into a hornet's nest of trouble, and might have to grab iron.

"Jim Potter." Two Wolves pointed out the gunslick as they rode into the small settlement. 'Who are those two with him?"

Bodine cut his eyes to the saloon. "Dave Agee and Nate Johnson. Texas gunhands. They're good."

"Better than you?"

"No. But if I have to face all three of them, they'll get lead in me."

"You won't be alone. We are brothers."

They stabled their horses and Two Wolves arranged for pack animals. They walked to the general store and started picking out supplies: bacon and beans and sugar and flour and tobacco and the like.

"The cook over at the cafe got any eggs?" Bodine asked the shopkeeper.

"Shore does. He's got him a flock of layin' hens. Best grub to be found anywheres."

Both men had been living off fish and rabbits for several days. The idea of a cafe-cooked breakfast of bacon and eggs and fried potatoes and lots of hot coffee got their mouths salivating and they put their boots in the street toward the cafe.

The man behind the counter didn't seem all that thrilled to see the pair of them, but he let his expression mirror his displeasure and using good sense, kept his flap shut. For about thirty seconds.

"Plenty of eggs and whatever else you're serving with

them," Bodine told the man as he pulled out a chair. "For the both of us."

"I don't want no trouble in here, fellers," the man said. "I seen them ol' boys come ridin' in the other day, the ones that wasn't dead was all shot to hell and gone, 'ceptin' for them two with their be-hinds all rubbed raw. And I know who both of you is. Bodine and Two Wolves. Now I'm tellin' you both, if trouble starts, take it outside. I'll get your grub."

Bodine and Two Wolves grinned at each other. That must have been quite a sight," Two Wolves whispered.

Then both of them laughed.

The sheriff picked that time to step into the cafe. He gave them both a look of disapproval and walked over to their table, pulled out a chair, and sat down. "Coffee, Bobby."

"You know where it is," the counterman told him, in exactly the same tone he'd used with Bodine and Two Wolves.

The sheriff grinned, got his coffee, and sat back down. "You might think Bobby didn't like you," he said, sugaring the black. "But he uses the same tone with everybody. He's a good cook, but I think if he bit hisself he'd die from rabies."

"Very funny, Sheriff," Bobby grumbled from the kitchen. The sheriff rolled a smoke and laid a sack and papers on the table. Help yourself, boys. You got a long ride ahead of you."

"Are we going somewhere soon?" Bodine asked innocently.

"Yep. Just as soon as you boys has et and resupplied, you're heading back to Johnson County. I don't want no trouble here."

"We have no intention of starting any trouble, Sheriff," Two Wolves assured him.

"I know that. But they's about ten gunslicks just hangin' around town. Makes me nervous. Since I know what the ante is on your head, Bodine."

"Then why don't you tell me and we'll both know. Last I heard it was between five and ten thousand."

"That's close enough." The sheriff sucked at his coffee mug. "Tom Thomas has a powerful lot of hate for you, Bodine. And let me tell you something else: he hates your father just as bad. He's got his eyes on your spreads." He cut his eyes to Two Wolves. "And yours, too, partner. That's why he's been suckin' up to you, him and that no-count woman them fool ranchers hired to teach their younguns."

The counterman brought their food and when he had left, Bodine asked, "You mean she isn't a schoolteacher?"

"She wasn't when they ran her out of St. Louis," he said flatly, then reached into his pocket and pulled out a dodger, laying it on the table.

Two Wolves picked it up, looked at the likeness, and read the information. "This doesn't say she's wanted for anything."

"Oh, she isn't. She's served her time."

"Time?" Bodine looked at the man. "For what?"

"Embezzlement, attempted murder, impersonation.

"Damn!" Two Wolves said.

"Impersonation of what?" Bodine asked.

"A schoolteacher," Two Wolves spoke before the sheriff could speak.

"You got it," the sheriff said.

"I feel like a fool," Two Wolves said.

The sheriff sort of figured he knew what Two Wolves was talking about, but a man's romancing was his own business—even a half-breed Injun—so the lawman didn't pursue that comment.

"How come you have this?" Bodine asked, holding up the dodger that Two Wolves had laid on the table.

"Well, boys, let me put it this way: the law is changin' as we progress. The telegraph wire and the mail is bringin' a lot of us to workin' closer together. But now let me warn you about this dodger here. You cain't use it agin that woman. She's free and clear as a bird. She's served her time and as far as I know, she might have gone back to school and gotten her teachin' certificate. I don't know. Take weeks or months to find out. The lawmen over in Missouri sent this dodger, or one like it, to the lawmen in Kansas—that's where she went after she got out of prison. Kansas sent it to Nebraska when she moved there, and so on as she pulled stakes and somebody got suspicious after she landed. She's a schemer and a conniver and a user, boys. And she's mighty slick. I got me a sneaky feelin' that she and Tom Thomas knowed each other 'way back down the line. Y'all watch that woman close. She's up to no good. But you tell anybody I showed y'all this dodger, I'm gonna say you lied. OK?"

Bodine and Two Wolves nodded their agreement.

"Fine. Now you boys finish up your breakfast and get your supplies and hightail it outta my territory . . ."

The door opened and a citizen stepped in, walking swiftly to the table. "Sheriff, Deputies Carson and Hankins had to go up to the Box T—rustlers. Three more of Tom Thomas's hardcases done rode in; made it plain they was lookin' for these two here." He cut his eyes to Bodine and Two Wolves.

"Damn!" the sheriff swore.

"I can get the boys together," the citizen said, but without a whole lot of conviction in his voice.

"Looks like we're a little late in leaving, Sheriff," Bodine said. "No point in your getting a lot of townspeople killed or hurt. Why not just pass the word to vacate the streets and let us handle it?"

"And then what am I supposed to do?" the man questioned. "Just sit back with my thumb stuck in my ear while the town gets shot up?"

"Beats getting killed, doesn't it?" Two Wolves made that point.

"There is no law against a stand-up gunfight, Sheriff," Bodine reminded the man. "There probably should be, but there isn't."

"You boys gonna be facin' 'bout eight or ten randy ol' boys."

Bodine and Two Wolves exchanged glances. "We're tricky," Two Wolves said with a smile.

The sheriff nodded his head. Looked up at the citizen. "All right, Harry. Get the people off the streets." He looked at Bodine and Two Wolves. "You boys better be more than tricky. You better have angels on your shoulders!"

Chapter 19

Bodine and Two Wolves finished their breakfast and enjoyed another cup of coffee before Two Wolves asked, "What's the drill, Brother?"

"We step out and walk right into that gun shop next door. Buy us a couple of express guns. I never have believed in a fair fight."

"Sure was a nice breakfast."

"Tasty."

"You ready to go to work?"

"Might as well. Those ol' boys sure aren't going to go away."

"Brother?"

Bodine met his eyes.

"You were right about Terri. I was wrong. I let my heart blind my eyes."

"Happens to the best of us, Brother."

"Even you?"

"I'll never tell!" Bodine replied with a laugh.

They paid for their breakfast and started for the door.

"Good luck, boys," the counterman called as they were leaving.

They both paused and turned around. The counterman was smiling at them. They returned the smile and stepped out onto the boardwalk.

Before entering the gun shop, Bodine and Two Wolves looked up and down the street. Two men, wearing their guns low and tied down, were lounging in front of the livery. Two more were at each end of the short street. They began walking toward the saloon.

"They certainly seem anxious enough," Two Wolves remarked.

"Yeah. Let's get loaded up."

They bought express guns: sawed-off, double-barrel, 12-gauge shotguns and a box of shells, stuffing their pockets. They checked their .44s and split a box, filling up the loops in their gunbelts. The shop owner watched them nervously. "You boys is damn fools!" he finally said. "There must be maybe ten or twelve gunslicks out there waitin' on you."

"What would you have us do?" Two Wolves questioned.

"Take the back door and work your way around to the livery," he suggested. "And get the hell gone from here. That's the sensible way."

"And the cowardly way," Two Wolves told him. "It will come sometime. Why not now?"

"Nuts!" the man said. "Both of you. Git on out of here. I'm lockin' this place up!"

Bodine and Two Wolves loaded up and once more stepped out onto the boardwalk. The street was empty. The doorlock clicked behind them and they heard the shades being pulled down. A few seconds later, they heard the back door slam.

"Nervous man," Two Wolves observed.

"Maybe he's got more sense than we have."

"There is that to consider."

"Where do we start?"

"I guess the saloon. I guess that's where those gunhands went. It appears to be the only place left open."

"Except for the undertaker's place of business."

"Let's go see if we can't send some customers his way."

They stepped off the boardwalk and onto the dusty street.

Bodine and Two Wolves carried the sawed-off shotguns in their left hands, the right hand of each close to the butt of the .44s.

As they walked, Bodine said, "We can't just go in shooting; might hit some innocent. So I guess we're going in blind."

Before Two Wolves could reply, the batwings were pushed open and men crowded the boardwalk. They began lining up, several feet between them. They stood with hands hovering over their guns, all of them smiling at the pair.

"An even ten," Two Wolves said. "You think they all work for Tom Thomas?"

"If they don't, they're sure in the wrong crowd. I think we ought to thin it, don't you?"

"You ready?"

"Now!"

Two Wolves and Bodine charged the line of gunmen, the move totally unexpected and catching the gunslicks off guard. As they ran the short distance to the boardwalk, Bodine and Two Wolves fired both barrels of the express guns, the heavy charges of nuts and nails and buckshot knocking four of the gunmen sprawling and sending the others diving for cover; two ran back into the saloon, two jumped off the boardwalk and ran into the alley, and the other two grabbed for iron.

Bodine's right hand dipped down and up, his fist filled with Colt. The muzzle lanced fire and smoke and a gunman screamed as the slug tore into his chest. Two Wolves' Colt was spitting lead and fire. His bullet slammed into the stomach of his target and doubled him over, dropping him to the rough boards.

"I'll take the alley," Two Wolves called, running for the alleyway.

The charge had not been bravado; Bodine and Two Wolves just didn't know what else to do.

Bodine was already running for the saloon, reloading the express gun as he ran. His boots slipped in the blood on the boardwalk and he lost his balance, literally falling into the saloon . . . which probably saved his life.

As he fell into the saloon, guns roared and lead sang deadly songs over his head, the slugs knocking holes in the batwings where he would have been had he not slipped.

On his belly, he cut loose the double-barreled, sawed-off, twelve gauge hand cannon and tore Dave Agee apart, the terrible charges striking the man in the belly and chest. Dave Agee's eyes were rolling back in his head and he was dead before he hit the sawdust floor.

Bodine rolled and came up with both hands filled with Colts.

"God*damn* you, Bodine!" Nate Johnson screamed at him.

Bodine started cocking and firing, on his knees on the floor, just as the sounds of shooting came to him from the alley. He poured round after round into Nate, but the gunman would not go down, clinging stubbornly to the bar, hanging there by one elbow. His guns had fallen from numbed fingers.

"Lucky," Nate muttered. "Luckiest man I ever seen." Then he closed his eyes and pitched forward, landing on his face in the sawdust.

Two Wolves had killed one gunny with his shotgun, and was now stalking the other one behind the row of buildings. A bullet blew splinters into his face as it tore off a piece of wood. Two Wolves dropped to one knee and leveled his Colt. He put three fast .44 slugs into the man, the last slug taking him in the throat and knocking him back against an outhouse. The outhouse collapsed and the man fell into the lime pit. He bubbled a couple of times and then was quiet as he sank into the mess.

When Two Wolves rounded the corner of the saloon, Bodine was standing on the boardwalk, reloading, talking to the sheriff, the dead and the dying and the badly wounded littered around their boots.

"I never seen nothin' like it," the sheriff said. "Not never in my born days. You boys *charged* them gunslicks. I never seen nothin' like it."

"Oh, mommy, mommy!" a gut-shot gunhawk called out, his voice filled with pain. "Help me!"

The sheriff looked at the man, contempt in his eyes. "Best thing your momma could have done was to take a pissel-mum branch to your butt about three times a day when you was younger." The sheriff looked at the bloody holes in the man's belly. "You ain't gonna make it. You hard-hit, gun-fighter."

The man opened his mouth to speak. He struggled to push the words out before death took him. He lost the race as the grim reaper rode up, grinning.

"Any charges against us, Sheriff?" Bodine asked.

"Nope. They braced you. That's the way I'm gonna write 'er up."

"We'll be getting our supplies now," Two Wolves said.

"Good," the sheriff told them.

"And leaving," Bodine added.

"That's even better," the sheriff said, smiling. "And boys? . . ."

They looked at him.

"Don't come back—please!"

It was an uneventful ride back to home country. But both young men knew the story of the gunfight would have reached home long before they did. Shoot-outs were not an uncommon thing on the frontier—with most of them going unreported—but when two men face ten men, and the two come away unscathed, that was news, and the story would grow and grow through the years. Reputations are made.

They stopped at the elder Bodine's spread on the Crazy Woman.

Bodine's father was standing on the front porch as they rode up, and after they stabled their horses, the elder Bodine was decidedly blunt.

"You boys played hell this time around," he told them. "Stories of that gunfight is bein' told all over the territories."

"We didn't feel like running." His son was equally blunt.

The father's gaze was bleak. "Do you realize, boy, that Nate Johnson is, was, one of the top gunslicks around?"

"He didn't seem like much to me, Dad. But he was tough going down, I'll give him that much. I must have put eight or ten holes in him before he gave it up."

"Your mother's been worried sick. Damn near had to put her to bed. You boys come on in the house. We got to talk."

They followed the elder Bodine toward the house. In his fifties, the older Bodine was still wang-leather tough, with a massive barrel chest and heavily muscled arms and thick shoulders. And bow-legged from nearly half a century on a horse.

His brother was on the range, and his sister visiting a friend over at the settlement on the Belle Fourche; her beau was also visiting the friend's sister. Most folks expected the engagement to be announced very soon.

Over coffee and pie in the kitchen, the elder Bodine said, "I keep gettin' word that this comin' summer is gonna be one to remember as far as the Indians is concerned. I hear that at the gatherin' some months back, they decided to make war."

"I hate to say I told you so," Two Wolves said. "But I certainly tried to warn people. The treaties have been broken too many times. By both sides," he added, the fairness within him surfacing. "My people . . ." He smiled sadly. "Sorry. I keep forgetting my father's words. The *Indians* still remember General Sheridan's words: The only good Indians I ever saw were dead. That is not a statement one is apt to forget easily."

"I'm sure the general has regretted saying that many times over," Sarah Bodine said.

"Begging to differ, Mrs. Bodine," Two Wolves gently rebuffed her. "I am equally sure he has not. The man despises all Indians. My father summed up the Indian situation very well just before we began our trek to the reservation. He told me, 'Our way has come and gone. The life that we have known for centuries will be no more. Not after the great battle. That will be the beginning of the end.' "

"What great battle?" the elder Bodine asked.

"I don't know. But one is surely coming. Even my brother has experienced the visions."

"Is that true, son?"

"Yes. In my vision it was the month of Moon Making Fat. June. I saw many soldiers falling upside down into an Indian camp. Custer was among them." He did not tell them what Medicine Horse had said about staying out of the valley of the Rosebuds. Bodine was not really sure what Medicine Horse had meant.

"You believe in these visions, son?" his mother asked.

"Yes, I do, Mother. I don't understand them, but I believe."

"Doesn't that fly in the face of Christianity, son?"

"I don't think so. Not if you accept that God made many different peoples with many different beliefs. I don't think it makes any difference how you perceive God, as long as you believe there is a God."

"I won't argue that," the elder Bodine said. "I just hope that He is looking after us all."

Chapter 20

It was one of those Wyoming winters that for days on end brought everything and everybody to a standstill . . . except for the cowboys. No matter what the weather, there is something to be done around a ranch. On mornings that would freeze a tin cup of boiling coffee before you could get it to your mouth, with the snow so deep it brushed the belly of your horse, the cowboys still had to step out of lineshacks, drop a loop on a very reluctant-to-leave-the-corral horse, climb into the saddle and endure the few seconds bucking game of who-is-the-boss-around-here, and then ride out to do what a cowboy is paid thirty a month and found for doing: work.

Holes had to be chopped into streams and creeks and watering holes so the cattle could drink. Hay had to be manhandled to those where the ice was so thick the cows could not dig down to forage. Newborn calves had to be located and picked up and carried across the saddle horn while the mother plodded along behind, back to a warm place so the little critter might stand a better chance of living. Sometimes that place was right in the bunkhouse. And if the mother didn't live through the birthing, it was find another cow who was fresh and would accept the calf, or else rig up a bottle, boys, and get ready for some long nights. And don't forget to bring a shovel in with you.

If you didn't just absolutely have to do it, nobody wandered from the fire on those days when the temperature dropped down to twenty or thirty below . . . at least not until cabin fever drove you out.

And anything to read was priceless. Cowboys had been known to have but one book in the bunkhouse, and before winter had blown its last icy breath, every one of them would have committed the book to memory; that and what was written on bean can labels, and anything else they could get their hands on.

And they were all hungry for news.

But the news that greeted Bodine during a break in the winter weather was anything but good: He found his cache of supplies was dangerously low. He had heard that the supplies at the general store at the settlement were so low the owner had closed its doors to all except those who lived there. There was that little settlement east of Bodine's spread, but they probably were in just as bad a shape as the rest.

Bodine smiled, feeling that old wildness fill him. Well, he thought, that left only one place.

"You want us to go *where?*" Two Wolves asked, almost dropping the coffee pot.

"You're out of supplies, aren't you?"

"Very nearly."

"So let's go to Cutter and get some before the weather closes us in again."

Two Wolves looked at his blood brother and then felt the same wildness overtake him that Bodine had experienced.

He laughed and sat down at the table in his small cabin on the knoll. "Why not?"

They pulled out within the hour, knowing they would have to sleep at least one night on the trail. But that didn't matter to them. They had made camp in blizzards before. Just give these two a few minutes' warning, and they could live through just about anything . . . or so their youth told them.

They hadn't seen much of each other during the hard and bitter months of deep winter, so they had a lot of catching up to do. Each had taken a pack horse to bring back the necessities. Providing they got out of Cutter alive, that is.

"Before you ask, Bodine," Two Wolves said, as they made their way almost due north toward the town of Cutter, and whatever fate lay in waiting for them there, "no, I haven't seen Terri."

"I wasn't going to bring it up. But since you did . . ."

"Hah! You're worse than an old woman, Brother. You thrive on gossip. But, very well. She is teaching school and seeing Mister Tom Thomas. I am told they are to be married."

"And that makes you feel . . . ?"

Two Wolves smiled. "I would be lying if I said it did not hurt my heart—at first. But now? . . . I feel good. She has been exposed, at least to us, for what she really is. So I consider myself fortunate. But I am told that Tom Thomas still hates us both. More so than he did."

"So that makes this sort of a stupid move, doesn't it?"

"Rather." Two Wolves held up his hand. "Listen, Brother."

Both of them heard the pound of hooves. Without exchanging a word, they swung their horses and rode behind a small hill, dismounted, and grabbed their rifles, running back to some brush. They relaxed when they spotted the blue uniforms. Bodine stepped out while Two Wolves went back for the horses.

"Bodine," Lieutenant Gerry said, reining up and halting the patrol. "What in the world are you doing out here by yourself?"

"Two Wolves is with me. Why, what's up?"

"With this break in the weather, Lone Dog and his bunch have begun wreaking havoc once more. He's been burning and killing and raping all around Cutter. Hi, Sam!" he called his greetings as Two Wolves stepped out, leading the horses. "Where are you two going?"

"To Cutter, for supplies," Two Wolves told him with a grin.

"Cutter! Man, have you taken leave of your senses? You'll never get out of that place alive."

"We will if the Army escorts us," Bodine said with a laugh.

Gerry looked at Sergeant McGuire. McGuire said, "The colonel did say for us to check out the town, Lieutenant."

"That he did, Sergeant, that he did. All right, why not?" He met Bodine's eyes. I've heard much of the talk about Miss Kelly, Bodine. I shall not tolerate any such malicious besmirchment of the lady's name while I am in command."

That the young lieutenant was very much in love with Miss Kelly was easy to see. Sergeant McGuire rolled his eyes and shifted his chewing tobacco, then spat, and kept his mouth shut.

Bodine shrugged. "You won't hear a bad word about her from me, Gerry."

"Good! We're all friends again. Let's ride, boys! We'll make camp at the springs."

Gerry was commanding a full complement of sixty men. And that was unusual for such a rank. During a break to let the horses water, Bodine asked him about it.

"Captains Mallory and Bishop were sent over east to join Custer's group. And before you ask, no, I don't know what's going on."

"None of our business anyway," Bodine said nonchalantly. But he was conscious of Two Wolves' intense glance.

Mallory and Bishop were both seasoned Indian fighters, with long years on the frontier. Old Iron Butt—as some called Custer, because of his ability to spend hours in the saddle and still appear fresh— might be thinking of a spring offensive against the Indians. He needed something to get back into President Grant's favor; recently Grant had been quite vocal about his displeasure with Custer.

Custer was an experienced and ruthless Indian fighter, albeit a tad on the arrogant side.

They mounted up and continued north toward Tom Thomas's town of Cutter.

They reached the springs an hour before dark and made camp, with the guard mount doubled. Bodine had noticed that about half of Gerry's command were green troops; a lot of fresh-faced kids from the East. And many of them apparently had falsified their age to join the cavalry, for the minimum age in 1875 was twenty-one. Over coffee, Bodine asked Gerry about that.

"I'm afraid you're correct, Bodine," the lieutenant admitted. He looked at Bodine in the gathering dusk. "Many of the seasoned troopers have been shifted over to Dakota Territory, Fort Abe Lincoln. Our garrison is due to close the last of June."

Perhaps the Army thought the Indian wars would be over by that time, Bodine mused. If they think so, then they're fools. But if that was their thinking, something very big was in the works. When we get back, I have to break my word to Medicine Horse and tell Colonel Travers about the visions and of Medicine Horse's warning to stay out of the Rosebuds come spring.

"You're quite pensive this evening, Bodine," Gerry said.

"I guess so," Bodine admitted, as Two Wolves sat down by the fire and poured coffee into a battered tin cup.

"How many of these troopers have seen combat, Gerry?" Two Wolves asked.

Gerry sighed. "Not many, I'm afraid. Most just got out here from the East. I've been worried about how they'll react when they do come under trial by fire."

"They'll be scared," McGuire said, squatting down and pouring coffee. "Just like any normal man. But they're good lads; I think they'll stand."

"Make certain they don't smoke while on guard duty, Sergeant," Gerry cautioned.

McGuire nodded. Gerry was learning fast and retaining it.

"You are aware that the town of Cutter is doomed?" Two Wolves asked.

"I keep hearing it," Gerry said. "But so far, no Indian attacks have materialized."

"But you say the attacks on settlers around the town have increased?" Bodine asked.

"Yes."

"Show me where." He handed the lieutenant a twig with which to draw in the dirt.

Gerry outlined a crude map, with the town of Cutter in the center. He began placing X's far out from the town, and then working in closer, in a loose circle. "I see what you mean," Gerry muttered. "Lone Dog is getting closer and closer to the town. And school is out for the remainder of the winter. She's . . . visiting Tom Thomas in Cutter at this moment."

Bodine started to tell the young lieutenant that Terri Kelly could damn well take care of herself. But knowing how the young man felt about the woman, Bodine kept his mouth shut.

"But I doubt the town is in danger," Gerry said. "Too many gunfighters there." He looked at Bodine and smiled. "Of course, that number has been drastically reduced, thanks to you and Sam."

"I imagine Thomas has hired more," Bodine told him. "What's the latest figure about the bounty on my head?"

"Talk is that Thomas withdrew it. The gunfighters who are still around are here out of pride or are looking to make a reputation. And there are plenty of them, Bodine."

"No doubt." Bodine's reply was dryly offered.

"Bodine." The whisper brought him awake and alert. Turning his head, he looked into the eyes of Two Wolves.

"We have company."

"How many?"

"Only a few, I'm thinking. They probably came to see if they could steal some horses."

Bodine eased out of his blankets and pulled on moccasins, leaving his boots beside the blankets. On hands and knees, the two men crawled away from the main body of sleeping soldiers and the nearly dead fire.

Bodine was not worried about anybody stealing Rowdy. If a stranger got too close to the big horse, Rowdy would either kick them to death or set up such a ruckus the entire camp would be awakened and the intruder would be frightened off.

Away from the sleeping and silent camp, the men rose to stand beside a huge boulder. They talked, using sign language in the dim light.

Guards? Bodine asked.

Unaware, Two Wolves answered.

Where to start?

Two Wolves shrugged and then signed, All around us. I think one guard is already dead.

Where?

In the timber.

We'll start there.

Two Wolves smiled his approval of that.

Moving slowly and making no sound, they entered the small stand of timber. Bodine smelled fresh blood. Two Wolves pointed. The body of a young trooper lay sprawled in death, his throat cut. He had been scalped and a small part of his skull shone ghostly white in the very dim light of the cloud-covered moon.

Bodine signed: Split up?

Two Wolves nodded and the men moved away, soon vanishing from the other's sight.

Bodine saw the brave, standing motionless by a tree. He slipped forward quietly, putting the wind to his face so the Indian could not smell him, then angled behind the brave, the long-bladed knife in his hand, held down beside his leg so the dim light could not reflect off it.

The Indian sensed someone or something behind him and turned. Bodine drove the blade into the brave's throat, the heavy blade stopping any sound before it was made. He drove the blade through the man's neck and tore it out one side. Then he drove the blade into the Indian's chest, piercing the heart.

Bodine lowered the body to the cold ground, wiped his blade clean on his jeans, and moved on, as silent as stalking death in the night.

Two Wolves had waited by a tree for his prey to come to him, and he knew they would, for the spot he had chosen was near the picketed horses. Two Wolves watched the guard advance, look around him, make his turn, and head back, walking his post as he had been taught. A very stupid move in Indian country, Two Wolves thought, then smiled at the irony contained within the thought.

He detected movement to his left and remained as still as

the tree trunk he crouched beside. The brave—and Two Wolves recognized him as one called Scabby Mouth—came closer, then for some reason, turned, putting his back to Two Wolves.

Two Wolves finished him with one heavy plunge of his knife, his hand over Scabby Mouth's lips to prevent any scream. He lowered the body to the earth and slipped back into the dark timber.

Two Wolves and Bodine spent two more hours in the brush and the timber, locating and killing the six Indians who had come to steal horses and instead found sudden and violent death. It was almost five o'clock in the morning when they finished and slipped back into camp. The sentries had never known they were outside the camp engaged in their deadly mission.

Bodine knelt down and shook Lieutenant Gerry awake. "Wake up, Gerry. You lost one sentry last night. Two Wolves and I killed the war party."

Gerry sat up on his blankets and rubbed the sleep from his eyes. "Wh . . . what?"

"Get your boots on. Come on."

The entire camp was up by this time, due in no small part to Two Wolves banging on a skillet with a large metal spoon.

"Now listen up, people!" Bodine yelled, getting everybody's attention. "You came close to losing some horses last night. You did lose one man. I don't know his name. He's right over there in the timber. Dead and scalped. He got careless, probably. Lieutenant Gerry tells me that most of you are from back East. This is not back East. This is Indian country and the Indians—a lot of them—are on the warpath. Come spring, they'll be a hell of a lot more on the warpath, I'm thinking. If you're going to survive out here, you're going to have to change a lot of thinking and forget a lot of the crap the Army has drilled into your heads."

Bodine noticed that Gerry stirred at his last comment, but kept his mouth shut. He knew that what Bodine said was true. He caught the burned down cigarette butt that Bodine tossed him.

"The dead man was smoking that when he was killed. He gave away his position just as clearly as if he'd blown a bugle and fired a flare. You want to stay alive in this country, you pick a protected spot, you very carefully and very slowly note everything around you. Don't just look at it—see it! You stay in that spot. You don't move. Move your eyes, not your head. Movement draws more attention than noise. You'll learn, or you'll die."

Bodine walked to the fire and poured a cup of coffee made the night before, hot and black and strong enough to melt nails.

Sergeant McGuire ordered a burial detail for the dead trooper. "What about the dead Indians, Lieutenant?"

"Cut off their heads," Bodine said. "And dump them out on the plains. That might convince Lone Dog his medicine is bad."

This time, Gerry did not vocalize any loud protestations over the barbarism of Bodine's suggestion. As Bodine had noted, the young lieutenant was learning that life on the frontier was rough.

As the town of Cutter came into sight, Lieutenant Gerry said to Bodine, "Attempting to steal horses from the Army, Bodine. That might suggest to me that Lone Dog was getting ready for a large-scale attack."

"It might. It could mean a lot of things. But I think you're right about the attack. And we're fast approaching the target."

"Our scouts have repeatedly reported that Lone Dog's followers have grown. Estimates range anywhere from three hundred to five hundred." He looked around him. "Where is Two Wolves? I haven't seen him for hours."

"Scouting. He said he had a bad feeling about this day; wanted to check something out."

"What?"

"His hunch that we were being followed. I've been feeling eyes on me for hours."

"You think it's Lone Dog?"

"Yes, I do. It would be quite a coup for him to catch Two Wolves and me in Cutter with the Army and wipe us all out."

Gerry was silent for a moment. "I can't believe that Lone Dog would be so brazenly foolhardy as to attack the town while the Army is in it."

Bodine smiled. "The Indians have been running circles around the Army for thirty years, Gerry. Fremont, Crook, Sheridan—a dozen more have chased the Indians over the long years. The Indian isn't afraid of the white man. Quite the contrary. And he certainly isn't afraid of the Army." Bodine looked toward the east. "Two Wolves coming."

Gerry halted the patrol, calling for a rest.

"Lone Dog and his warriors have circled us and are paralleling us," Two Wolves said. "Staying miles away, in small bands, so we won't see the dust. I'd say they're waiting for us to enter Cutter and then they'll attack."

"You saw them?" Gerry asked.

Two Wolves fixed him with a cool gaze. "I saw enough of them to know what is going on, Lieutenant, and I've been reading sign since I was old enough to walk. What direction did I take when I left, Lieutenant?"

"I . . . ah . . . did not notice you leave."

"Right. I rode west, Lieutenant. And when I returned, I came in from the east."

"I get the point, Sam."

"I hope your lack of attentiveness doesn't get you the point of an arrow or lance or knife, Lieutenant."

Gerry might have had a response to that. If he did he kept it to himself. He got up from his squat and moved to confer with Sergeant McGuire.

"How many, Brother?" Bodine asked.

"I'd say three to four hundred. They're painted for war, Bodine."

"Cutter is our only shot, isn't it?"

"There is nothing else within a fifty- to seventy-five-mile radius. I hate to think I'm going to be fighting to save Tom Thomas's worthless hide."

Bodine couldn't resist it. With a smile, he said, "Then just consider it a fight to save the fair, virtuous Terri Kelly."

Two Wolves groaned. Then he removed Bodine's hat, filled it up with water from the creek, and placed it back on Bodine's head—while the troopers stood around and laughed.

Let them laugh, Bodine thought, while the water ran down his neck. Chances are, it'll be the last laugh for many of them.

Maybe for all of us.

When they rode into Cutter, Tom Thomas stepped out of his office and stared in disbelief at Bodine. The man's eyes bugged out, his face turned red and when he finished jumping up and down, he looked like he might keel over from an attack of apoplexy.

He pointed a finger at Bodine and began to stutter as Bodine reined up and dismounted in front of his office building. You . . . you . . . you . . ."

"Oh, shut up, Thomas!" Bodine told him. "I don't have time to whip you again. Where's your private army?"

But Thomas was too angry to even speak.

Whacker Corrigan stepped out and said, "In the field, Bodine. What's going on?"

Bodine very quickly explained.

That calmed Thomas down in a hurry. "Destroy *my* town!" he roared. "The hell they will!"

Bodine lifted his eyes to the second floor of the building. Terri was standing by a curtained window, looking down at him. She wore a robe that Bodine suspected had nothing under it except Terri. He smiled at her.

She jerked the curtains closed.

Thomas caught the direction of Bodine's eyes and his own gaze was filled with raw hatred as their eyes met and locked.

"No time for that now, Thomas," Bodine told him. "Right now you'd better concentrate on staying alive."

"I will be in my living quarters with my fiancée," Thomas said, then spun around and entered his office building.

Bodine joined Two Wolves just as Lieutenant Gerry was walking up.

"I have absolutely no knowledge of or experience in defending a town," the Army man admitted. "My training was solely dedicated to fighting hostiles in the field."

"This will be something new for the Indians, as well," Bodine said. "I don't recall them ever taking on an entire town."

"They will probably slip warriors in close," Two Wolves advised. "They'll shoot fire arrows into the buildings. Then once the town is burning, they'll hit us."

"I'll split my command," Gerry said. "Then . . ."

"No!" Bodine's interruption was sharply given. "That would be suicide. Your command is too small for that." He pointed toward stone buildings on a hill overlooking the town. "The old mining operation. There's water, a place for the horses, and a good field of fire. We can hold for a long time there." He looked at Two Wolves. "Think you can make the garrison?"

"As soon as it's dark."

"If they catch you, Brother, you'll die hard."

Two Wolves smiled. "I would not give them that satisfaction ."

Chapter 21

The old mining operation, the first in this part of the territory, had turned out to be a total bust. But the men who financed the boondoggle had put up buildings to last. Gerry led his command to the hilltop and began assigning positions. Bodine went to the cafe where the waitress had been friendly.

"Lucy," he told her. "You and the cook fix as much food as you can and get up to the old mine buildings with the Army."

"Why are you doing this, Bodine?" she asked.

"Because I think you and the Chinaman are about the only decent people in this town."

"And the rest of the people can go to the devil?"

"That's about the size of it."

She stared at him for a few seconds. "I was on my way to Oregon. On the same wagon train with Loo Boo. The wagon master deserted the train. As it turned out, me and Loo Boo run out of money at the same time. We ended up here. I hate this town and I hate Tom Thomas and so does Loo Boo.

We've made some money here. Maybe enough to start up another cafe somewhere else."

Bodine smiled at her. "Get your savings and the food and head out the back door, Lucy. I know a little settlement down on the Clear that could sure use a good eatin' place. Move, people, I just don't know how much time we have."

The Chinaman bobbed his head up and down in agreement and spoke words that sounded to Bodine like loose gravel rattling around in a bucket. Bodine stepped out onto the boardwalk. Several people were hurriedly piling up possessions in wagons. He walked over to them.

"You'll never make it, people," he warned them. "Your chances are much better staying here."

"You go to hell, mister!" a woman bluntly told him. "We're pullin' out."

"I can't stop you."

"You shore can't," the man with her said. "So stand outta the way."

Bodine turned his back on them and started to walk off. Then he stopped and turned around. "Mister, when the Indians attack, kill the two women before Lone Dog takes them."

One of the women, an older, hard-faced veteran of the soiled dove trade, cursed him. "Mister Hot-Shot Gunfighter, there ain't nothing them Injuns can do to me that ain't already been done by so-called civilized white men a thousand times over down through the years, from St. Louis to Frisco."

Bodine looked at her, no emotion in his cool eyes. "That's what you think."

He walked off, his eyes taking in the activity in the town as the citizens made ready to meet the Indian attack. They were filling water barrels to use against fires. Rolling wagons in and turning them over to make barricades. Smashing out store windows to avoid flying glass when the attack came.

They might last a day and a night, Bodine thought. Maybe.

He rode out from the town and looked around. The rolling hills could, at this moment, contain several hundred warriors, just waiting to attack. And probably did, he concluded.

He circled the small town and rode once up the short main street, stopping at the livery and ordering the man to take a wagonload of corn up to the old mine buildings. He said he'd do it, but he didn't like it. Just do it, Bodine told him. As he passed Thomas's office buildings, he looked up at the second floor. Thomas and Terri were standing in a window, staring down at him. Their expressions were very hostile.

The man who would be king is about to have his kingdom, or at least a large part of it, destroyed, Bodine thought. He put Tom Thomas and Terri Kelly out of his mind and rode up the hill to the old mining complex.

Gerry had put his men to work and at this, at least, the lieutenant knew his business. Gerry had three lines of defense, the third being the three stone buildings where his men would, as the battle heated up, be forced to fall back to.

"How's the water?" Bodine asked.

"It's good. And it's protected," Gerry told him. "We've filled every barrel and bucket and container we could find. I had men out with the horses, letting them graze to their fill. That corn you had sent up was a godsend. I signed for it. I suppose eventually the man will get his money."

"He probably won't have much use for money in the grave, Gerry. That town is going to take a lot of misery, I'm thinking."

"I feel like we've betrayed the citizens by coming up here. In a way I feel that." He sighed. "I really don't know how I feel."

"Didn't Colonel Travers declare this town off-limits to his troopers?"

"Yes. Some months ago."

"Then don't worry about it."

Bodine and Lieutenant Gerry watched as several wagons began pulling out from the town.

"Fools," Gerry muttered.

"They'll get three or four miles, probably. It might be a blessing for us."

"How do you mean?"

"Once they're taken, the Indians will probably delay their attack on us while they're having fun torturing the prisoners."

"Good God, man! That's a *blessing?*"

"That's reality, Gerry. I warned them not to leave. They chose to ignore me."

"I wonder what will happen to them?"

"Lone Dog will probably show us a couple of them . . . after they've finished with them."

Judging by the expression on Gerry's face, the young lieutenant was not looking forward to that. "The hostiles are . . . quite inventive, so I'm told."

"That is one way of putting it."

Two Wolves joined them. "Lone Dog will not attack this night," he said. "He and his braves will be having too much fun with those unfortunates who chose to leave the town." He spoke with his eyes on the fading wagons. "The attack will come at dawn, and it will come hard. By that time, I should be close to the fort. I would like one of your men to ride with me, Gerry."

"Of course, but why?"

Two Wolves kept his expression stoic. "Because I am a half breed, Lieutenant. Colonel Travers, or more probably, Major Dawson, might think it a ruse on my part; an effort to pull them away from the fort. Colonel Travers might refuse to leave."

"I suppose," Gerry said. "Pick your man, Sam."

"I have. He's the smallest and lightest man in your command. We shall be riding hard. We'll leave at dusk, riding south for a few miles and then cutting west until we reach Dead Valley. From there we'll cut northwest and head for the fort."

Two Wolves looked at the sky. "It will be dark in three hours. We shall rest until then."

Bodine looked at him. "May your medicine stay good, Brother."

Two Wolves smiled, a twinkle in his eyes. "There was a Jewish fellow in one of my classes at the university. We became friends. He used to say, 'And a little bit of luck wouldn't hurt nothin', either.'"

The sounds of the gunfire drifted to those in the now silent town and the men on the hill. It was a very brief battle. Soon the rolling hills became very quiet.

"I hope the men killed the women before the hostiles got to them," Sergeant McGuire said, as he stood by Bodine's side.

"I doubt if they did. We'll know just after dark."

"How?"

"Lone Dog will move the prisoners in close enough for us to hear them screaming. It's a good psychological move on the Indians' part. Very demoralizing to a lot of people."

"But not to you, Bodine?"

"I've heard it before."

"In the camp of Medicine Horse?"

Bodine looked at him to see if the sergeant was serious. He was. "Oh, no, Sergeant. Medicine Horse is a very civilized person. He was educated back East. While he chose to return to the old ways, he retained many of the white man's ways. But don't ever think he wasn't a great warrior before and after he married white. Because he was. Medicine Horse rejected torture because it wasn't civilized and didn't prove anything. That is in direct conflict to many Indian beliefs. They believe that the longer a man stands torture, the better his dying. If he dies well, they will sing songs around the campfires, praising his bravery."

"Even if he was an enemy?"

"Oh, yes."

"I will never understand the Indian, Bodine."

"Probably not. And neither will I."

"But you lived with them off and on for fifteen years!"

"That's true. You may live with wolves all your life, but that doesn't make you a wolf."

As full night spread its dark cloak around the hills, Gerry came to stand beside Bodine at the stone fence around the complex on the hill.

"It's about time for Two Wolves to be pulling out, don't you think?"

"He left about a half hour ago."

"He told you goodbye?"

"No."

"You saw him leave?"

"No."

"You heard him leave?"

"No."

"Well, hell, man!" The lieutenant's voice held a note of exasperation. "How do you know he's gone?"

"I know."

Before Gerry could retort, the screaming began. It drifted in to them, touching hidden emotions among them all, peeling back the skin and exposing the raw nerve endings.

"Mother of God!" Sergeant McGuire hissed. "Is that a man or a woman?"

"I don't know," Bodine said. "At this point in that poor

being's life, it doesn't matter. They've been reduced to something less than a human being. That was deliberately done out of our earshot."

"Do you suppose the women were, ah, molested?" Gerry asked.

"Probably. It's best not to think about that."

"Why do they want us to hear all that awfulness, Lieutenant?" a young trooper asked, walking up.

Gerry looked at Bodine.

Although there probably was not five years' difference between Bodine and the young trooper, Bodine was frontier-toughened and more experienced than most men many years older. "You'll see in about five more minutes, troop."

It didn't take quite that long. The first screaming had scarcely bubbled off into a merciful death when another yowling took its place. This time it was plain to all that it was a woman.

She began begging for someone, anyone, to please God come and help her.

"Sergeant McGuire," Lieutenant Gerry said.

"Sir."

"Pass the word up and down the line: I will order the court-martial of any trooper who leaves his post without orders."

"Yes, sir."

"The savages want us to come out there, don't they, Lieutenant?" the young trooper asked. "So they can kill us."

"That's it," Gerry pushed the words through tightly compressed lips.

The screaming and crying and begging intensified. Gerry looked at Bodine. The man's face was impassive. His eyes as cool and unreadable as always. Gerry wondered if he would ever possess that type of coolness in the face of adversity. Then he wondered if he wanted to.

"Any minute now," Bodine said. "That screaming will prove too much for somebody in town."

The sounds of galloping horses reached them as men from the town went to the rescue of the tortured.

"They're going to rescue them!" the young trooper cried.

"No, they're not," Bodine told him. "All they're going to do is insure the torture goes on all night. With their own bodies."

The young trooper swallowed hard.

Chapter 22

Those townspeople who went charging into the dangerous darkness with hopes of aiding the prisoners only succeeded in riding to a horrible death. Lone Dog's braves took them without firing a shot; and now they had enough prisoners to fill the night air with painful shrieking until the dawning. Then they would destroy the town.

"Try to get some sleep," Bodine told Gerry.

"How in God's name do you expect people to sleep with that painful screaming in one's ears?"

Bodine looked at the man, then walked to his bedroll, laid down, put his head on the saddle and his hat over his face, and was asleep in less than a minute.

"Damn the man!" Gerry muttered. "Sometimes I don't think he's human."

"He's human," Sergeant McGuire said. "He was born out here, Lieutenant. Twenty-five years ago there weren't fifty whites for a hundred miles in any direction. Maybe not that many. He's wang-leather tough, both in body and mind."

For a moment, the screaming abated, and both men could breathe a little easier. Then it began again.

"Will this night ever end?" Gerry wiped sweat from his face, even though the air was cold.

"I imagine them folks under the knife out yonder are wondering the same thing, Lieutenant."

Bodine was up long before dawn, walking among the troopers, many of whom had not slept a wink all night. But the screaming had finally stopped.

"Brace yourselves," Bodine told Gerry and McGuire and a few other troopers. "At first light you're going to see with your own eyes what Lone Dog did to some of those people last night."

"I do not believe that the Indians could have crept into the town and left the bodies without someone down there in town seeing them," Gerry said.

McGuire spat on the ground.

"You are not one with the earth, the sun, the wind, the sky, or the night, either, Gerry," Bodine told him.

"All that nonsense is Indian hooey!"

Bodine smiled. "You'd be surprised how many people believed just like that, Gerry. They changed their minds seconds before they died."

The lieutenant walked away, his back stiff.

"He's a fine officer, Bodine," McGuire said. "Really cares about his men. He's just a little wet behind the ears yet."

"Lone Dog is just about an hour away from drying him off," Bodine told the sergeant.

"How do you get to be one with all those things you mentioned, Bodine?"

"You believe, Sergeant. You fast, you pray, you endure pain, you seek visions."

"And you did all that?"

"Yes."

"Was it worth it?"

"Oh, yes." Bodine pointed to a barely discernible object lying in the middle of the wide street in town. "Come into the light, get your field glasses, Sergeant. I want the men to see just how, as Gerry put it, inventive the Indians can be. I think it'll make them fight better."

Several of the newer and younger troopers lost their meager breakfast after viewing the tortured remains lying in the dirt. Others had already steeled themselves. But all took a look through the long lenses.

"Jesus, God, and Mary!" Lucy breathed, her face pale as she lowered the glasses. "I knowed that woman. I didn't like her, but no one deserves to be treated like that."

Bodine remembered the tortured body of the man he'd found not far from Cutter. "There are some people in that town down there just as bad, Lucy. If it comes to it, Lucy, I won't let them take you alive."

"Don't let me see you do it, Bodine," she requested. "Just shoot me and let it be."

"All right. But I don't think it'll come to that. Two Wolves should be reaching the fort within the hour. Say it'll take Travers an hour to gear up. It's a full fifteen to twenty hours forced march from the fort to here; and they've got to spare their horses for the march back." Gerry and McGuire were listening. "We've got to hold out today and tonight."

"That's providing Sam made it," Gerry tossed cold water on the statement.

"That is correct."

"How many Indians does Lone Dog have, Two Wolves?" Colonel Travers asked the weary man.

"At least four-hundred, Colonel. And they're well armed, mostly with repeating rifles."

Travers had not hesitated. He had listened to Two Wolves, and immediately ordered a company to gear up. He would lead the unit personally, leaving Major Dawson at the garrison with less than a company of mostly green and untrained troopers.

"We'll pull out in about an hour, Two Wolves. You're not thinking of returning, are you? You're beat, man."

"I'll sleep until time to leave. That's my brother back there, Colonel."

During the night, Lone Dog's braves had crept close to the town. Usually low on ammunition, the warriors normally did not waste their shots. They picked their targets carefully and conserved ammo. And they did not immediately try the Army dug in on the hill, concentrating first on the town and its badly rattled citizens. The bodies of the tortured lay in the street, bloody and naked and hideous to the eyes of the defenders.

Which was Lone Dog's intention. The Indians did not know the word and could not pronounce it had they known it, but they were masters in the use of psychological warfare.

By eight o'clock in the morning, several buildings of the small town had been burned, set afire by flaming arrows. Many of those people who ran for safety didn't make it, being cut down by gunfire from the hills. And fighting the fires proved far too costly in human life, for the Indians were very close and their aim was true.

On the hill the Army occupied, only a few shots had been fired at the elusive enemy, and Bodine had fired most of them.

He was sitting behind the stone fence, motionless, his eyes on a bush on the side of a hill, about two hundred yards away. Lieutenant Gerry lay beside him.

"What do you see out there, Bodine? I can't see a damn thing except empty land."

"There's an Indian close to that bush, Gerry. But I don't

know, yet, which side he's on. He's dug in, sometime during the night, and covered himself with dirt, breathing through a tiny airhole. Might be using a reed from the creek or a hollowed out stick. I'm sure there are others much closer to us than him, but I just haven't been able to spot them."

A strangled yell cut Bodine's eyes. A brave had obviously crept up to the fence line during the night, laying close to the stone, and waiting for his chance to kill.

A young trooper had presented himself just in time to die with his throat cut.

The brave ran toward an outbuilding. Bodine's rifle barked, the bullet taking the brave in the side, dusting him through and through. Bodine shot him in the head for insurance.

"Sneaky bastards!" Gerry said, as the body of the dead trooper was dragged off by other soldiers, staying low as they pulled their dead comrade's body from the fence.

Bodine smiled. "Just good fighters, Gerry. That's all."

"Don't you hate them, Bodine? These Indians, I mean. Lone Dog's bunch."

Bodine shook his head. "No. They were here before we came. They're just fighting for a way of life. You can't hate somebody for fighting for land that has been theirs for hundreds of years."

Gerry shook his head. "I don't understand you, Bodine."

Bodine chuckled. "You're not part of this country, Gerry. If you live here the rest of your life you won't really be a part of it. Although you'll be closer than you are now."

"Whatever that means," the young officer said wearily.

Bodine glanced at him and laughed at the expression on Gerry's face. His eyes cut away from Gerry to watch the arc of a fire arrow as it came soaring from behind a low hill behind the main street of the frontier town. It landed on the roof of a building. A careless Indian stuck his head up and

Bodine snapped off a shot. He didn't know whether he scored a hit or not, but he probably caused the brave a few anxious seconds either way.

Bodine looked back at the roof of the building. A small fire had been started by the arrow. The building would be gone in ten minutes, with more people pouring out onto the street.

A sentry stationed belly down on the roof of the old headquarters of the mining company yelled, "Here they come. Jesus Christ, there must be five hundred of them!"

The pounding of hooves reached the ears of the men on the hill as Lone Dog's braves thundered over the hill and galloped into the few smoky streets of Cutter. A few soldiers began firing their single shot carbines.

"Hold your fire!" Gerry yelled. "Cease firing. The range is too great. You're wasting ammunition."

A bullet clipped the stone fence, stinging Gerry with tiny shards of rock splinters. He quickly went belly-down, cussing.

Those on the hill could but watch as those in the town closed with the Indians, in many cases a hand-to-hand battle.

Gerry looked at Bodine, questions in his eyes.

"You're in command here, Gerry. But if I were you, I'd move some sharpshooters over there," he pointed, "to protect on that most vulnerable side, and then send some troops down the hill far enough to put them in range of the town. When the Indians attack, pull them back. We're going to have some townspeople up here very shortly and we need to give them some covering fire."

Lieutenant Gerry nodded and glanced at Sergeant McGuire. "Do it, Sergeant."

When the Indians saw what the Army was doing, several groups broke off from attacking the town and charged the hill, exactly what Bodine hoped they would do. The troopers slaughtered the first wave of mounted Indians and, the Indian concept of warfare being what it was, Lone Dog waved his braves back rather than lose another twenty or thirty men to the withering fire from the troopers.

Bodine had already moved to his horse and saddled up. In the saddle, he made sure his Winchester was loaded up full and checked his Colts. Sergeant McGuire and a dozen other troopers were in the saddle, doing the same.

Bodine looked at a young trooper with a bugle hanging from a cord over his shoulder. "Can you blow that thing, Troop?"

"Yes, sir!" the young man said, grinning.

Smoke from the burning town was billowing, the cold winds whipping it in all directions, smarting the eyes. The screaming from those trapped in the town was intensifying.

"All right, McGuire," Bodine said. "Let's do what the Indians don't expect us to do."

With the reins in his left hand and his right hand around the butt of a six-shooter, McGuire yelled the orders: "Charge!"

The young trooper lifted the bugle to his lips and blew the command as loudly as he could as the small force galloped down the hill, screaming and yelling at the top of their lungs.

Because of the smoke, the Indians had no way of knowing whether they were being attacked by ten or a hundred cavalrymen. Many of them broke and galloped away from the fire and smoke and confusion and death, heading for the cover of the hills.

An Indian holding a bloody scalp leaped out of a storefront just as Bodine reached the first short block of the village. Bodine shot the brave in the chest, the slug knocking him back into the burning building.

An Indian jumped behind the saddle of McGuire's horse. The sergeant threw him off and another trooper shot the brave before he could rise.

Bodine spotted Tom Thomas and Terri. "Get up to the hill!" he shouted at them. "Move, damnit!"

He struggled to see through the acrid smoke. Whacker Corrigan rode up to him, mounted on a huge mule, a long-barreled pistol in one hand. The New York City man grinned at him. "I want to keep you alive so I can give you a proper whipping, Bodine, so I'll stay with you. We'll watch each other's back."

"Glad to have you, Whacker," Bodine yelled over the roaring of combat and the wild screaming of the wounded and the frightened and the dying. "But don't count on whipping me."

The former shoulder-striker laughed and lifted his pistol, shooting a painted brave in the back as he tried to run into an alley.

Bodine watched as Simon Bull and Stutterin' Smith came charging up the middle of the bloody and smoky street. The reins in their teeth and both hands filled with six-guns. They were guns for hire, to be sure, but there was no questioning their bravery.

The pair of gunslingers rode right up to and through the jaws of death, each with a red-light lady behind them, the powdered arms around the waists of the gunfighters, clinging tightly, the rouged lips saying prayers they hadn't uttered since childhood.

"To the hill!" Bodine yelled at them.

The gunfighters nodded and galloped up toward safety.

"To the hill! Sound the call!" McGuire yelled at the bugler.

As they gathered around the sergeant, Bodine could see that several of the troopers had been wounded, but all were still in the saddle as they began battling their way back to the hill and safety; safety at least for a time.

Bodine stabled Rowdy and stripped the saddle from him, giving him a bucket of water and a bucket of corn. He carefully inspected the big stallion for any wounds he might have received and, finding none, patted him on the rump, moving quickly as Rowdy tried to step on his boot and then tried to give him a little sign of affection by kicking him in the butt.

Bodine moved to the stone fence and squatted down, looking at the town, now totally consumed in flames. No live Indians in sight, but Bodine knew Lone Dog had them surrounded; surrounded and outnumbered. Using the billowing smoke, the Indians would be moving closer and closer to the buildings on the hill. The charge could come at any time.

Lone Dog would have suspected a rider had been sent to the fort, and he would know within an hour's accuracy how long it would take Travers to reach the town. There was no way the relief column could arrive before nine or ten o'clock that night, and Travers would be rightly hesitant about launching any attack at night. The people on the hill would have to hold out this day and through the coming night.

Staying low to present a smaller target to the hidden Indians stationed on the hills around the complex, Bodine made a slow circle of the makeshift fort.

Only about thirty or so people had made it out of Cutter alive.

"Twenty-two men and ten women," Gerry told him "I figure they took about seventy percent casualties. But the men came out heavily armed and with plenty of ammunition. They brought some food and water and medical supplies with them. We're in pretty good shape." He consulted his pocket watch. "Colonel Travers should have two hours' march behind him by now."

"Peterson just died, Lieutenant," McGuire said, walking up. "Shot through the lungs."

"How are the wounded?"

"Mackey is not going to make it. The rest did not suffer serious wounds. They're being patched up and will be back on duty."

"Lieutenant!" the sentry on top of a building called. "Here they come!"

Chapter 23

Lone Dog and his braves spent the next hour taunting the men and women on the hill. The Indians would ride to just outside rifle range and yell and scream at the besieged band behind the low stone walls.

But Bodine quickly picked up on what Lone Dog was doing. He pulled Gerry and Sergeant McGuire to one side. "Lone Dog wants all our attention focused in one direction, Gerry. Switch some men around to cover the other directions and tell them to be alert for infiltrators. I'm thinking there'll be a rush in a few minutes. Tell your men to hold their fire and let them bunch up."

McGuire nodded and moved away, beginning the shifting of his troopers.

"God, if we only had some artillery." Gerry did some wishful thinking.

"We can make it," Bodine said, as Tom Thomas walked up. "We're just going to have to be on our toes at all times." He looked at Thomas. "Where is that rag-tag so-called army of yours, Thomas?"

"I don't know," the man replied tightly, his hatred for Bodine scarcely concealed behind the words.

"More Indians joining the group, Lieutenant!" the rooftop sentry called, looking through field glasses. "And they're dressed . . . odd."

Gerry uncased his binoculars and took a look, a grim expression altering his face. He handed the field glasses to Bodine.

"Walker's Militia is no more, Thomas," Bodine said, after quickly looking through the long lenses. He handed the glasses to Thomas. "Take a look at those shirts the braves are wearing."

Thomas looked and cursed. Many of the bucks were wearing brown shirts, and fresh scalps adorned the manes of their ponies and reins and rifle barrels. Thomas slowly lowered the glasses. He had seen the destruction of his town, and now it seemed his army had been wiped out. The man seemed to age before their eyes.

"You son of a bitch!" The female voice sprang at them from behind. They turned, looking at Terri Kelly.

"Now, Terri . . ." Thomas spoke.

"Oh, shut up, you windbag!" she spat at him, just as Sergeant McGuire walked up. Then Terri cut loose with a stream of profanity that would have shocked any saloon operator on the Barbary Coast. She traced Thomas's ancestry back to where he was sitting in a tree, scratching himself and picking fleas off his brothers and sisters.

"My word!" Lieutenant Gerry said, shock and awe in his voice.

"I told you this scam wouldn't work, you big ox," she yelled at him.

"Terri, shut your mouth!" Thomas shouted, regaining some of his composure.

"No way, buffalo-butt!" she squalled at him. "I'm not going to die with this on my conscience."

Thomas lifted a hand to hit her and Bodine blocked the blow and busted Thomas in the mouth with a hard right fist, knocking the man down. He looked at Terri. "What's on your conscience, Terri?"

"Keep your damn mouth shut, you slut!" Thomas struggled to get to his boots.

Bodine kept him on the ground with a boot in the man's belly. Thomas groaned and twisted on the cold earth.

Sergeant McGuire motioned for several troopers to come over. He pointed to Tom Thomas and they nodded heads, standing close to the man.

"It was Walker's army who attacked and killed the people at the settlement where I was teaching," Terri said.

Thomas called her a very ugly name.

"Women prisoners were taken. I guess they were raped and then killed by the men in Walker's army."

"Disgusting!" Lieutenant Gerry said. "Why was the settlement attacked?"

"You see, for a time, Walker and his men had been working with Lone Dog. Lone Dog and Thomas had a deal going. Thomas would give him guns in return for being left alone. But Thomas tried to cheat Lone Dog. The raid was done to make it appear Lone Dog did it so the Army would hunt him down."

Thomas cussed her, low and long.

"Lone Dog said he would kill Thomas and destroy Cutter. But Tom never thought he would really do it. Guess he was wrong, huh?"

"Place this . . . creature under arrest, Sergeant McGuire," Gerry said, pointing at Tom Thomas. "And Miss Kelly as well. Tie them securely and place them in that shed over there."

Whacker Corrigan and Stutterin' Smith had stood by silently, listening to the story. Corrigan's sigh was audible. "You tell them the truth about me, Thomas," the huge man said. "Or I'll stomp you to death before the Army can do anything about it."

Thomas nodded his head. "Corrigan and Smith and the others had nothing to do with my arrangement with Walker or Lone Dog. They're clear."

Corrigan met Bodine's eyes. "If I had known about Thomas's involvement with Lone Dog, I would have killed him myself."

Stutterin' said, "I hire my g . . . g . . . gun, Bodine. I don't believe in rapin' w . . . w . . . women and killin' k . . . k . . . kids."

Bodine nodded at the men; he knew that many gunfighters operated under an odd but very strict code of honor.

"Lone Dog's ridin' up, Lieutenant," a sentry called. "He's comin' under a white flag."

"Hold your fire!" Gerry shouted. "We'll honor the truce flag."

"I'll walk out with you," Bodine said. "Lone Dog's English is not good."

Bodine and Gerry walked out to meet with Lone Dog on the slope.

"Bo-dine," Lone Dog said. "Give me Tom Thomas and the woman and you all may leave."

"I wish I could, Lone Dog. They deserve no better. But they are prisoners of the Army. I can promise you that they both will be tried and probably hanged for what they've done."

Lone Dog's smile was a grim baring of the teeth "If you do not give them to me now, you will all die with them, Bodine."

"Give it up, Lone Dog. You can't overrun us on the hill. All you will succeed in doing is losing a lot of warriors."

"I could kill you both now."

"Then that would mean you have no honor. Your wife

would throw your belongings from the tipi, you would never see your children again, and you would be forever banished from the tribe. They would tell stories around the fire about what a coward you are. You would be known forever and ever as Cowardly Dog, The Man Who Could Not Be Trusted To Keep His Word."

That stung Lone Dog, for he knew the truth in Bodine's statement. "I did not say I was going to do that, Bo-dine. Only that I could."

"We will not hand the prisoners over to you, Lone Dog. That is my final word"

"Then return in safety to your fort, Bo-dine. And sing your death songs. I will personally hang your scalp on my rifle." Lone Dog swung his pony and rode down the hill.

"Let's get back up the hill before he changes his mind," Bodine said. "They'll be hitting us in a few minutes."

Bodine and Gerry just made the safety of the stone buildings before the Indians opened fire, the slugs sending everyone diving for whatever cover they could find. The Indians kept up the fire all that day. Obviously, as Bodine pointed out to Gerry, Lone Dog and his braves had taken a lot of ammunition from the dead men who had made up Walker's Militia. And this fight was worth the expelling of it, for if Lone Dog were victorious, it would mean he would be a great chief and a wise and very courageous leader in battle. And his medicine would be good so many more braves would join him.

Two of Gerry's troopers were downed by the gunfire from the hills and ridges, with one of them dying. One civilian was wounded, another killed during the long day.

And Bodine knew that Lone Dog's braves were inching closer and closer to the complex on the hill. They would probably attack from the west side just as the sun was going down, leaving the defenders on the west side nearly blind.

The town of Cutter was completely gone; not even a privy

had escaped the raging flames, and only a few wisps of smoke drifted into the air, to mark the end of Tom Thomas's evil scheming.

Then the chanting began, wafting to the ears of the defenders on the cold hill.

"What are they doing?" Corrigan asked Bodine.

"Preparing themselves for a great battle. Asking for courage in the upcoming fight and for the strength to die well."

"Then they're about to attack."

"It won't be long. They'll be sending in fire arrows first, to demoralize us. Or try to. Lone Dog knows these stone buildings won't burn. But his thinking is that they might get lucky and set some of us on fire. Maybe kill some horses."

"Charming fellow," Corrigan said.

"What are your plans when this is over?" Bodine asked.

"You mean if we live through it?"

"We'll live through it."

"I like this country, Bodine. I think I'll stay. Hell, I might even try to farm." His laughter was genuine. "I don't know nothing about it, but I can learn. It's not like New York City. Man, this air is so clear and fresh out here!"

"No more shoulder-striking?"

"Who am I going to strike, a buffalo?" Again, the big man laughed and Bodine smiled with him. "No, Bodine. I'm tired of all that. I'm tired of the stink of saloons and of the smell of crooked men. I want to put all that behind me and start over. I just want to live and let live and be a good neighbor. Actually, I came out here to do that. But I let that slick-talking snake Thomas talk me into joining him. We all make mistakes."

Bodine stuck out his hand and the man shook it. "Welcome to the frontier, Corrigan."

A bullet sent them both diving to the ground, bringing this comment from Corrigan: "It would seem that not everyone is as happy to see me as you, Bodine."

* * *

Lone Dog's braves came just as Bodine had predicted, the main thrust coming out of the sun on the west side, and they came in a silent, deadly rush.

Bodine and Corrigan and Stutterin' Smith joined the defenders on the west side of the complex and managed to beat back the first wave. But Bodine knew that many Indians still lay hidden near the stone fence. They would wait until dark and try again.

Stutterin' looked at Bodine in the gloom of cold night. "I ain't g . . . g . . . got nothin' personal agin you, B . . . B . . . Bodine. I just think I'm b . . . b . . . better than you. So when this is all over, I'm gonna b . . . b . . . beat you."

"There's no point to it, Smith."

"There really never is, B . . . B . . . Bodine." The gunfighter turned and walked away.

"Keep a sharp eye out, men." Bodine heard the lieutenant's voice. "What was that all about, Bodine?" Gerry asked, stepping out of the darkness.

"Professional pride, I suppose," Bodine told him. "Utah Jack Noyes was supposed to be one of the best around."

An agonizing cry split the darkness. "They're in the compound!" the call went up.

The trooper standing next to Gerry went down with an arrow through his neck, to die on the cold ground, choking his life away.

Bodine felt a buckskin-clad arm around his neck and the prick of a knife blade at his side just as he turned and twisted, using brute strength to toss the brave to the ground. Bodine leveled his Winchester and shot the buck in the chest. He brought the butt of the rifle straight back and into the belly of an Indian, then turned and clubbed the warrior on the side of the head with the stock.

Bodine did not have time to check how badly he had hurt

the warrior, for the compound had suddenly filled with Lone Dog's men.

Bodine lifted his rifle and began shooting. He really did not have to aim, for Indians were pouring over the stone fences in human waves.

"Into the buildings!" Lieutenant Gerry's cry was just heard over the crash of guns and the screaming of the hostiles and the cries for help from the wounded.

Bodine took a war club against his head, knocking him sprawling. He rolled and managed to knock down an Indian who was grappling with a civilian from the town. Bodine stuck his rifle barrel into the brave's face and pulled the trigger, the slug tearing away part of the man's jaw. The civilian helped Bodine to his feet and the two of them stumbled toward the stables, figuring that the buildings would soon be filled to overflowing.

As they raced for the dubious safety of the stables, the civilian gave a small cry and collapsed, falling to the ground on his side, a bullet hole in the center of his back and another in his chest where the bullet had exited. It took only one look for Bodine to see that the man was dead.

Bodine reached the stables in time to see an Indian trying to lead away a few horses. Bodine shot the buck and re-stabled the horses, almost stumbling over the body of a young trooper who had been assigned to guard the huge old barn.

"Bodine?" a man called.

Bodine recognized the voice as belonging to Sergeant McGuire. "Mac. You all right?"

"Got a crease on my noggin from a bullet. It's nothing. You?"

"Knot on my head."

"I've got four men at the far end of the barn. Let's you and me climb up into the loft and take the other end."

"Sounds good. Did Gerry make it?"

"I think so. But I saw him take a bullet in his arm."

"Going to be a long night, Mac," Bodine said, after climbing up into the loft and taking a position just inside the second floor hay door.

"Long it may be," the man replied. "I just hope we make it through it."

Chapter 24

Long before midnight struck its toll, the fight had turned into a stand-off.

Lone Dog's warriors could not breach the stone buildings and the men and women inside the buildings could not drive the Indians off the hilltop. Lone Dog's braves had taken cover behind the stone fence and the battle had now been reduced to a few sporadic shots from either side. Just enough to keep both sides on edge and allowing no sleep.

"What's the time, Bodine?" Mac whispered.

"My watch got busted. I figure it's close to midnight."

"The relief column should be out there close. If the riders made it," he added.

"Travers won't want to lead a charge at night. I'll expect them at first light. Right now I'd give a double eagle for a hot cup of coffee."

"I try not to think about that. Damn, but it's getting cold!"

A bullet that came singing its deadly tune out of the night and whined close to his head moved the sergeant around some and increased his circulation. It also produced some pretty fancy cussing from the man.

Bodine smiled. "Did that warm you up some, Mac?"

"That it did, lad. That it did." The man cut his eyes to the hills behind those that had been occupied by Lone Dog's braves. "Well, I'll be damned, Bodine. Take a look!"

Bodine crawled to the opening and looked out. The hills were dotted with small fires. He made his way to the other end of the barn. The same sight greeted his eyes. It was Travers' way of letting them know they were not alone.

"Another time, Bo-dine!" the call came from out of the night. From the mouth of Lone Dog. "We will meet again, Bo-dine."

"Running away, Lone Dog?" Bodine shouted. "I always knew you were a coward."

Lone Dog returned the slur, tracing Bodine back to the belly of a rabid prairie dog.

Bodine laughed at the man, the taunting laughter infuriating the man.

"You will die hard, Bo-dine. This I promise you."

Bodine told him where he could put his threat. Sideways.

Long before first light, Bodine and a few others had prowled the grounds, seeking confirmation that Lone Dog and his braves had indeed pulled out. The Indians were gone. The many fires had convinced Lone Dog that he was facing many more soldiers than he really was, and he had no taste for total defeat.

Lieutenant Gerry had lost eight men with more than a dozen wounded, three of the wounded not expected to make it. The body count of the civilians could not be completed until the Army had the opportunity to inspect the charred ruins of the town.

Bodine's eyes were gritty as he squatted down beside the stone fence, a welcome cup of scalding coffee in his hands and waited for the first silver streamers of dawn to cut the darkness.

Lieutenant Gerry came out to join him, one arm in a sling. The front of his coat was dark with dried blood. He held a cup of coffee in his good hand. "Up until this time, my experience with Indians had been limited to what I now see as only minor skirmishes with what I perceived to be very cowardly fighters. I have changed my mind about their courage."

"They aren't afraid to die, Gerry. Many of them would prefer death to life on a reservation."

Gerry nodded his head. "I . . . think I understand." He was silent for a time, enjoying the silence of the pre-dawn. "I wonder if Sam came with the column?"

"I'm sure he did. We're brothers."

Gerry looked at the dark bulk of the man. "Did you and Two Wolves really beat each other to a bloody pulp by the river?"

"Oh, yes. It was just something we had to get out of our systems. We've been fighting since we were boys. We've always competed against each other."

Again, Gerry nodded his head. The sky was growing lighter in the east. "Talk is that you and this Stutterin' Smith person are going to have a gunfight very soon."

"Only if he pushes it. I have nothing at all against the man."

"But you will fight if he calls you out?"

"I have to, Gerry. That's the way it is out here.

"You could just turn your back and walk away."

Bodine stood up from his squat to face the lieutenant. "That's something I can't and won't do, Gerry." He drained his coffee cup and tossed the dregs onto the ground. "Here comes the column."

Gerry looked around him in the dull grayness of early dawning. "I don't see a thing. Or hear anything."

"They'll be coming over the ridge in about a minute. You'll want your people in formation, I suspect." Bodine walked away.

Gerry watched him walk away and shook his head. "The man is impossible," he muttered. "I doubt the Colonel has even rolled out of his blankets."

Then he heard the faint drum of steel-shod hooves on the hard-packed road leading to the burned-out town of Cutter. "Someday," Gerry muttered, "I'm going to be around when he's wrong."

A few wagons, only slightly fire-damaged, had been located, the burned wheels or tongues replaced, and the women and wounded placed into the wagons after a quick breakfast on the cold hillside.

Gerry had informed Travers about the upcoming gunfight and the colonel had been appalled.

"After all of *this!*" He waved a hand toward the burned-out town. "And this Smith person wants a gunfight?"

"That's the talk, sir."

"And Bodine says what?"

"He'll fight if he's pushed."

Two Wolves walked up.

"Can't you stop Bodine, Sam?" Gerry asked him.

"I would sooner to attempt to stop the wind. But Bodine will not call Smith out. My brother is willing to ride out and forget it. It will all be up to Smith."

"Someday there will be laws against this sort of barbarism," Gerry predicted.

"We will be middle-aged men before that happens," Two Wolves told him. "There is Smith."

The two officers and the half-breed turned as Stutterin' Smith stepped out of the barn. He had taken off his jacket and removed his right hand glove.

"Bodine!" Smith called.

Bodine stepped out from beside the wagon that contained Lucy and the Chinaman. His jacket was brushed back, exposing his Colts.

"It doesn't have to be this way, Smith."

"Yeah, it d . . . d . . . do, Bodine. I c . . . c . . . cain't have no talk about you bein' b . . . b . . . bettter than me. I m . . . m . . . make my livin' with a g . . . g . . . gun."

"You're too good a man to end it like this, Smith. You're a brave man. You fought well. I'd like you to be my friend."

A surprised look came onto Smith's face. "B . . . b . . . but we is friends, Bodine. I ain't g . . . g . . . got nothin' agin you p . . . p . . . personal."

"You men stop this immediately!" Colonel Travers shouted.

"You shut up, soldier b . . . b . . . boy," Smith told him. "This ain't none of your affair."

"Stay out of it, Travers," Bodine told the man without taking his eyes off of Stutterin'. "This is something you don't understand."

"My price just went up, B . . . B . . . Bodine," Smith said with a smile. "Sorry it had to b . . . b . . . be you."

"Dead men don't earn money, Smith."

Simon Bull was leaning up against the stone fence, watching intently. He knew that someday he would face Bodine. He wanted to see just how good the man was. Nobody could be as good as the rumors implied. He'd never seen a gunfighter yet who lived up to his reputation.

Simon Bull felt eyes on him and he cut his gaze. Two Wolves was watching him. The breed's buckskin jacket brushed back, exposing the butt of his six-gun. Simon smiled and crossed his arms over his chest, showing Two Wolves that he was out of this showdown.

Two Wolves left the side of the officers and walked over to lean against the fence, beside Simon.

"What's the matter, Breed—don't you trust me?"

"No more than I would trust a cornered puma."

Simon chuckled softly. "That's probably best."

"Time for t . . . t . . . talkin' is over, Bodine!" Smith called. "M . . . m . . . make your play!"

"That's up to you, Smith. I really wish you wouldn't force this."

"You yellow?"

"No. I just don't see the point."

"The p . . . p . . . point is this!" Smith yelled, then grabbed for iron.

He never cleared leather on his first try. Bodine's Colt roared and bucked and spat smoke and lead and death. The slug took Smith in the gut, knocking him back but not putting him down.

"B . . . b . . . bastard!" Smith snarled the word.

Bodine let him pull iron. Smith cocked his Remington .44 and the muzzle rose slowly.

Bodine shot him twice in the chest, the slugs so close together a silver dollar would cover the holes. Smith's boots flew out from under him and he landed hard on the cold, rocky ground, his pistol slipping from fingers that would never hold another gun.

Bodine reloaded as he walked over to the dying man and looked down at him.

"F . . . f . . . fast," Smith said. "Always k . . . k. . . knowed I'd see the varmint. Never t . . . t . . . thought it'd be this soon."

"You got kin, Smith?"

"Nobody who'd g . . . g . . . give a damn. Wrap me up g . . . g . . . good, Bodine. I never did like the cold. Take my watch, Bodine. It's a g . . . g . . . good one."

"All right, Smith."

"You ought to . . . you ought to . . ."

Whatever it was that Smith figured Bodine ought to do

died with the man. The gunfighter slipped into that long sleep with his eyes open, staring up at the new dawn, the last dawning he would see on this earth.

"Stupid," Bodine was heard to mutter. "It didn't have to be."

Bodine dropped his Colt back into leather and hooked the hammer thong. He knelt down and took the blanket that was handed him by a trooper, spreading it over Smith.

Two Wolves glanced at Simon Bull. "Still want to try him, Bull?"

The big man smiled. "I'm a lot bigger than Stutterin'. I can soak up more lead. I believe I can stay on my boots long enough to kill him."

Two Wolves shook his head. "But you would both be *dead!*"

"But can you think of a better epitaph than the man who killed Matt Bodine?"

"Yes, I can. How about: He lived a long and noble life?"

"You good with a gun, Breed. But you ain't no gunfighter. You don't understand us no more than I understand Injuns."

"Perhaps not." Two Wolves walked over to his brother and helped him pick up Smith and carry him over to the shallow mass-grave hole that the burial detail had chopped out of the cold earth.

"Senseless," Two Wolves muttered, as he helped lay the body beside the others.

Bodine said nothing as he buttoned up Smith's shirt and placed his hat on his chest. He removed Smith's watch and slipped it into his pocket. It was a good one.

"How come I cain't go through their pockets and look for change?" a man called from a wagon.

"Shut your damned mouth!" Colonel Travers told him. "Scum!" he muttered. Then he waved to the burial detail. "Cover them up."

The cold wind picked up, moaning softly over the hillside as the earth and rocks began filling the hole.

Chapter 25

"Sam," Terri said, finally catching his eye as he started to ride past the open wagon.

"I have nothing at all to say to you, Miss Kelly. Civilization would have been better served had you died back in Cutter."

"You don't mean that, Sam!"

But his cold eyes told her that he most certainly did mean it.

"I've made mistakes, Sam. But don't we all? I deserve another chance."

"I know all about your past, Terri. I know you have been a criminal all your life. You've been run out of every town you've ever tried to settle in. You and Thomas deserve each other."

"Sam! What a horrid thing to say. Not gentlemanly at all. Certainly not a bit like you. I must say that I am really very disappointed in you."

"Terri?"

"Yes, my darling Samuel?"

"Go right straight to hell!"

He lifted his horse into a stiff canter just as Terri opened her mouth and let the foulness roll forth like sewage into a cesspool.

Two Wolves rode away with a small smile of satisfaction on his lips. He was still smiling as he slowed at Bodine's side.

"Was that you responsible for for that caterwauling back yonder?" Bodine asked.

"I certainly was."

"She sure has got a filthy mouth. She try to butter up to you?"

"For a very short time. I told her to go to hell."

Bodine looked at him for a moment and then bursted out laughing. Soon Two Wolves was laughing along with him. Gerry rode back to see what was so funny. Bodine told him. The lieutenant tried to look stern but he could only hold it for a few seconds before he broke into peals of laughter.

At the head of the column, Colonel Travers shifted in the saddle in an attempt to ease his sore butt. He glanced at Sergeant McGuire. "Mac, what in the devil is so funny back there with those three?"

Mac spat before replying. "Oh, they're just young, sir. And full of it." He hid his secret smile. He knew damn well what they were laughing about.

They rode on for about a mile before Travers broke the silence. "I might as well tell you now, Mac. Your request for transfer to the 7th Cavalry was turned down. I tried, Mac."

"I know you did, sir. Just as well, I reckon. I was trying to get with Major Reno. I know him well. But they'd have most likely put me with Custer; he takes too many chances to suit this old soldier."

"You're probably better off right here with me, Mac."

"Yes, sir, you're probably right."

* * *

Bodine and Two Wolves broke off from the column and headed south, toward their ranches.

"We best stop at Dad's and pick up some supplies. Say, why don't you come on down and spend some time with me. I haven't beaten you at checkers since the last time we played."

"You haven't beaten me at checkers in years, Brother. But I shall pay you a visit for a time. I want to look over that mean, miserable hovel you call a home."

"Hovel! Just for that, by God, you can do the cooking."

"Thank you. At least I know now that neither of us will starve during the remainder of the winter. Since you seem to have so much difficulty in even getting water to boil."

They were still arguing, with Bodine waving his arms and shouting, and Two Wolves smiling and shaking his head in disagreement as they rode onto their home range.

The hard Wyoming winter hit them again before spring managed to shove winter aside. But the two blood-bonded brothers stayed snug and warm in Bodine's house near the Powder, venturing out only to hunt, to chop wood, and to break ice for the cattle and horses to drink.

As the days began to warm, Slim Man, a breed like Two Wolves, rode up to the cabin and swung down from the saddle. He was welcomed in for food and coffee and for any news he might have. And he had plenty.

After eating his fill, and over a second cup of coffee, Slim Man pushed back his chair and rubbed his belly. "Good grub. You didn't cook it, did you, Bodine?" His dark eyes twinkled with good humor as Two Wolves laughed.

"I ought to make you wash the dishes for that remark," Bodine said with a laugh. "You got any news worth telling?"

Slim Man's smile faded. "Yes. And none of it good. Crow King, Sitting Bull, and Gall have been on their hunting grounds for some time now. The Army ordered them back to the reservation two and a half months ago. They refused to go. The Cheyenne have agreed to join the Brule, Ogalalla, Sans Arc, Blackfeet, Miniconjou, and Hunkpapa in their fight against the Army."

Two Wolves and Bodine exchanged glances, Two Wolves asking, "Where are they now, Slim Man?"

"Heading for the Rosebuds. They plan to make their camp close to the Little Bighorn."

Slim Man paused.

"What's the matter?" Two Wolves asked.

"I was talking to some Crows two, three days ago. They've been told to make ready for an expedition around the middle of May. It has to be against the Sioux and the Cheyenne"

"Who will be leading it, Slim Man?"

"Iron Butt."

Lieutenant Colonel George Armstrong Custer, known also as Yellow Hair, Long Hair, and Ringlets. And Custer was known as a ruthless, if a brash and sometimes reckless, Indian fighter.

"What other wonderful news do you have for us?" Two Wolves asked.

"Tom Thomas and Terri Kelly have escaped from confinement and linked up with the Texas gunfighter, Walker."

"I thought Walker was dead," Bodine said.

"So did everybody else. Not so. Most of his army was slaughtered, but he escaped, along with maybe ten or twelve men. Thomas and Terri have formed their own little outlaw army with Simon Bull, Pete Terrance, Jim Wilson . . . to name a few."

"Where are they?"

"No one seems to know for sure. But this much is known, Bodine: Thomas has sworn to kill you. I think Thomas has taken over that little settlement on the Yellowstone; right where the Bighorn starts. He's got fifteen or twenty hardcases working for him."

"Probably working the river, robbing and raping and murdering."

"You got it."

"Any news about Corrigan?" Bodine asked

Slim Man grinned. "He filed on land just south of your spread, Bodine. Just had equipment shipped in and he's going to farm and live in peace. I believe he's really sincere."

Bodine nodded his head, but his thoughts were not on farming. They were remembering his dreams about the great battle near the Little Bighorn.

Slim Man thanked them for the food and left; said he was going north now that spring was here. He had him a job lined up punching cows.

The two blood brothers stepped outside the cabin to stand in the warming early spring air.

"What are your thoughts, Bodine?" Two Wolves asked.

"Breaking my word to our father."

"I don't think he would be disappointed if you did. I think he felt you would mull over his words and then choose the white man's ways. As he pushed me to it. But do you think you will be believed?"

Bodine sighed "Probably not, Brother. But I have to try."

"I'll saddle up. Are we going to see Travers?"

"Yes. Well stop by Dad's and see if he's heard anything."

They pulled out within the hour, making sure they carried plenty of ammunition. Bodine did not take Thomas's threat lightly. The man was about half-crazy, and Bodine knew Thomas blamed him for his downfall.

They rode toward the Crazy Woman, spending the night at Bodine's parents' house.

"It's been quiet around here, son," the elder Bodine told

him. “Although others have reported seeing bands of Indians now and then.”

“They’re on their traditional hunting grounds.”

“Making ready for war,” Two Wolves added, a grim expression on his face.

Both father and son knew that Two Wolves was torn emotionally between two sides, and they also suspected he was wondering if his father was among the Cheyenne who had chosen to fight the Army.

Two Wolves sighed and shook himself out of his reverie. “I wonder if Lone Dog is in the Rosebuds?”

“Not from what I’ve heard,” the father said. “He and his band have been working much farther north; up north of the Musselshell. And they’ve been causing a lot of grief up there.”

“He’s quite mad, you know?” Two Wolves said. “He always was unstable.”

“And has always hated you,” Bodine reminded his brother.

“Envious. And I never understood that.”

Bodine had not told his father why he was going to the fort, and the elder Bodine did not push it. But his son confirmed his own thoughts when he said, “Stay out of the Rosebuds, Dad. You’ve got some holdings up close to the border, I know. It would be best if you sent some hands up there to push the cattle south.”

“Any particular reason, boy?”

Bodine smiled. “Maybe the cows would like a change of scenery?”

By dawn they had crossed the Crazy Woman and were heading for the Clear. From the Clear, the garrison was a good three days’ ride away.

When they had crossed over into Montana Territory, they began seeing small bands of Indians. They were challenged several times, but once the Indians recognized them, they veered off and Bodine and Two Wolves were left alone.

"Odd," Bodine said. "They won't even ride close enough to talk."

"They don't want us to spoil their medicine," Two Wolves pointed out. "This confirms in my mind that they are preparing for war."

"They're also telling us that we are not welcome at the main camp."

"Yes. For the first time in my life I truly do not feel like an Indian. It is very distressing to me, Brother. I want to go to the Rosebuds to see if my father is there. But I have been forbidden by him to do that. I feel like a traitor going to see the Army. But Medicine Horse ordered me to fully adopt the white side of me. So if I am to do that, I must think and act like a white man. It is very confusing."

They rode in silence for a time, crossing a flat and fording a small creek. As they rode up the bank, they came close to a band of Cheyenne, led by a sub-chief named Strong Bull.

The Cheyenne braves all lifted their hands, shielding their eyes from Bodine and Two Wolves. As they drew nearer, the Cheyenne turned their ponies, refusing to look at the blood brothers. Angry, Two Wolves reined up.

"Why do you treat me this way, Strong Bull? Have I not always been your friend? Have I not shared your food as you have shared mine. Am I not still the same person that I have always been?"

Strong Bull waved his band forward and rode away, without saying a word.

"Damnit!" Bodine spat the word. "They've left the reservation to join the Sioux."

"That means my father has joined Gall and the others in the Rosebuds. He is going to fight."

"I don't believe that!"

Two Wolves' words were sad as they left his mouth. "Bodine

is forgetting that Medicine Horse is still a great and powerful warrior of the Cheyenne. I knew it would come to this. My father was shamed. For years we lived in peace with the whites, on land given us by the government. To save his people, Medicine Horse agreed to be shifted to new lands, allowing humiliation to be heaped on his head. He has left the bulk of our people on the new lands, and brought only the older warriors like Strong Bull with him to the Rosebuds. Chiefs, sub-chiefs, shamans, and war chiefs. They are going to die, Bodine. That is the only way they can save face."

Bodine slumped in the saddle. "Then . . . there is nothing we can do."

"Nothing."

But Bodine did not like the look in Two Wolves' eyes. "What are you thinking, Brother?"

"Things that are of interest to me alone, Brother." He rode past Bodine to take the lead.

But Bodine was not to be put off that easily. He cantered to Two Wolves' side. "You know in your heart that the Indians cannot win. Your father did the right thing by ordering you to adopt the white man's ways. You know that the words I speak are true ones."

"I know only that at this moment I am confused. And your talking is an irritant I can do without."

"Do you want to go to the mountain, Brother?"

Two Wolves reined up. Looked at Bodine. "Yes."

"Then go. I'll be back in three or four days. Meet me at the creek where we saw Strong Bull."

Two Wolves stared at Bodine for a very long moment. "And if I don't?" There was clear defiance both in the question and in his eyes.

"What are you trying to get me to say, Brother? I meant only that I would meet you at the crossing. Nothing more."

"You might never see me again, Bodine. Except on the field of battle."

"Don't be a damn fool!" Bodine lashed out at him. "You could no more kill a soldier than I could. So stop being so goddamned noble."

"Are you saying that I am doing this to be a martyr?"

"Of course. Damnit, Brother, the ways of the wild are going and soon they will be gone. When are you going to realize that?"

"These words are coming from the mouth of a gunfighter?" he questioned sarcastically.

The question shocked Bodine. "Sam . . . you can go right straight to hell!"

Bodine turned Rowdy's head and galloped off.

Chapter 26

Bodine did not expect his brother to follow him, and Two Wolves did not. Bodine camped alone that night just south of Pyramid Butte. His sleep was restless, his dreams troubled ones, visionary in content: of great battles in which the Army was slaughtered, cut down by thousands of Indians. He dreamed it over and over again, until finally, long before dawn, he was up and drinking strong coffee. First light found him on the lonely and silent trail, working his way north, and at noon, he rode into the garrison.

Lieutenant Gerry walked toward him as he was stabling Rowdy. Bodine greeted him and asked, "How's the arm?"

"Oh, I'm fit as a fiddle. Good to see you. What brings you this far into hostile country?"

"I've got to see Colonel Travers."

"I'm sure he'll see you immediately. You heard about Tom Thomas and Terri?"

"Yes. And about what they're doing along the Yellowstone."

"They didn't escape from our custody, thank God. U.S. Marshals had picked them up and were transporting them to

Nebraska to stand trial when Walker and some other men hit the wagon."

"They're definitely at the settlement on the Yellowstone?"

They talked as they walked to the CO's office.

"Yes. But it's a civilian matter, Bodine. We can become involved only if the territorial governor requests our assistance."

"I'm not faulting, Gerry. You don't have the men to go looking for outlaws."

"I'm glad you feel that way. There are many who don't. Here we are. Let's see if the colonel is busy."

Travers waved Bodine in and to a chair. "You stay, Lieutenant." He sat down behind his desk and looked at Bodine. "What's on your mind, Bodine?"

Bodine could detect something in the colonel's eyes and tone of voice that gave him a precognition about the outcome of this meeting. The colonel probably knew that a major push was being planned over at Fort Abe Lincoln, Dakota Territory, and he wasn't going to be very receptive to anything Bodine said about the Indians.

"Not going to be a friendly meeting, huh, Colonel?"

"We'll talk about the pleasant weather, Bodine. I'll ask how your herds look and the health of your family and so on and so forth. We'll keep it light."

"I didn't ride three days for chit-chat, Colonel."

Travers leaned back in his chair. He lit a cigar and smoked it for a moment, keeping his eyes on Bodine all the while. "All right, Bodine. But I cannot discuss military matters with you."

Bodine smiled. "Why not? The Indians already know that Custer and the Seventh Cavalry are leaving Fort Abraham Lincoln in mid-May to lead an assault against them on their hunting grounds in the Rosebuds."

Travers almost jumped out of his boots. His cigar fell out of his suddenly-opened mouth and he frantically brushed sparks from his tunic. "God*damnit!*" he roared, slamming his hand down on his desk. "That was one of the best-kept secrets of this entire campaign!"

Lieutenant Gerry looked awfully uncomfortable under the colonel's outburst.

Bodine simply shrugged his shoulders. "Not anymore, it isn't."

"I demand to know where you got that information, Bodine!"

"I got it from an Indian who goes by the name of *Mohk sta wo ums'ts.*" Which was Northern Cheyenne for Starving Elk. Bodine also knew that the colonel did not know a word of the nearly incomprehensible-to-the-white man Cheyenne language and would have no idea whether Bodine was lying or not.

Travers picked up a pen and dipped it into an inkwell. "How do you spell that?"

"How the hell do I know?" Bodine told him honestly.

Travers sighed and put down his pen. "All right, all right, Bodine. But you better keep your mouth shut about this upcoming campaign. And that is not a threat from me, by the way. Just a friendly piece of advice."

"I'll take it as such. Stay out of the Rosebuds, Colonel. And that is not a threat from me. Just a friendly piece of advice that might save your life."

"What do you know that I need to know, Bodine?"

"The Army is going to lose."

Travers stared at him for a moment, then burst out laughing. He wound down to a chuckle and then took a linen handkerchief from his pocket and wiped his eyes. "Thanks, Bodine. I needed a good laugh." He pointed a finger at Bodine. "Now you listen to me, young man: the Army is not going to lose. Custer is probably the best Indian fighter on the frontier. Now tell me, why do you think we're going to lose?"

Here goes nothing, Bodine thought. "Visions, Colonel. Visions in the minds of many people, all of them the same. Including a vision of mine."

Gerry laughed and so did Travers. Bodine had expected that reaction and maintained a straight face.

"Indian hoo-doo, Bodine. Do you actually expect me to act on your dreams?"

"No. But I had to tell you. My conscience is clear. I tried."

Travers waved that away, signaling the topic was concluded. "Where is Two Wolves?"

"I don't know."

"Have you said everything you came here to say, Bodine?"

"I suppose."

Travers stood up. The meeting was over.

Two Wolves was not at the crossing when Bodine arrived at the creek, nor was there any sign he had been there. Bodine rested for a time at the creek, allowing Rowdy to drink and graze. He stood for a time, looking toward the west. The Rosebuds were a half a day's ride away, but Bodine knew better than to ride there. He had been warned, and warned fairly, to stay out.

He built a small fire and made coffee, then rolled a cigarette and thought about his options. He had done his duty as an American citizen by trying to warn Colonel Travers at the fort. He could do no more than that. What he should do, he knew, was go on back to his spread and forget it. Let what he was sure in his mind was going to take place in the Rosebuds happen.

But he didn't want to return home; he was too restless for that. Bodine had four very capable hands working for him, so the ranch was in good shape. It was just a little early to start pushing the cattle up onto new graze.

However, he knew very well that he was behaving foolishly by staying out here by himself. If the Ghost Dancing had begun, the blood might become so hot among the braves that they could easily kill him before they knew who he was.

And who he was just might not make any difference anymore.

His thoughts turned to Two Wolves. Just how far did his responsibility toward his brother go? Two Wolves was a grown man, not a child. If he had made up his mind to disobey his father and return to the Indian way . . . so be it. Bodine had no right to interfere.

With a sigh, Bodine carefully put out his small fire and saddled up. He would go home. He had done all that he could do.

March drifted into April, and April moved with warm days and cool to sometimes downright cold nights into early May. Bodine had neither seen nor heard from Two Wolves. He had stayed close to his ranch, making sure all the work was caught up.

Bodine was getting very restless toward the middle of the month. Rowdy was about to tear down the barn with his antics, telling Bodine he was tired of all this lollygagging about. The big stallion was ready to once more hit the trail, and it'd better be damn soon.

On May 16th, 1876, Bodine saddled Rowdy, stopped by to tell his parents he'd see them when he got back, and headed for the spirit mountain.

On May 17, 1876, on a foggy dawn some 425 miles east of the Rosebuds, Lieutenant Colonel George Armstrong Custer took his position at the head of the column just as the Army band struck up Custer's favorite battle tune: the stirring "Garryowen." As the column pulled out, the band slipped into the emotionally touching "The Girl I Left Behind Me" as the wives and girlfriends stood in doorways and waved goodbye to the men.

Some twenty-six of the women were seeing their husbands for the last time; Elizabeth Custer, who would accompany her husband and the two-mile-long column during the first day of the march, was uneasy. She felt she was seeing her husband for the last time. As the sun's new dawning played over the long column, she felt she was witnessing a mirage of specter-like mounted horsemen, ghost-riders moving upward into the sky.

At that same moment, far to the west, Sitting Bull, leader and medicine man of seven bands of Lakota Sioux, was experiencing the same vision he had seen months before—that of many soldiers falling upside down into an Indian camp.

"Yellow Hair comes," Sitting Bull announced.

Bodine sat up in his blankets, shaking and drenched with sweat from his terrible dreams. He had witnessed in his mind a bloody, terrible massacre; a wholesale slaughter of Army troops.

Bodine stripped and jumped naked into a creek, the shockingly cold water cleansing his body and calming his mind. He dressed and made coffee, then cooked a breakfast of bacon and potatoes. But his mind would not erase the horrible dreams he had experienced.

Something monumental was taking place this day. But what? Then it came to him. It had to be: Custer had left Fort Abe Lincoln over in the Dakotas with his cavalry regiment, his infantry, and his artillery.

Bodine relaxed a bit as he ate his breakfast. It would take Custer a good thirty to forty hard days to complete the march to the Rosebuds. He had plenty of time to find Two Wolves and talk some sense into him. Or knock some sense in him, whichever the case might call for.

Bodine sopped up the grease in the pan with a hunk of bread, ate that, then drank the last of the pot of coffee. He saddled up and continued his searching for his blood brother.

He would go first to the spirit mountain; but he had a hunch his brother had left the mountain. To where, Bodine had not a clue. But he would find him. He had time. That's what he kept telling himself.

He searched the mountain, finding signs of where his brother had camped; finding a crude spirit lodge Two Wolves had built, where he had fasted, seeking guidance in visions. Two Wolves had shifted locations many times over the months, always staying on the mountain. But Bodine could find no recent sign of him.

Bodine stayed on the mountain for five days, until he was nearly out of supplies and he had convinced his mind that Two Wolves was gone.

Bodine left the mountain and headed north, working his way toward the Yellowstone.

He stopped at a newly-founded little four-building town on the Rosebud River. The people in the town would be gone in less than a year, all traces of the buildings gone in a few more years.

Bodine resupplied and was just lifting a glass of beer to his mouth when he heard the horses coming. He noticed the quick fear that jumped into the store owner's eyes.

"What's the matter?" Bodine asked.

"They come for their due," the man told him.

"Due? What are you talking about, man. Who's coming here?"

"Don't say nothin', mister," he warned Bodine. "Them's mighty mean people. That's some of Tom Thomas's bunch. They collect fees from us ever' month for protection from the Injuns."

"And you pay them?"

"Got to pay 'em, mister. Them that don't gets burnt out or worse. Wimmin has been taken off. Ain't never seen 'em since. You just don't say nothin'. I'm tellin' you, keep your mouth shut and live."

Bodine set the glass of beer down on the rough counter and dropped his hands to his Colts. "You tell them that you just sold this place to me, mister. That you're working for me now. You do that."

"You're crazy, man! They'd kill you. That bunch is meaner than a sack full of snakes."

Bodine met the scared eyes. "You want to get clear of this bunch?"

"Hell, yes!"

"Then you do what I tell you to do. And when the shooting starts, you hit the floor."

"I don't need to be told that twice, mister. I tell you what I'll do: I'll read over your grave personal. Even if you are a crazy man. You got a favorite passage from the Good Book?"

When Bodine did not reply, the man asked, "You got a name, mister?"

"Bodine."

"Oh, Lordy!" the man moaned, just as the door was pushed open.

Chapter 27

Bodine had seen six men ride into town. If the other four were as ugly as the two who stepped into the store, they could all make a living haunting old houses.

One of the two glared at Bodine. He jerked a thumb toward the door. "You—out!"

Bodine told him where he could put his order—five words plus a very ugly comment concerning the man's ancestry.

The extortionist looked at Bodine, disbelief in his eyes. "What the hell did you say, cowboy?"

Bodine repeated his original suggestion.

The ugly man spread his boot on the rough plank floor and dropped his hands to his sides. "Nobody calls me that and lives."

"I just called you that and I'm still alive," Bodine told him.

"Not for long, you ain't!" The man grabbed for iron.

Bodine put two holes in the man's chest before ugly's hands even touched the butts of his guns. The second man was just clearing leather as Bodine's slugs tore into his body, knocking him backward out the warped door and into the muddy street.

Without looking back, Bodine ran out the back of the general store to where he had tied Rowdy and jerked his Winchester from the saddle boot, levering a round into the chamber. He ran up to the end of the four-building town and peeked around the corner of the last building. A man with both hands full of guns and a face full of pure ugly was walking up the boardwalk.

Bodine stepped out and shot him in the belly with the rifle, the .44 slug doubling him over and dropping him to his knees.

A slug from the only building on the other side of the street, the barn, knocked a chunk of pine from the facing and sent splinters into Bodine's face. Bodine ran back to the rear of the buildings and ducked into the back door of a home. The lady of the house was standing by a slant-backed bathtub in the kitchen, full of hot water. She didn't have a stitch on. She didn't exactly brighten Bodine's day, either. He couldn't remember ever seeing so many ugly people in one place.

"Excuse me, ma'am," he said, doffing his hat with his left hand and running on through the house, stopping in the parlor.

"Come back anytime!" she called after him.

"Safer outside," Bodine muttered, peering out a window. He located the man in the barn loft, gently eased open the door, and knocked him back with one shot, the man dropping his rifle with a scream.

Bodine was out the door and running up the muddy side of the street. He'd made up his mind he'd rather do that than go back and look at that ugly woman in her all-togethers.

There were two of Thomas's men somewhere, but where?

Movement from a window caught his eyes and sent

Bodine sliding belly-down in the muddy ground just as gunfire blasted the air where he'd been standing. Lifting his rifle, he made a mess out of the window and a bigger mess out of the face of the man who had been standing there.

Bodine rolled out of the mud and into a space between buildings. He got to his feet and caught his breath.

"Bodine!" came the call. "What's your interest in all this?"

"I don't like to see folks robbed," Bodine called.

"I ain't got no truck with you, Bodine. Lemme ride on out."

"What's your name?"

"Pete Grant. I mean it, Bodine. I know that's you. I seen you one time afore. Lemme ride on out."

"I see you again, Pete, I'm gonna kill you."

"I believe you, Bodine. I'm gone, Bodine. Headin' south back to Texas. You ain't gonna see me around here no more. That's a promise."

"Ride on out, Pete." Bodine stepped out from between the two buildings.

Pete hadn't been kidding. Once in the saddle he went foggin' it, without even a glance back. People began coming out of the buildings, to stand and stare at Bodine.

Bodine cleaned the mud off his clothing at a horse trough and checked and cleaned his guns. He walked back to Rowdy and made sure his supplies were tied down securely, then stepped into the saddle. As he rode past a building, the back door opened and the woman whose bath he'd interrupted smiled at him. Bodine noticed she had put on a robe—thank God!

"Leaving so soon?" she asked.

"I got to go, lady."

"Pity. We could have a real good time. My old man run out on me."

I can't imagine why, Bodine thought. "Your town's safe now, lady. I gotta go."

"Hell, them fellers never bothered me!" she yelled at his back.

"I can believe that," Bodine muttered, then rode out of town. Rowdy seemed as anxious to leave as Bodine did. Hadn't been a decent-looking mare in the whole damn town.

A week later, Bodine had still not been able to pick up Two Wolves' trail. It seemed as though his brother had dropped off the face of the earth.

Bodine had turned east, searching from the Rosebud to the Tongue, and then traveling the vast and lonely emptiness between the Tongue River and Mizpah Creek. There, he stopped.

He just didn't see the point of going on.

There was no doubt in his mind that Two Wolves knew he was looking for him. Bodine had seen a hundred or so Indians during the past week, talking with some of them. But whenever he mentioned his brother's name, they would either clam up or change the subject.

All right, Bodine thought. If that's the way it is to be, Brother—so be it.

"Looking for me?" the voice came from behind him.

Bodine did not look around from his cooking bacon over the small fire.

"Why should I look for a person who has no more sense than a goat?"

"If you are not looking for me, why are you so far from home?" Two Wolves walked down the embankment, leading his horse. He picketed the horse next to, but not too close to Rowdy.

"I grew restless with all the inactivity." He looked at Two Wolves. He was wearing boots and jeans and a beaded buckskin shirt. His hair was cut short, but he wore a headband.

Two Wolves caught the direction of his eyes. "I do not know who I am. So I will dress as what I am. A halfbreed."

"That's all right with me. As long as you behave like the intelligent person I know you are."

"Bah!" Two Wolves poured a cup of coffee. "It is the act of an intelligent person to enter into a gunfight with six of Tom Thomas's men?"

So Two Wolves had been following him. That would account for the occasional dust Bodine had seen on his back trail.

"I did not say I was intelligent. I merely stated that you were."

"For once, you speak the truth."

"Why don't you eat. That's one way of shutting your mouth."

"I thought you would never ask. I thought you might have forgotten your Cheyenne upbringing."

"As long as I wear the scars on my chest I shall never forget."

"True." Two Wolves broke off a piece of hard bread Bodine handed him and sopped it in the hot grease. He speared a strip of bacon with the point of his knife and let it dangle there, cooling.

"I thought I'd follow the creek down a-ways and then cut east over to the Powder and take that on down to home range."

"I might decide to ride with you. I might not."

Bodine let the subject drop with that remark from Two Wolves. He wasn't going to push him.

"Have you been to the Rosebuds?" Two Wolves asked after a long silence.

"No. You?"

"No. I wanted to go. I wanted to see my father one more time. But I was afraid he would turn his back to me. I would not want that as my last memory of him. I have dreamed." He abruptly shifted subjects.

"My own dreams have not been pleasant."

"I prayed and fasted on the mountain, seeking guidance. But nothing came to me. I believe I am a nonperson. I do believe I am no longer a human being."

"If you are not, then I am not."

"That may also be truth."

Bodine looked up at the sun. "Six, maybe seven hours of daylight left. We could cover a lot of ground in that time."

"That definitely is the truth."

Bodine poured another cup of coffee and refilled Two Wolves' cup, emptying the battered and blackened old pot. He tossed the grounds away and set the pot aside. They finished the bread and bacon and Two Wolves carefully put out the fire.

Both young men stood up.

"There is something you should know, *I tat an e.*"

Cheyenne for brother. Bodine waited.

"General Crook has left Fort Fetterman with a large force. There have already been small battles between Crook and the Cheyenne and Sioux. It is believed among my . . ." He paused. Sighed. ". . . the Indians, that Crook and Custer believe they can trap the Indians, with Crook coming from the south and Yellow Hair from the east. They will not trap the Indians. They will die instead."

"I tried to convince Colonel Travers of this. He would not listen."

"Then you have done all that you can do."

"How many Indians are camped along the river in the Rosebuds, *I tat an e?*"

"Crow King says they are plenty as the leaves on the trees."

"You have spoken with Crow King?"

"I have spoken with a few warriors from the Hunkpapa, yes. Seven thousand in the Rosebuds, Bodine."

"Seven *thousand!*"

"Yes. That would mean more than three thousand warriors. At least."

"And you think we should do what with this information?"

Two Wolves shrugged. "I do not plan to do anything with it. What you do with it is your concern."

"We could ride to the fort; tell Colonel Travers."

"We could ride to the fort. *You* could tell the colonel."

"Of course, he wouldn't believe me."

"Probably not."

"What is the date, Brother?"

"I do not have any idea. May something or the other. I have lost track of time."

"As have I."

"We could ride north and try to intercept Custer's columns."

"This is also true."

"Going north would be closer than trying to ride for the fort."

"It would certainly be the humane thing to do to try to reach Iron Butt. A man should know that he is going to die."

"Of course, he won't believe us either."

"Probably not."

They walked toward their horses and saddled up. Then both returned to the creek and filled their canteens.

"This could be a dangerous ride for you," Bodine said.

"I would not feel right if I let you go riding off alone, Bodine. You might get lost and wander around forever and ever. Then I would have to come looking for you. Better I ride along."

Bodine smiled and Two Wolves returned the smile. Then both young men laughed as they mounted up.

"I remember when you got lost when you were about

fourteen," Bodine said, pointing Rowdy's nose toward the north.

"Me? Lost? Bah! I have never been lost."

They were still arguing as they rode away from the creek, on their way to try to alter destiny.

Chapter 28

The two young men angled toward the northwest, following trails and paths that only the Indians and a few mountain men knew of. This was raw, rugged, beautiful, and untamed country. A land where a misstep or the taking of the wrong trail could mean a quick death. But already settlers were moving in, trying to carve out some sort of existence from the wilderness. Most had not lasted. Crude crosses above shallow graves offered silent and lonely testimony to that hard fact of frontier life.

The men lost track of the days as one blended into another and they began riding more west than north.

"We may have missed him," Bodine finally had to admit, standing up in his stirrups and scanning the horizon.

"According to the braves I talked with, the column was several miles long and with infantry, moving no more than ten miles a day. I think we've come too far west." He twisted in the saddle and pointed to a butte in the distance. "Let's make camp up there and sit it out for a couple of days. The horses can use the rest."

On the flat, they found an overhang that was blackened

from the countless fires of those the Indians call The People Who Came Before. Past the overhang, in a cave, they found a small stream that bubbled out of the rocks, a stream with cold clear water. Two Wolves killed two rabbits for supper while Bodine built a fire and heated water for coffee, dumping in the grounds when the water boiled. It was evident to them both that they were the first humans to use this flat in many years. How many, neither of them cared to venture a guess.

They slept soundly that night, knowing their horses would alert them if danger was near. They could only stay for two days, for their supplies were dangerously low and they would have to ride for a settlement on the Yellowstone very soon.

On the afternoon of the second day, Two Wolves spotted the dust.

Bodine and Two Wolves hurriedly broke camp and saddled up, riding in an easy lope toward the long column. As soon as they were spotted, several of the forty Indian scouts, mostly Crow and Ree, broke from the column and raced toward them. Bodine and Two Wolves did not stop, but instead rode right through the cursing and yelling scouts and headed for the front of the column.

"See what those two men want, Marcus," Custer said to Major Marcus A. Reno.

Reno broke from the column and loped over to Bodine and Two Wolves. "Just hold up right there, gentlemen," the major ordered. "What's the big hurry?"

"I'm Matt Bodine, Major. This is Sam Two Wolves, son of Medicine Horse."

Reno rocked back in his saddle and studied the pair for a moment. "I've heard of you both. Now what do you want?"

"To see Custer."

"Why?"

"To try to save his life," Bodine said bluntly. "And yours, as well."

"You have news of the hostiles?"

A hundred years after the west was tamed, Indians would still bristle at the term: hostile. Two Wolves sat his saddle and chuckled.

"Perhaps you would like to share the humor with me, Sam?" Reno questioned.

"Some other time, Major. Providing you have that much time left you."

They all heard Custer shout the column to a rest. He loped over to join Reno. Reno backed up his mount and spoke quietly with Custer for a moment. Custer moved forward to look at Bodine and Two Wolves.

The colonel's long flowing hair had been cut short even for that time. His mustache was thick and bushy, hanging well over his mouth. He wore a red tie, fringed buckskins, and a wide-brimmed campaign hat. He was thirty-six years old.

Custer waved Reno back to the column and faced the two men alone. "State your business, Bodine."

"You're riding into a death-trap, Colonel. You have vastly underestimated the strength of the Sioux and the Cheyenne in the Rosebuds."

"You saw the encampment?"

"My news comes from Crow King."

"Then I must place no credence in your warning, sir. But I do thank you for your concern. Is there anything else?"

"We've had a hard ride to warn you, sir. We could do with some supplies."

"How many days?"

"Three should do it."

"See the quartermaster. Good day, gentlemen."

Custer wheeled his mount and rode back to the column. Bodine stared at Custer's back, a disgusted expression on his face. "On second thought, I think we can do without his supplies. We'll hunt what we need. That sound all right with you?"

But Two Wolves did not reply.

Bodine glanced at him. His brother was staring at the long column intently, an odd expression on his face. "What do you see, Brother?"

"Death. Pain. I do not want their supplies, Bodine. Let's ride."

They rode on to a settlement on the Yellowstone, on the way living on rabbits and berries and fish. At the settlement, which some were already calling Rosebud, because of its location at the mouth of the river, they bathed and had a shave and a haircut and enjoyed food they did not have to cook themselves. They soon found that the people in the village were very excited about Custer's coming to once and for all deal with the hostiles.

It was here, at the mouth of the Rosebud, that General Alfred H. Terry, the commander of the Department of Dakota, had ordered Custer to turn south to find the hostiles, believed camped in the Rosebud Mountains, probably along the Little Bighorn.

Bodine and Two Wolves spent one night camped just outside the tiny settlement and pulled out before dawn the next morning, following the Rosebud down to its gentle curving toward the southwest. There, they angled off on a trail that would take them to the Tongue. Both had decided they would camp for a time along the Tongue and do some hunting.

Both knew that was not the real reason for their staying close to the Rosebuds; but neither one spoke that reason aloud.

They loafed for several days, fishing, hunting, sleeping,

and acting like a couple of kids, swimming barebutted in a deep cold pool of the Tongue.

They were fixing their supper under a late afternoon's dying sun when a call came from the gathering shadows.

"Hello, the fire! We're friendly but slap out of grub."

"Come on in," Bodine called, drawing a Colt and rearing the hammer back, knowing the sound would reach the distance. It wasn't being unfriendly, just cautious.

"We'll be right back," the man called. "Got to go back and get our horses. We didn't know who the fire belonged to."

They were a couple of young cowboys who were just drifting after having spent the winter in a line shack just south of the Missouri.

"Made the mistake of wanderin' into the Rosebuds," one said. "Man, I never seen so damn many Injuns in all my life."

"It's a good thing they didn't see you," Bodine told him.

"You shore got that right!" the man's buddy said. "When we seed what we was gettin' into, we got out of it, in a hurry!"

Bodine poured them coffee and began dishing up the food. It was venison fried in wild onions with beans, but to the hungry young cowboys, it was a feast.

Two Wolves eyeballed how fast the plates were emptying, smiled, and began slicing more meat to fry.

"I better tell y'all," one cowboy drawled his Texas speech. "They's some bad ol' boys about a day behind us. Headed by a gent name of Bull. Simon Bull."

"We've heard of him," Two Wolves said.

"They're lookin' for the gunfighter, Bodine. I hear he's a bad one, too."

"Yeah," his buddy spoke around a mouthful of food. "He's got quite a name for hisself. Simon Bull's a-ridin' to kill him. That's what we heared."

"He won't do it," Bodine said softly.

"How come you to say that?"

"I'm Bodine."

Both young men stopped eating and stared.

Bodine jerked a thumb toward his brother. "That's the son of the Cheyenne war chief, Medicine Horse. Sam Two Wolves. We're brothers in blood."

"Pleasure to meet you gentlemen," Two Wolves said, smiling at the awestruck young punchers. "Eat, eat, please. No one is ever turned away from food at a Cheyenne fire."

"Ch . . . ch . . . Cheyenne?"

"Of course," Bodine stuck the needle a little deeper with a straight face, "the trick is to get away after you've eaten and rested."

"And always eat everything an Indian gives you," Two Wolves told them. "It's very bad manners to leave food uneaten. Not to mention being a great insult."

The boys went to gobbling.

Both Bodine and Two Wolves realized they had taken the joke too far and tried to calm the young men. But the young punchers weren't having any of it.

With their plates shiny clean, the punchers thanked them for the food, and backed out of the camp. They mounted up and rode out, quickly.

"Shame on you!" Bodine admonished his brother. "You wild Indian."

"Shame on *me!* I'm not the one with the reputation. You're the big, bad gunfighter who frightens young cowboys. What about Simon Bull?"

"What about him? I don't have any quarrel with Simon."

"He's riding to kill you."

"He's got it to do."

They broke camp at dawn and moved south, staying on the west side of the Tongue. They took their time as they headed for a trading post on the river.

"It's the only trading post for seventy-five miles, Brother," Two Wolves pointed out. "Bull will probably be there."

"I know it. But we need supplies and I need to find out what the date is."

"You have an appointment?" Two Wolves smiled the question.

"We both do," Bodine said somberly.

"Yes. But only one of us will keep it."

"We'll see."

Two Wolves gave him a curious look and did not immediately respond. They rode on for a few miles in silence.

"What would you do, Bodine, if I decided to ride to the Rosebuds?"

"I'd stop you."

"You would try."

"I'd stop you."

"Very well. But why?"

"Because you don't belong there. You don't hate the white man, Sam. Neither does Medicine Horse. You don't hate the Army. They're just men following orders . . . and a lot of them don't like it, either."

"But my father is by the river, waiting to die with his people."

"With *some* of his people, Brother. You admitted that yourself."

Two Wolves grunted. "Pointless argument. Each of us will do what we think is best."

"This is truth. Trading post is just up ahead."

"And Simon Bull is probably waiting for us."

"Waiting for me, Brother."

"Us, you jackass!"

"Always meddling."

"I promised your mother and father I would look after you."

"When did you see them?"

Two Wolves smiled. "While you were camped on the

mountain looking for me, I was enjoying the hospitality of your mother's cooking and your father's conversation."

Bodine called him some very ugly names.

Two Wolves laughed at him.

Chapter 29

The trading post was a big, low, and long building, securely built and fortified against Indian attack. The stables and corral were in the back.

"That's Simon Bull's horse," Two Wolves pointed out. "I recognize it from the fight at Cutter."

"This should be interesting. Five men with him, at least. If all those horses are from the same bunch."

"The way your luck runs, they probably are."

Bodine and Two Wolves stabled their horses and told the boy to give them a bucket of corn. The stable boy gave them odd looks.

"If your name's Bodine, them hardcases in yonder is waitin' for you."

"How many are there?"

"Six."

Bodine and Two Wolves took their rifles from the saddle boots, levered rounds into the chambers and eased the hammers down.

"You know the date, boy?" Bodine asked.

"June the 18th."

Bodine nodded and walked out of the stable, Two Wolves by his side.

Custer and his men were headed south, toward the Rosebud Mountains.

The Cheyenne camped along the Little Big Horn were in the midst of their Ghost Dance.

Bodine pushed open the door of the trading post and stepped in, Two Wolves right behind him.

Two of Bull's men were at the rough plank bar, drinking whiskey. Simon Bull and three of his men were at a table, playing poker with a greasy deck of cards. Bull looked up, a surprised expression on his face. He had not heard Bodine and Two Wolves ride in, and that irritated him.

Bodine and Two Wolves walked to a table, sat down, and told the barkeep to bring them something to eat.

"Venison stew and fresh-baked bread is what we got."

"That'll be fine."

"You boys eat hearty now," Bull said, a dirty grin creasing his unshaven face. "A man shouldn't go to meet his maker on no empty stomich."

"Then you better eat up, Bull," Bodine told him. "And tell your rabid skunks to do the same."

Jim Wilson and Pete Terrance, the two men at the bar, stirred at this, but carefully kept their hands away from their guns. Bodine's Winchester was lying on the table, the muzzle pointed at them. Two Wolves' Winchester was also on the table, the muzzle pointing in the direction of Simon Bull.

"I thought you boys were all tied up with Thomas and Walker?" Bodine asked.

"Somebody come along and wiped out about half of Thomas's bunch," Bull said, a twinkle in his eyes. "Little two-bit town up in Montana. Took the heart right out of the rest of the boys. We decided to drift."

"Why don't you keep drifting?"

"Oh, I probably will, Bodine. After you and me settle up our differences."

"I have no quarrel with you, Bull. None at all. Never have."

"It's just something that has to be, Bodine. One of those things, I reckon you'd call it."

"Why?"

"Too damn many people sayin' you're the best there is. I can't have that. You're good, all right. But not as good as me."

"Seems like I heard the same thing from Stutterin' Smith."

"It do, don't it?"

Bodine and Two Wolves ate the stew and it was good. When their plates were empty, Bodine and Two Wolves stood up, rifles in hand, their thumbs on the hammers.

"Where you boys think you're goin'?" Bull asked.

"Back on the trail, Bull. I told you, I don't have any quarrel with you."

"Damn you, Bodine! What's it take to make you stand and fight?"

"Admittedly, not much, Bull. So I guess I'll just have to even out the odds some." He thumbed back the hammer on his Winchester and one-handed, pulled the trigger, shooting Bull in the center of the chest, the slug slamming the big man out of the rickety old chair and dropping him to the floor.

Two Wolves put a slug into the belly of Pete Terrance and shifted the muzzle, shooting Jim Wilson in the chest.

Bodine was busy working the lever of his Winchester, clearing the table of gunslicks with .44s at very close range.

The sound was deafening and the room quickly filled with gunsmoke.

Simon Bull crawled to his knees, cursing as he was dying, and pointed a .45 at Bodine. Bodine shot him between the eyes just as a slug burned Bodine's arm and turned him around, facing the bar.

Terrance was on his knees, both hands filled with guns. Bodine and Two Wolves fired simultaneously, the .44s striking the man in the chest and jarring him back against the bar, dead.

"Holy Christ!" the owner of the trading post said, peering out from behind a barrel of pickles, which had several holes in it, leaking sour pickle juice onto the dirty floor.

"That was good stew," Bodine told him, shoving .44s into his Winchester. "How much do we owe you?"

"Fifty cents." The man found the words.

"Take it out of his pockets," Two Wolves said, pointing to the dead Bull.

"Yes, sir."

Bodine and Two Wolves ignored the sprawling bodies and walked around the trading post, picking up supplies. The post owner busied himself going through the pockets of the dead men, transferring the contents to his own pockets.

After taking a wad of greenbacks from Simon Bull he rocked back on his heels, grinned, and said, "On second thought, boys, the stew was on the house."

"That's so kind of you," Bodine told him, tossing some money on the plank bar. "Here's money for the supplies."

The post owner waved that off without even looking around. "Fine, boys, fine. Come back anytime." He was busy admiring a pocket watch taken from Pete Terrance. It chimed the hour and he grinned through his tobacco-stained beard.

Bodine and Two Wolves walked out of the death-stinking trading post.

Dawn found them camped on the Tongue, about ten miles from the trading post.

Bodine poured coffee and grinned at Two Wolves.

"Why are you smiling like that? What have you got up your sleeve this time?"

"We better stick together from now on, Brother. Your reputation as a gunslick is fast approaching mine."

"Reluctantly, I will have to agree. I knew I should never have allowed you to help me from under that pony. Something told me you would bring me much grief over the years."

Bodine drank his coffee and tossed the grounds away. "You ready to drift?"

"I'm going west, Bodine. It would be best if you don't ride with me."

"Oh, I think I'll tag along, Brother. Somebody has to look after you."

"My mind is made up, Bodine. I think you knew that several days ago."

"I saw a change come over you, if that's what you mean."

"If my father will have me, I am going to stay with the Cheyenne on the Little Bighorn."

Bodine slowly nodded his head, then surprised Two Wolves when he said, "All right, Brother. I won't interfere this time."

"Your word on that?"

Bodine leaned over and stuck out his hand. Two Wolves took it. "Will you obey your father if he orders you out of the camp?"

"Certainly. But the words will have to come from his mouth."

"I'll wait at the Rosebud, at the point where it angles south. I'll go no farther west than that."

Two Wolves packed up swiftly and swung into the saddle. He looked at Bodine, lying on the ground with his back against a log. Two Wolves lifted his hand and rode toward the west.

Bodine waited several minutes before digging another cup out of his pack and placing it on a rock next to the fire. A war-painted Cheyenne stepped out of the bushes and walked to the fire. He squatted down and poured coffee, declining the bread Bodine offered him.

"Last Bull," Bodine spoke.

"Do not go past the river, Bodine," the chief warned him. "Wait there for your brother. Medicine Horse will order him out of the camp."

"I was wondering if that hunting party took my message back to my adopted father. It's been several weeks."

"You have been observed. We have seen the signs you left along your back trail. Medicine Horse thanks you for your concern."

"He is my brother."

Last Bull drank his coffee slowly. "You do not hate us, Bodine?"

"No. You're doing what you think is best."

"And you did what you thought was best when you rode to warn Yellow Hair." That was said with a smile and with the dark eyes twinkling.

Bodine knew then that he had been under constant observation from the Cheyenne and the Sioux. He had suspected it all along.

"Yes. I felt it my duty."

"That is understood in the camps. There are no hard feelings against you for your doing what you thought was best." Last Bull drained his coffee cup and stood up. "Ride carefully, Bodine. There are many young braves among us who do not know you for what you really are. And Lone Dog has promised you a very long and painful death. He has made this pledge to the spirits, with the dust as your flesh, carried by the winds over the fire."

"I expected that."

Bodine rose and the two men gravely shook hands. No more words were spoken between them. Last Bull turned and walked away, quickly disappearing into the thick brush.

Bodine did not even hear the sounds of his pony's hooves as the chief rode away toward the west, toward the Rosebud Mountains and the river called the Little Bighorn. It was the 19th day of June.

Bodine carefully put out his fire and packed his gear. He took his time, allowing Two Wolves plenty of time to put miles between them.

Last Bull had been right. Bodine would have to ride very carefully as he moved west. The Ghost Dancing would have begun for some and be over for others, and for the latter, their blood would be hot and savage, and they would be painted for war.

Bodine stowed his boots and spurs and slipped on high-topped moccasins, tying them securely over his pants' legs. He changed clothes, dressing all in buckskin except for his hat, then swung into the saddle.

He had not gone two miles before Rowdy's ears perked up; Bodine could feel the tension in the big stallion's powerful body.

He moved quickly off the trail and into the brush, dismounting and whispering quietly to Rowdy, as he stroked the nose of the horse.

Bodine watched as four Indians came into view, only a few hundred yards off. They were Crow, on a scouting mission for the Seventh Cavalry, searching for the Sioux and the Cheyenne. Custer and his men would be only a few days' ride away. Maybe even closer than that, and probably miles farther to the west.

Bodine remained motionless. He was not well-liked by the Crow, since they all knew him, knew he had been adopted into the Cheyenne ways, and the Cheyenne and the Crow were bitter long-time enemies.

Bodine silently cursed his luck as the scouts reined up, swung down, and prepared to rest for a time.

Bodine knew it was only a matter of time before the horses scented each other. It would be best to play this as openly as possible.

He mounted up and rode directly into the Crow camp.

Chapter 30

The Crow scouts looked up, distrust bordering hate in their eyes and their hands full of guns as Bodine approached, riding slowly, with his Winchester across the saddlehorn, the reins in his left hand.

"Cheyenne dog droppings!" one of them said, loud enough for Bodine to hear.

"What a terrible thing to say to someone who means you no harm," Bodine told him.

"Your mouth speaks the words, but we do not know what is truly in your heart, Bo-dine."

"My heart is heavy this day. I have lost my brother."

"What do you mean?"

"He has gone to join his people."

"Then he will surely die with the rest of the Sioux and Cheyenne when Yellow Hair attacks."

"But first you have to find them, don't you?" Bodine smiled the taunt.

The Crow did not take the bait. "We have already found them, Bo-dine. They are by the Little Bighorn. This news has been sent back to Yellow Hair. So there is nothing you can do to change what will soon be history."

The Crow did not know how prophetic his words really were.

"I am not here to change anything. I don't think anything can be changed. It's too late for that."

"This is truth. Bo-dine might be considered trustworthy after all. I was told you came to warn Yellow Hair. We were gone at the time."

"Yes. I felt it my duty to do that."

The Crow signaled Bodine to dismount and join them. He did so, carefully, never taking his eyes from the scouts. He passed around his tobacco sack and papers and the Crows nodded with approval.

The spokesman said, "We have tried to warn Yellow Hair that he is wrong about the numbers of Cheyenne and Sioux. I do not think he believed us."

"I did the same some days ago. He did not believe me, either."

"This is also true. We heard. But it makes no matter. The Army will be victorious." He shrugged philosophically. "If not this time, then the next time."

"You are not joining Custer?"

"We have been ordered to Fetterman."

Bodine slowly rolled a cigarette, licked it and lit up. In his mind, he was choosing his words carefully, wanting to know just how the scouts felt. "That order just might have saved your lives."

"This is also truth," the Crow scout spoke the words softly.

Bodine continued west, riding carefully, staying away from well-defined trails, choosing to make his own trail as he rode toward the Rosebud.

He arrived at the curve of the river on June the 23rd. Two Wolves was waiting for him.

"My father ordered me out of the camp and threatened to disown me if I did not obey." He looked hard at Bodine. "You knew he would do this, didn't you?"

"I suspected he would."

"Custer and his forces are very near. Wolf That Has No Sense told me this; he has seen them. There will be a great battle, Bodine. Tomorrow or the next day."

"Then we'll ride closer, Brother. We may be able to help with the wounded."

Two Wolves looked at him, suspicion and doubt mingling in his eyes.

"On both sides," Bodine added.

Two Wolves nodded. "Then let us ride."

They made a cold camp that night, not wanting to light a fire and give away their position. They chanced a fire just at dawn, for coffee, building the fire under low-hanging branches so the smoke would dissipate. They had cold biscuits with their coffee, and then mounted up, heading west.

"Is this Sunday?" Two Wolves asked.

"Saturday. June the 24th."

"We have heard no gunfire, so this must not be the day of the battle. So would Yellow Hair attack on a Sunday? On your God's day?"

"Troops don't pay much attention to that, Two Wolves. I expect he would attack if it seemed the thing to do."

"Odd way to worship one's God," Two Wolves commented.

About this time Custer's scouts were reporting to him that a large force of Sioux and Cheyenne were camped in a valley near the Little Bighorn. The scouts did their best to convince the brevet general that the Indians were too large in number.

"We attack in the morning," Custer told Reno and Benteen.

Major Reno pointed out that the pack train was much slower than the mounted troops and would be at least two hours behind them with much needed food, ammunition, and equipment.

Custer waved that away. He was eager to get into battle. Much too eager, for he had badly misjudged the Indians' strength and ferocity, for to them, this was no ordinary battle. This was a holy war.

"We attack in the morning. Get some rest and have the men check equipment. We'll be in the saddle before dawn."

The Sioux and the Cheyenne were anticipating the battle, and they were more than ready for it. Later in the day, a band of Arapahoes came into the camp. The Cheyenne believed they were scouts from the army and disarmed them, ready to kill them. But Black Wolf and Last Bull intervened, and ordered them taken to the lodge of Medicine Horse. After talking with them, he decided they had come to fight with them and ordered their weapons returned and for them to be fed at his lodge.

"It is to be a great battle," Medicine Horse told them after they had eaten. "Be prepared not only to fight, but to die."

They assured him they were ready.

Medicine Horse left his lodge to stand outside. He had made peace with his gods and with himself. He smiled and hefted his Winchester. It was much lighter now that he had emptied it of shells.

"This is as close as we'd better go, Brother," Two Wolves said, pulling up.

They were about three miles east of the valley of the Little

Bighorn. They watered their horses and filled their canteens at a small spring and then backed off some distance, allowing the animals a chance to come in at night and drink without being alarmed by human scent.

The two young men had been silent most of the day, riding very carefully and cautiously. That, and the fact that they both felt the battle was only hours away. They made a cold camp and rolled up in their blankets.

"Bodine?" Two Wolves whispered from his blankets.

"Yeah?"

"I feel a great sadness in my heart."

"I know. I feel . . . some of what you feel. But not to the degree that you're experiencing."

"I plan to ride closer in the morning."

"We'll ride together."

Colonel Travers stepped out of his quarters and stood in the cool darkness. He lit a cigar but it did not taste good and he snubbed it out against the porch railing. He turned to his orderly.

"Find Lieutenant Gerry for me, please. Tell him I want to see him."

"Yes, sir."

Lieutenant Gerry stepped out of the night into the dim light on the porch. "Sir?"

"I have no orders to do this, Gerry. But I do have some leeway in the orders from Dakota Command. We'll leave two companies at the garrison, under the command of Lieutenant Walters. You and I will lead four companies out of the fort at three o'clock in the morning. We're heading for the Rosebuds."

"Yes, sir."

"Each man will have four days' hard rations. One hundred rounds for his carbine and twenty-four rounds for his sidearm."

"Yes, sir."

"Order the garrison to quarters and tell the sergeants to roll the men out at two o'clock. You will meet me at my quarters at that time."

"Yes, sir."

"And God have mercy on our souls if Bodine was right."

"Permission to speak, sir?"

"Of course."

"He probably was right, sir."

Travers sighed. "I know, son. That's what's got me so worried."

On June the 22nd, General Alfred H. Terry had ordered Custer to take his men, about six hundred and fifty soldiers plus scouts and pack train drovers, to go to the southern end of the Little Bighorn Valley. And to wait there.

General Terry and his men were to reach the northern end of the valley on June the 26th, thus putting the Sioux and Cheyenne encampment in a box.

Custer had been advised to take it easy; be careful and don't be greedy. To wait for them.

Then General Terry gave Custer permission to depart from his written orders if Custer found "sufficient reasons to do so."

The dawning of Sunday, June the 25th exposed a very hot, dry, and dusty day. By dawn, Custer had been on the march for over an hour, pushing straight toward the Little Bighorn River.

Colonel Travers, at the head of four companies of cavalry, was just entering the eastern edge of the Rosebud Mountain range.

Bodine and Two Wolves had ridden to within a mile of

the river and picketed their horses in a natural corral. They proceeded on foot, carefully, toward a ridge that overlooked the valley of the Little Bighorn.

"Jesus God!" Bodine whispered, as he looked at the encampment that stretched for nearly four miles.

"I told you," Two Wolves returned the whisper.

"There must be seven or eight thousand down there."

"Yes. About thirty-five hundred warriors. The Ghost Dancing was concluded last evening. They are ready."

Bodine took his field glasses and watched several Indian boys fishing along the banks of the Little Bighorn. A man wearing a war bonnet joined the boys, but the distance was too great for Bodine to make out the man even with the aid of the binoculars. One of the boys, Spotted Hawk, would later relate that it was another boy's uncle, White Shield, a war chief, who had left his dressing for war when he became concerned about the boys' safety along the river.

"It looks so peaceful," Bodine said, laying aside the field glasses.

"It is anything but that. Brother, what can we do to stop this tragedy?"

"Nothing. I tried to warn Travers. You and I tried to warn Custer. There is nothing we can do except watch it unfold."

As the morning progressed, the day grew warmer and the young men on the ridge, overlooking what would soon be one of the bloodiest battlefields in all of the Indian wars, dozed under the sun, waiting for history to unfold before their eyes.

By midday, Custer's scouts had firmly located the Indian encampment and reported back to him.

Again, they warned him that the Indians were many. As Crow King had said, "Plenty as leaves on the trees."

Custer again ignored the warnings and prepared to attack.

He ordered a detour from his set route and set his new route to attack from the ridge overlooking what is now called Reno Creek.

Then, making a decision that many military officers thought he should have been court-martialed in absentia for doing, Custer split his command.

Custer sent Captain Frederick W. Benteen with about a hundred and twenty men to scout for Indians to the southwest. He sent Major Marcus A. Reno with one hundred and forty men to attack the southern end of the huge encampment that Custer could not adequately see because of dust, hills, and trees.

"I'll continue north along the bluff," Custer told his officers.

Custer then sent a trooper back to the pack train to hurry it along. The pack train carried nearly thirty thousand rounds of ammunition, various equipment, and food and water.

"Dust," Two Wolves said, poking Bodine in the ribs and bringing him out of his doze.

"Hell, there's dust everywhere," Bodine griped, trying to see something through his field glasses. All he could see was a blisteringly hot day filled with haze and dust.

"My father's people are at the north end of the village, near the ravine at the curve of the river. See what is happening there if you can."

Bodine again lifted the glasses and brought the Cheyenne encampment into focus through the dust and the haze of the hot Sunday afternoon. "Lots of activity down there. But nothing hurried."

"More dust over there," Two Wolves pointed out. He put his ear to the ground. He could hear nothing.

Bodine lifted his glasses, focusing on the Hunkpapa Sioux village camped near timber along the curving Little Bighorn.

"They sure are getting ready for something," he said.

Two Wolves glanced up at the sun. "It's about two o'clock."

Less than one hour remained until Custer and his men of the Seventh Cavalry would ride into destiny.

Chapter 31

Colonel Travers halted his column and consulted a map. He had been following the river, but where in the hell was Custer and his Seventh? He took out his watch and clicked it open. Three o'clock. And how many more miles to go?

Travers waved his companies forward.

Major Marcus Reno told his bugler to sound the charge and they hit the Hunkpapa Sioux village, catching them completely by surprise. This village was under the leadership of Chief Gall. During the first charge of the cavalry, two of Gall's wives and several of his children were killed, and that action probably spelled Reno's downfall. Gall rallied his warriors and drove Reno and his men back into the timber along a curve of the Little Bighorn. But that position was anything but secure. Gall, furious over the killing of his wives and children, pressed the attack and according to many survivors' own words, the cavalrymen became panic-stricken at the size and fury of the Hunkpapa force and left the timber, crossing the Little Bighorn in something of a rout and taking up positions on the high bluffs on the north side of the river where they dug in deep. But since the pack train was more than an hour behind them, the men were forced to dig in with knives, spoons, and tin cups.

Major Reno had already lost forty men, thirteen were wounded, and many were missing. Some of them would never be found.

Gall said the killing of women and children "made his heart bad." After that, he fought with a small axe, swinging it with a vengeance.

Upon hearing the gunfire, Benteen and his command returned to find a badly shaken Reno and what was left of his mauled command.

Bodine and Two Wolves were helpless to do anything except lie on the ridge and watch the slaughter.

Not knowing that Reno and Benteen were under such heavy attack, Custer and his five companies—numbers vary between two hundred and ten and two hundred and forty men—had galloped north. They were out of sight of the village, along the ridge on the other side of the Indian encampment and the battles.

Sioux and Cheyenne scouts, who had been sent out to spy on General Crook's command, had returned, and they saw Custer and his men. They raced back to the village with the news. More than two thousand Sioux and Cheyenne were mobilized and set out to intercept the troops coming toward them from the lower end of the village.

Few among them knew it was Yellow Hair until the battle was over.

But Medicine Horse knew.

The Sioux and Cheyenne were armed with at least forty-one different types of rifles and pistols, many of them with Winchester repeating rifles, some with muzzle-loading muskets, others with the traditional bows and arrows and lances. As the army retreated, the Indians gathered up the weapons from the dead and from the ground where panic-stricken men had thrown them in their haste to get the hell out of that area. Some were armed with only coup sticks. As was Medicine Horse.

The combined forces of Sioux and Cheyenne spotted Custer as he and his command topped the ridge just north of Reno's embattled position. Because of the dust and the haze in the gunsmoke-filled air, Custer did not see what dire straits Reno was in and continued on north, on the ridge, pursued by at least two thousand hostiles.

Custer tried to get off the ridge and did manage for a time to fight briefly near the river, but within minutes was forced back onto the ridge and continued on north, losing men with each Indian assault.

By this time, most of the Indians who had been fighting Reno and Benteen had left the creek to pursue the companies of cavalry on the ridge. Only Captain Thomas Weir and his few men stood in their way.

With most of the pressure off Reno and Benteen, they managed to fortify their positions on what would come to be known as Reno's Hill.

They did not know what was happening to Custer.

Bodine lowered his binoculars. "I can't see anything, Brother. I don't know what's happening over there."

"I do," Two Wolves spoke the words grimly. "It is as my father said: the beginning of the end."

All the soldiers who had been along the river, from all commands, had now pulled back to the ridges, many of them losing their horses and many of them losing their rifles, forced to fight with six-shooters, and since they only were issued twenty-four rounds of ammunition for their sidearms, conditions were becoming somewhat more than desperate for the men of the Seventh Cavalry.

Bodies of cavalrymen littered the ground between the river and the ridges.

Bands of Cheyenne, led by Contrary Belly, Yellow Nose, and Chief Comes In Sight, began leading charges up the ridges, getting very close to the soldiers. Yellow Nose actually got inside the perimeter of the troops and grabbed the company guidon from the hands of a soldier and counted coup on the man with it, striking the soldier with the staff and then riding off, leaving the man alive and bewildered.

After that charge, the badly frightened horses of the cavalrymen broke and ran free. Out of the seven companies of troops on the ridges, only four companies still had mounts. With no place to run.

Two Wolves had the field glasses and through the murky haze could see the frightened horses galloping riderless down the ridges, across the river, and tearing through the Indian village. He pointed that out to Bodine.

"If that means what I think it does," Bodine said, "it's a slaughter over there."

More shooting and screaming were heard from the top of the ridge, and as more Indians left to pursue Custer and his troops, that much more pressure was taken off Reno, Benteen, and Weir. They were now able to recover somewhat and take better stock of their situation, which was still very grim.

Custer and his men had now retreated to a point just above the Miniconjou and Blackfoot camps in the village. Custer dispatched a man with orders to locate Benteen and return with help.

The courier did not make it and Benteen, Reno, and Weir would not know what had happened to Custer and his men for another thirty-six hours. No one is really sure what happened to the courier. The courier may have been part of the twenty-six troopers of Company E who presumably died in and around what is known as Deep Ravine. No one knows. Their bodies would never be found.

Custer and his troopers had now crossed what is known as Deep Coulee and ran right into Gall and his hundreds of warriors. Medicine Horse was with Gall and through the dust and gunsmoke and confusion, recognized Yellow Hair, but was unable to reach him. Meanwhile, a band led by White Shield was attacking soldiers led by Tom Custer, George Custer's brother and commander of Company C. White Shield thought this was Colonel Custer and pressed the attack, slaughtering them all and counting coup upon the badly mutilated body of Tom Custer. He was so badly mutilated that later he could only be identified by the initials tattooed on his arm.

With the men of Company C now dead or out of action, White Shield led his group of braves toward George Armstrong Custer's besieged band of cavalrymen, who had now retreated to Calhoun Hill. They were not far from where they would make their last stand.

Boston Custer, a civilian scout, died a few hundred yards from his brother, Tom. Their nephew, eighteen-year-old Harry Reed, who had come along for the adventure of it, died a few feet away from Boston.

From Reno Creek to Calhoun Hill, dead soldiers were being stripped of their clothing and then mutilated so their spirits would not be able to enjoy a final resting place, but would instead be forced to wander forever and ever.

Now, with many Indians dressed in army clothing, a Cheyenne, Lame White Man, was shot and killed and scalped by his own people, who mistook him for an army scout.

Custer and his men had now reached Last Stand Hill, with the warriors of Crazy Horse and Gall all around them.

Brave Wolf, who was the fighting chief of the Cheyenne, would later state, "I saw such brave men as those who fought and died with Yellow Hair on the hill. It was hard fighting; very hard fighting. They did not panic but fought well and stayed together. I have been in many battles. But I never saw such brave men in all my life. They died well on the hill."

Benteen and Reno were still pinned down, but they had suffered no more deaths; mostly they were under observation from the Indians who surrounded them. They had been strengthened by the arrival of thirteen more men—twelve soldiers and one civilian scout. They had been hiding in the timber along the river.

"It can't go on much longer," Two Wolves said. "Surely all the soldiers must be dead by now."

Bodine agreed, with neither of them able to know about Reno and Benteen and the troopers still on the ridges above the Little Bighorn.

Bodine looked up through the dusty haze at the sun. "About five o'clock."

At Last Stand Hill, the fighting had intensified with the Indians closing in.

Medicine Horse charged up the hill, waving his coup stick. Custer looked up, surprise in his eyes as he recognized Medicine Horse. Custer lifted his pistol and shot Medicine Horse through the chest. The chief tumbled from his horse and crawled up the hill. He whacked Custer on the leg with his coup stick, rolled over, and died with a smile on his lips.

Custer and his few remaining troopers held to their battle formation to the last.

On the ridge above the valley of the Little Bighorn, Two Wolves screamed and threw his hands to his head as a great pain filled his brain, almost blinding him with its intensity. He put his head to the earth and moaned as the pain began to lessen.

Bodine looked around to see if someone was shooting at them. He could see no one.

"What's wrong, Brother?"

"My father is dead."

Lieutenant Colonel George Armstrong Custer fell to his knees after being shot through the left side. Bleeding badly, Custer summoned all his will and struggled to rise to his boots. He continued fighting until moments later he was shot through the temple. Without uttering another sound, he fell to the hot, dry earth and died. Many Indians have stated that he was the last in his command to die on Last Stand Hill.

Custer's body was stripped naked, but he was neither scalped nor mutilated. A sign of respect from the Indians who fought him and killed him.

Last Stand Hill grew quiet as the Indians left and the blood of the dead was soaked into the hot, dry earth.

It was almost over.

Chapter 32

The Sioux and Cheyenne warriors left Last Stand Hill to the women and the children, who stripped and mutilated many of the bodies. Many of the soldiers were mutilated beyond recognition.

Money was taken from the bodies, but since the Indians had no use for it, it was given to the children to play with.

Buttons were cut off the uniforms as trinkets, and all the weapons and ammunition and what horses were left were taken.

The battle now shifted to the ridges where Reno and Benteen and their men were trapped. But they had grown in number, with more soldiers wandering in from their hiding places and the pack train reaching them, finally coming over the ridge about two hours behind the main body.

Bodine and Two Wolves ran back to the horses and mounted up, riding around the valley and coming up to Last Stand Hill from the west. They sat their horses and stared at the scene, total shock and disbelief in their eyes. All bodies of slain Indians, including that of Medicine Horse, had been taken away.

"God have mercy on their souls," Bodine finally whispered.

Bodine and Two Wolves stared in shock at the bloody awful sight on the hill.

Bodine finally swung down and walked to where Custer lay. Medicine Horse's coup stick lay beside Custer's body. He pointed to it and looked at Two Wolves, questions in his eyes.

Two Wolves shook his head and broke the silence. We are in great danger here, Brother. It will not matter who we are. If we are found by either side on this hill, we will die."

Bodine mounted up and they rode away from the slaughter, heading first west and then, when they were well away from the valley, they headed south, following the river.

It was well after dark when they reined up, seeing many small fires along the river.

"A dollar says that's Travers heading north from the fort," Bodine said.

"No bet. Brother, no one must ever know that we were on the ridge overlooking the battle. For many reasons."

"I know. Do we ride into Travers' camp?"

"Might as well."

As they rode, they tidied up the story they would tell.

A few hundred yards from the encampment, Bodine called out to the sentries and they were waved in.

Over coffee, Bodine told the story to a stunned Travers and Gerry and other officers and sergeants.

"All I know is that it was a hell of a battle. It was pretty well over by the time we decided not to go any farther into the Rosebuds. Really all we could see was a lot of dust in the air."

"But you did see the Indian camp?" Travers pressed the question.

"Yes. Early this morning. By the number of lodges, I would guess about seven thousand or so Indians. Perhaps as many as three thousand braves."

"Dear God in Heaven!" Sergeant McGuire breathed. "And you think they're still in the valley?"

"I would have no reason to think otherwise."

Travers looked at Gerry. "We'll try to link up with Terry and Gibbon. It would be suicide for us to ride in there alone." He looked at Bodine. "Will you ride with us—both of you—and scout?"

"All right."

Bodine found Terry's column and stayed with it while Two Wolves rode back to Travers to guide them in. The two forces linked up on the afternoon of June the 26th just as the sun was setting. They were only a few miles from the valley of the Little Bighorn.

Benteen and Reno had watched the Sioux and the Cheyenne break camp that afternoon and start their pull-out. Not knowing whether the Indians were trying to trick them into leaving their positions, the surviving members of Custer's forces stayed behind their breastworks and waited it out, knowing that Terry and Gibbon could not be far away.

On the morning of June the 27th, Bodine and Two Wolves led the column to Last Stand Hill, coming up from the south end of the valley. The stench was awful. Many a hardened trooper leaned out of the saddle and vomited. Several of the younger troopers fainted at the stench and again at the crest of the hill when the hideousness came into full view.

Bodine and Two Wolves found the position of Reno and Benteen and led them to the generals, who listened to their stories in stunned silence.

Burial parties had few tools, so very shallow graves were scooped out for some; only sagebrush covered other bodies. The burying was soon over.

Daisies and mariposa lilies and tiny roses bloomed in a pinkish purple blaze as the still-stunned survivors and rescuers who came too late rode away from the silent, blood-drenched hills above the Little Bighorn.

Bodine and Two Wolves drifted away from the column and went their separate ways. Each had to somehow erase the sight of the massacre from their mind, and each had to do it in his own way. Somehow.

Sam August Webster Two Wolves rode in search of his father's burial site, and Matt Bodine rode to search for peace of mind. Both quests would prove to be very elusive for the young men.

For the Cheyenne and the Sioux, the victory at the Little Bighorn would be their last. Within two years, the majority of the plains tribes would be on reservations, for the Army, after the humiliation at what was being called Custer's Last Stand, would become relentless in their pursuit of the Indians . . . but that's another story.

Bodine spent the summer alone, riding aimlessly along the Montana/Wyoming border.

Two Wolves finally located his father's burial site—after speaking with various bands of Indians—his father's body wrapped in a blanket, suspended high in the air on a lonely ridge. Two Wolves picked sweet sage and sprinkled it around the site and on himself, to purify both. Then he prayed and fasted.

Bodine and Two Wolves met again in the valley of the Little Bighorn. Both had been drawn there by the many visions they suffered alone through the long nights. They camped there for several weeks, and it was a balm to soothe invisible wounds. When they finally pulled out, they knew they could now live with the memories of that day back in June, 1876.

The ghosts that still ride the ridges and would do so forever spoke to them. They would never mention those ghostly riders to anyone, and they would seldom talk about them to each other. But both knew what they saw, and they knew better than to question the order of nature.

And Tom Thomas, his empire shattered, his men scattered, and Terri Kelly gone to only God knew where, decided to ride west.

He awakened one morning with fear clutching his heart with cold fingers.

He was surrounded by Indians, Lone Dog smiling down at him.

"Tom Thomas," Lone Dog said contemptuously. "Do you believe it is a good day to die?"

Chapter 33

Bodine and Two Wolves returned to their home range as summer was waning. Bodine's parents took one look at the young men and knew they had been forever changed. They did not know the how or the why of it, only that it had happened.

And being people of the West, who minded their own business, they did not press the point.

Over coffee on the front porch, the elder Bodine said, "The Army found what was left of Tom Thomas. The scout with the patrol said, from the looks of things, he did not die well."

"Lone Dog?" Two Wolves asked.

"The scout thinks so. Did you boys stop by the battleground at the Little Big Horn?"

"We stopped." His son told him that much and nothing more.

The man looked at Two Wolves. "Was your father . . . ?"

"Yes."

"I'm sorry."

"I was for a time. I am no longer in sorrow. My father

died a warrior's death, counting coup. I believe he went on the hill to die."

"What makes you so sure?"

"Because I have talked to Indians who were in the battle." This was true. "My father was armed only with a coup stick." That was also true, but no Indian had told him that.

"Well," the elder Bodine said with a sigh, "I reckon you boys will settle down now and ranch, right?"

The young men exchanged glances. "Wrong," his son told him.

"Boy!" The father half rose from his chair, a note of exasperation in his voice. "You're twenty-five years old, damnit! You both have ranches that could be money-makers; are money-makers. What in the Sam Hill are you two going to do?"

"Drift," Two Wolves took the heat off his brother. Mrs. Bodine stamped her foot on the porch floor and crossed her arms under her breasts. She looked like she wanted to cuss.

"Drift," the father said disgustedly. "Two twenty-five-year-old kids."

Bodine and Two Wolves said nothing in rebuttal.

"It won't be forever, Dad," Bodine assured him. "And I wish I could tell you the reason, reasons, for our feelings. But that's going to have to stay locked up for a time. I'm truly sorry."

"Are you wanted by the law, boys?"

"No, Dad. No. That isn't it. Both of us have got to go up into the timber and the High Lonesome. We've got to ride the rivers and see what's over the next mountain. Call it an . . . inner search, if you will."

"Your sister is getting married next month," his mother told him.

"I'm glad. But I won't be here."

His mother said no more about it. She knew her son;

knew that when he said he was going, even though he might have to move heaven and hell, he was going.

"What about your ranch, boy?"

"I'll give Carl a working interest in it. I'll draw up the papers all legal-like and you can witness it."

"That's fair," the father conceded. "The boy needs to get out of this house and stand on his own. Two Wolves?"

"Slim Man is on my place now. I will hire others to help him. It is settled."

"I reckon it is," the father spoke the words. "I only hope that someday you boys will tell me why you're doing this."

Bodine drew up the papers giving his brother a share in the ranch in exchange for his staying on it and running the sprawling spread. A large responsibility for one so young, but in the West, one grew up quickly.

"You boys picked a hell of time to get itchy feet," the elder Bodine pointed out. "What with winter lookin' us in the face. Where are you headin'?"

"We honestly don't know, Dad. South, for sure, but how far south is up for grabs."

"I have never been to Arizona," Two Wolves said. "I have talked to people who have told me about the deserts there. I would like to see them."

The father grunted. "Way I hear it, it's too damn hot for my tastes. You boys be sure to post Mrs. Bodine a letter every now and then. Wimmen get right touchy about things like that."

"I shall write her regularly," Two Wolves promised. "That way I know that she will at least hear from one of us."

"Very funny," Bodine groused, tightening down the cinch on Rowdy. "I'll write."

"It'll damn sure be the first time," his father said dryly.

* * *

They got to the west side of the Powder and looked at each other.

"You serious about heading south?" Bodine asked.

"I certainly have no desire to ride north with winter coming."

They pointed the noses of their horses south. They would follow the Powder all the way down to the South Fork of the river and then leave the river, heading into the Rattlesnake Hills and then over to cross the Sweetwater, staying to the east of the Green Mountains and the Great Divide Basin, which was not the most hospitable place in which to wander. They took their time, but always riding alert for trouble.

They lost track of the days as they drifted, but they were forever being reminded of the slaughter they had witnessed at the Little Bighorn. Nearly every person they met on the trail, Indian and white, when they learned Bodine and Two Wolves were from the upper Wyoming country, wanted to know if they knew anything about the great battle between Custer and the Sioux and Cheyenne. Bodine and Two Wolves would tell them no and let the subject die.

Then they began hearing about this beautiful blond lady who was running a bar down on the North Platte in the Medicine Bow Mountains. Young, people said. A real looker, others told them. It was worth the price of a drink just to look at her.

"Has to be," Two Wolves said.

"Yeah. Terri Kelly. Want to drop in for a drink and some friendly conversation?"

Two Wolves shrugged. "Why not?"

They were still days away from the Medicine Bow range, with no plan to hurry along just to see Terri.

"She's got some gunslicks with her," a grizzled old trapper told them over the fire one night. "Story is she robbed some rich man up in Montana; used to own a whole town up there, he did. So the talk goes. She grabbed his poke and run one night, she did. Her and some Texas gunfighter named Walker. He's a bad one, boys. And mighty jealous of that blond-haired woman. I'd fight shy of that place was I you."

"You said gunhands. How many?" Bodine asked.

"No tellin'. They come and go. Maybe ten, maybe thirty. Salty bunch. That place of hers is worser than them joints out on the Barbary Coast. Lots of folks gone in there alive through the batwings and come out dead through the back door, they pockets all turned inside out, if you know what I mean."

As they rode south, Two Wolves asked, with a smile on his lips, "What are we striving to be, Brother: the Robin Hoods of the West?"

"I'm on no mission of mercy, Two Wolves. If folks want to get robbed and beat up and tossed in the alley, that's their business. I want a hot bath, some food that you or me didn't have to cook, and some corn for Rowdy. But we don't have to get it in Terri's town."

"I'd never hear the end of it if we didn't. You'd be complaining about it all the way to Arizona."

They were still arguing when they rode into the little town.

They rode in quietly, stopping first at the stables and seeing to their horses, then walking across the street and checking into the hotel. They left clothes at the laundry for the Chinaman to wash and iron and then went to a barber shop for a haircut and bath in tubs out back of the shop while they sent a boy over to the general store for fresh long-handles and jeans and shirts and socks.

Scrubbed clean of dirt and any fleas they might have gathered during the long dusty days on the trail, the two young men resupplied for their journey, took the supplies back to the hotel, and then walked across the street to a cafe for a hot meal.

They had wiped the dust from their guns and checked the action carefully, loading the cylinders up full. Two Wolves had taken to wearing a second gun, the left-hand gun butt-forward. He had been practicing his draw, since, as he put it, "If I am to be in the company of a notorious gunfighter, I'd better practice if I plan to stay alive."

"Very funny, Brother," Bodine had told him. "You're a real comedian."

They ate well and polished off a pot of coffee, conscious of the cafe's counterman eyeballing them. "I know you," he finally said. "You're Bodine."

"That's right."

"And you'd be the half-breed, Two Wolves."

"Correct."

"Thought it was you, Bodine. I seen you when you was just a kid; back when them hardcases braced you after that stagecoach run when they tried to rob you of that gold you was guardin'. That was some mighty fine shootin'. Mighty fine."

Bodine rolled a cigarette and leaned back in his chair. He knew the counterman was leading up to something.

"You boys headin' over to the saloon after your smoke?"

"We might be," Two Wolves told him.

The man smiled. "Thought that might be the case. I'll just close up early and head on over there for a drink. The meal and the coffee is on the house."

"That's very kind of you," Two Wolves acknowledged. "But why the generosity?"

"This used to be a right nice little village. Had us a church and a little school for the kids to learn. Then that damn Terri woman and them gunslicks of hers come in. Must have been twenty-five or thirty killin's over the past few months. Probably more than that; sometimes men go in that place and don't nobody ever see them agin. Lots of miners drift in here with a hefty poke. Don't nobody ever see them drift out agin. That woman is evil, boys. And that Walker is a devil. He's supposed to have been kilt a dozen times over the years. But he's still standin' in his boots and still raisin' Old Nick with them guns of hisn."

"I never heard of anybody or any gang ever treeing a western town," Bodine said.

"Oh, the town wasn't treed right off. Terri and them gunhands of hers was too smart to just ride in and do that. First the town marshal was kilt; shot in the back one night. We got us another one and he went out the same way. Nobody else wanted the job. The church and the school was burnt down. The mayor got hisself all in-volved with that blond-haired witch. It kinda went downhill from then on—if you know what I mean."

"Only too well," Two Wolves said softly. He looked at the counterman. "Can you handle a gun?"

"Shore can. I rode cavalry in the War between the States. They's about a half dozen of us in town who still got the belly for some gunplay."

"You round them up," Bodine told him. 'We're going to go back to the hotel and sit in the lobby; read the papers. Give us a sign when you're ready. How many people does Terri have on her payroll?"

"Twenty-five or thirty."

"Damn!" Two Wolves said. "All gunhands?"

"Most of 'em, yeah. She's into all sorts of things: robbin,' rustlin,' killin.' You name it, and she's got her finger in the pie."

Bodine and Two Wolves stepped out onto the boardwalk. Two Wolves said, "Well, here goes Robin and his Hood to the rescue."

"Which one of us is the Hood?"

"I think we'd better leave that up to history."

"Let's go read the papers."

"Right. Nothing like dying with a full stomach and a mind full of current events."

Chapter 34

The counterman—he'd said his name was Max—walked by the hotel and nodded at the young men. He had a six-gun belted on and wore it like he knew how to use it.

It was early in the afternoon but the saloon—the only one in town—was jumping with business.

Bodine nodded at Max and the man walked on. Bodine waved a boy over to his side; the boy should have been in school and would have been had not Walker and his thugs burned the school—on Terri's orders.

Bodine handed the lad a note. "Go into the saloon and give this to Walker." He gave the boy a silver dollar and that put wings on the boy's feet.

Bodine had written: WALKER, YOU BIG BLOWHARD. YOU'VE BEEN FLAPPING THAT BIG FAT MOUTH ABOUT HOW YOU'RE BETTER WITH A GUN THAN I AM. NOW IS THE TIME TO PROVE IT—PROVIDING YOUR BIG FAT BUTT HASN'T OVERLOADED YOUR MOUTH.

He had signed it "Bodine".

"You do have such a way with words, Bodine," Two Wolves told him.

"Thank you. I thought it was quite good myself." Two Wolves rolled his eyes.

The boy ran back into the hotel, almost out of breath. "Mister!" he panted. "I don't have no idea what you wrote on that paper, but you shore caused Mister Walker to lose his temper and cuss. Lordy, did he cuss!"

"Fine, boy. Now you get over there with the desk clerk and the both of you stay away from the windows."

Bodine and Two Wolves walked to the windows and looked out. The street was barren of any kind of life, human or animal. Max and his men should be getting into position on the rooftops. Bodine and Two Wolves slipped the hammer thongs free and stepped out onto the boardwalk.

Walker and a dozen of his men stood on the boardwalk in front of the saloon.

"You were expecting Walker to meet you alone, Brother?"

"One can always hope," Bodine replied.

"Bodine, the eternal optimist."

"I have a plan."

"I would certainly hope so!"

"It just came to me."

"I don't doubt that, either."

"Max and his people are in position on the roofs, right."

"We hope."

"Well, why don't we shorten the distance by about half a block and just start shooting into the mob of them all bunched up there on the boardwalk?"

"Bodine, that's positively brilliant!"

Bodine smiled and glanced at him. Two Wolves' eyes were twinkling despite the danger that faced them. "You ready?"

"Lead on, Bodine."

They began walking up the boardwalk, spurs jingling.

When they were about seventy-five feet from the knot of hardcases, Bodine yelled, "Now, Max!" and grabbed for his guns.

The men on the rooftops opened fire with rifles, pistols, and shotguns just as the guns of Bodine and Two Wolves roared.

But at Bodine's yell, Walker had dived back through the batwings, into the saloon.

A half a dozen gunhands were killed during the first volley and the others were down, wounded and moaning.

"I'm going around back!" Bodine told Two Wolves, punching empties out and reloading. "I'll see you in a minute."

"I certainly hope so. It would be a lonesome ride to Arizona without you."

Bodine grinned and ran into the alley.

One of the wounded lifted a gun and pointed it at Two Wolves. Two Wolves shot him, the bullet taking the man directly through the nose; if he'd had any sinus problems, Two Wolves just cured them . . . and any other problems he might have been suffering during his short stay on this mortal plain.

Bodine rounded the corner and ran right into a gunslick, knocking him sprawling. Bodine kicked the man in the head and went in through the back door of the saloon. He threaded his way through the murk of the dark storeroom, which was filled with kegs of beer and cases of whiskey. The door suddenly flew open and a man stood there, a sawed-off shotgun in his hands.

Bodine shot him twice and grabbed up the shotgun, fanning the man for shells and finding a handful. He checked the weapon and slipped away from the door.

None too soon. For just as he changed positions, half a dozen guns barked from within the saloon and the door was riddled.

Bodine fired through a small, dirty window, giving several gunnies standing at the bar both barrels and making a big mess behind the bar with various parts of them.

He again shifted locations, reloading the sawed-off as he moved.

Bodine spotted stairs leading to the second floor and took them quietly, just as the storeroom was shattered with lead. The stench of beer and whiskey was very nearly overpowering.

He stepped out onto a balcony, lifted the shotgun and blew two more of Terri's toughs out of this world. He dropped the shotgun and filled his hands with Colts just as Walker stepped into view.

Bodine literally filled him with lead. The man jerked and stumbled each time the lead struck him, the bullets driving him back against the bar. He died with his elbows hooked onto the bar railing and his blood leaking into a dirty spittoon.

"You rotten son of a bitch!" Terri squalled at him.

Bodine had the strangest sensation that he'd done all this before.

"You can't do this to me!" Terri hollered as her butt hit the seat of the wagon and the reins were pressed into her soft, pretty hands. Reins that were attached to two mules.

The bed of the wagon was filled with wounded gunhands, patched up by the local doctor. Without benefit of laudanum.

Bodine slapped a mule on the rump. "See you around, Terri!" he called.

"I'll get you for this, Bodine!" she screamed. "You and that damn half-breed! I'll see you both in hell for this."

She was still squalling and cussing and raining down dire threats upon their heads as the wagon lurched out of town.

Two Wolves had been burned on the arm by a bullet and Bodine had his new jeans torn by a ricochet. He cussed the hole in his jeans more than he did the burn on his leg.

They swung into the saddle and headed out, with the cheering of the townspeople ringing in their heads. But with it, they both knew another notch had been carved deeply into their already growing reputations.

"Do you suppose, Bodine," Two Wolves said, "that when our luck begins to turn bad, we'll have enough sense to hang it up and go back home?"

"I sure hope so, Brother. I surely do."

"Get off the road, quick!" Two Wolves said. "Good God, there's the wagon and Terri!"

"She's got a pistol!" Bodine warned.

They just made it out of pistol range when she opened up on them, standing up in the front boot and banging away. Fortunately for them, hitting nothing but cool fall air.

"I'll get you, damn you both!" she hollered. "Ill find you, Bodine. You too, you damn Godless heathen!"

"Godless heathen?" Two Wolves said, as they galloped away. "I guess I forgot to tell her my mother had me baptized into the Presbyterian church."

The two young men laughed and with wild whoops out of their throats, they galloped south, letting their horses run for a time, carrying them into the unknown. But both of them knew that while they might square off and bust each other in the mouth and cuss each other, and argue from dawn to dusk, they were Brothers of the Wolf, bonded by blood. And if you chose to fight one, you had to fight the other. For that was the way their fathers had wanted it, and that was the way it was to be.

And they knew that destiny pulled them south. Unknown, but real.

They slowed their horses and walked them.

"Look, Bodine!" Two Wolves pointed. "A message from the Other Side."

A huge old Lobo wolf stood on a knoll, watching them through wise eyes.

He threw back his head and howled.

AFTERWORD

Notes from the Old West

In the small town where I grew up, there were two movie theaters. The Pavilion was one of those old-timey movie show palaces, built in the heyday of Mary Pickford and Charlie Chaplin—the silent era of the 1920s. By the 1950s, when I was a kid, the Pavilion was a little worn around the edges, but it was still the premier theater in town. They played all those big Technicolor biblical Cecil B. DeMille epics and corny MGM musicals. In Cinemascope, of course.

On the other side of town was the Gem, a somewhat shabby and run-down grind house with sticky floors and torn seats. Admission was a quarter. The Gem booked low-budget "B" pictures (remember the Bowery Boys?), war movies, horror flicks, and Westerns. I liked the Westerns best. I could usually be found every Saturday at the Gem, along with my best friend, Newton Trout, watching Westerns from 10 A.M. until my father came looking for me around suppertime. (Sometimes Newton's dad was dispatched to come fetch us.) One time, my dad came to get me right in the middle of *Abilene Trail*, which featured the now-forgotten Whip Wilson. My father became so engrossed in the action he sat down and watched the rest of it with us. We didn't get home until after dark, and my mother's meat loaf was a pan of gray ashes by the time we did. Though my father and I were both in the doghouse the next day, this remains one of my fondest childhood memories. There was Wild Bill Elliot, and Gene Autry, and Roy Rogers, and Tim Holt, and, a little later, Rod Cameron and Audie Murphy. Of these newcomers, I never missed an Audie Murphy Western, because Audie was sort of an antihero. Sure, he stood for law and order and was an honest man, but sometimes he had to go around the law to uphold it. If he didn't play fair, it was only because he felt hamstrung by the laws of the land. Whatever it took to get the bad guys, Audie did it. There were no finer points of law, no splitting of legal hairs. It was instant justice, devoid of long-winded lawyers, bored or biased jurors, or black-robed, often corrupt judges.

Steal a man's horse and you were the guest of honor at a necktie party.

Molest a good woman and you got a bullet in the heart or a rope around the gullet. Or at the very least, got the crap beat out of you. Rob a bank and face a hail of bullets or the hangman's noose.

Saved a lot of time and money, did frontier justice.

That's all gone now, I'm sad to say. Now you hear, "Oh, but he had a bad childhood" or "His mother didn't give him enough love" or "The homecoming queen wouldn't give him a second look and he has an inferiority complex." Or "cultural rage," as the politically correct bright boys refer to it. How many times have you heard some self-important defense attorney moan, "The poor kids were only venting their hostilities toward an uncaring society?"

Mule fritters, I say. Nowadays, you can't even call a punk a punk anymore. But don't get me started.

It was "Howdy, ma'am" time too. The good guys, antihero or not, were always respectful to the ladies. They might shoot a bad guy five seconds after tipping their hat to a woman, but the code of the West demanded you be respectful to a lady.

Lots of things have changed since the heyday of the Wild West, haven't they? Some for the good, some for the bad.

I didn't have any idea at the time that I would someday write about the West. I just knew that I was captivated by the Old West.

When I first got the itch to write, back in the early 1970s, I didn't write Westerns. I started by writing horror and action adventure novels. After more than two dozen novels, I began thinking about developing a Western character. From those initial musings came the novel *The Last Mountain Man: Smoke Jensen.* That was followed by *Preacher: The First Mountain Man. A* few years later, I began developing the Last Gunfighter series. Frank Morgan is a legend in his own time, the fastest gun west of the Mississippi . . . a title and a reputation he never wanted, but can't get rid of.

For me, and for thousands—probably millions—of other people (although many will never publicly admit it), the old Wild West will always be a magic, mysterious place: a place we love to visit through the pages of books; characters we would like to know . . . from a safe distance; events we would love to take part in, again, from a safe distance. For the old Wild West was not a place for the faint of heart. It was a hard, tough, physically demanding time. There were no police to call if one faced adversity. One faced trouble alone, and handled it alone. It was rugged individualism: something that appeals to many of us.

I am certain that is something that appeals to most readers of Westerns.

I still do on-site research (whenever possible) before starting a Western novel. I have wandered over much of the

West, prowling what is left of ghost towns. Stand in the midst of the ruins of these old towns, use a little bit of imagination, and one can conjure up life as it used to be in the Wild West. The rowdy Saturday nights, the tinkling of a piano in a saloon, the laughter of cowboys and miners letting off steam after a week of hard work. Use a little more imagination and one can envision two men standing in the street, facing one another, seconds before the hook and draw of a gunfight. A moment later, one is dead and the other rides away.

The old wild untamed West.

There are still some ghost towns to visit, but they are rapidly vanishing as time and the elements take their toll. If you want to see them, make plans to do so as soon as possible, for in a few years, they will all be gone.

And so will we.

Stand in what is left of the Big Thicket country of east Texas and try to imagine how in the world the pioneers managed to get through that wild tangle. I have wondered about that many times and marveled at the courage of the men and women who slowly pushed westward, facing dangers that we can only imagine.

Let me touch briefly on a subject that is very close to me: firearms. There are some so-called historians who are now claiming that firearms played only a very insignificant part in the settlers' lives. They claim that only a few were armed. What utter, stupid nonsense! What do these so-called historians think the pioneers did for food? Do they think the early settlers rode down to the nearest supermarket and bought their meat? Or maybe they think the settlers chased down deer or buffalo on foot and beat the animals to death with a club. I have a news flash for you so-called historians: The settlers used guns to shoot their game. They used guns to defend hearth and home against Indians on the warpath. They used guns to protect themselves from outlaws. Guns are a part of Americana. And always will be.

The mountains of the West and the remains of the ghost towns that dot those areas are some of my favorite subjects to write about. I have done extensive research on the various mountain ranges of the West and go back whenever time permits. I sometimes stand surrounded by the towering mountains and wonder how in the world the pioneers ever made it through. As hard as I try and as often as I try, I simply cannot imagine the hardships those men and women endured over the hard months of their incredible journey. None of us can. It is said that on the Oregon Trail alone, there are at least two bodies in lonely, unmarked graves for every mile of that journey. Some students of the West say the number of dead is at least twice that. And nobody knows the exact number of wagons that impatiently started out alone and simply vanished on the way, along with their occupants, never to be seen or heard from again.

Just vanished.

The one-hundred-and-fifty-year-old ruts of the wagon wheels can still be seen in various places along the Oregon Trail. But if you plan to visit those places, do so quickly, for they are slowly disappearing. And when they are gone, they will be lost forever, except in the words of Western writers.

The West will live on as long as there are writers willing to write about it, and publishers willing to publish it. Writing about the West is wide open, just like the old Wild West. Characters abound, as plentiful as the wide-open spaces, as colorful as a sunset on the Painted Desert, as restless as the ever-sighing winds. All one has to do is use a bit of imagination. Take a stroll through the cemetery at Tombstone, Arizona; read the inscriptions. Then walk the main street of that once-infamous town around midnight and you might catch a glimpse of the ghosts that still wander the town.

They really do. Just ask anyone who lives there. But don't be afraid of the apparitions, they won't hurt you. They're just out for a quiet stroll.

The West lives on. And as long as I am alive, it always will.

Turn the page for an exciting preview of the next book in William Johnstone's BLOOD BOND series:

BROTHERHOOD OF THE GUN

Coming in February 2006

Wherever Pinnacle Books are sold

Chapter 1

They were blood-brothers, bonded by the Cheyenne ritual that made them as one. And more importantly, they were Brothers of the Wolf.

Two young men, Matt Bodine and Sam August Webster Two Wolves. The two men could and had, many times, passed as having the same mother, which they did not. Both possessed the same lean hips and heavy upper torso musculature. Sam's eyes were black, Matt's were blue. Sam's hair was black, Bodine's hair was dark brown. They were the same height and very nearly the same weight.

Both wore the same type of three-stone necklace around their necks, the stones pierced by rawhide. Both were ruggedly handsome men.

Both had gone through the Cheyenne Coming of Manhood, and each would carry the scars on his chest until death turned the soulless flesh into dust.

They were both Onihomahan: Friends of the Wolf. Both revered the great Gray Wolf, and both had raised wolf cubs as boys. The Indians did not have the fear of the wolf that the white man possessed, probably because the Indians took the time to understand animal behavior. Matt had learned the white man never took the time—any animal he didn't understand he wanted to kill.

"Are we going to have to ride forever to reach Arizona?" Two Wolves asked, shifting in the saddle.

"I think we are. in the territory, brother. I also think we are being followed."

Neither one of them knew it, but they were already in Arizona, having crossed the border two days back.

"You think? Hah! I have known about that for at least two hours."

"Nice of you to say something about it."

"I was waiting for you to dig the sand out of your eyes and ears and discover it yourself. You would have probably noticed something amiss just before they—whoever they might be—conked you on the head."

Matt grunted. "At least four of them, I figure. Maybe more."

"I would say four. But you're right; maybe more."

"There are Apache here," Matt said. "But there are a lot of Navajo and Zuni too. Hualapai and Kaibab are to the west of us."

"Those behind us are not Indians," Sam said. "We'd probably have never spotted an Indian." He smiled. "At least you wouldn't have," he needled his friend.

Matt silently agreed with the first part of Sam's statement. He ignored the second part. The blood brothers were always sticking the needle into each other and had been for years. Neither took it seriously. Matt pulled his Winchester out of the boot, shucked a round into the chamber, eased the hammer down, and rode with the rifle laid across his saddle horn. Sam Two Wolves did the same.

Sam pointed to the west and Matt cut his eyes. The ruins of an ancient pueblo could be seen. "Navajo?" he asked.

Sam shrugged and gave the reply that most Indians of any tribe would. "Those who came before us."

"Let's cut straight south," Matt suggested. "Keep your eyes open for Los Gigantes Butte. We want to swing to the west of that."

"We're running low on water. This would not be a good time for us to get caught up in a trap."

"Lukachuka Creek is south and west of the butte." Then Matt remembered what a drifting cowboy had told him a long time back. "There's supposed to be a tank in the rocks just up ahead," he told Sam. "If the cowboy knew what he was talking about and it isn't dry."

"Your words are so comforting, brother."

Matt twisted in the saddle, looking behind him. Those following them were no longer trying to hide their presence. The dust trail was clearly visible. "I don't like it," he stated.

"Neither do I. Let's find that tank and find it quick."

"And full," Matt added.

It wasn't full, but there was more than enough water to fill their canteens, water the horses, fill a coffee pot, and still have enough for several days should they have to defend the place.

The tank was located high in the rocks, with graze for the horses and good cover for both man and beast.

Neither Matt nor Sam were too worried about the men following them. If anything, the men following should be worried about what would happen should they catch up with Matt and Sam. Matt's reputation as a gunhandler had begun when he was just a boy. He killed his first man at age fourteen; the bully prodding the boy into a fight. The bully had not even managed to clear leather.

Less than a year later, the bully's brothers came after Matt Bodine. They got lead in the boy, but when the smoke drifted away, Bodine was standing over their bodies, his hands filled with Colts. When he was sixteen, rustlers hit his father's ranch. Bodine's guns put two more in the ground and left two others badly wounded and wishing they had taken up farming for a living.

At seventeen, Bodine went off to live with the Cheyenne for a year. He'd been spending forbidden time with them since he was a boy—often for weeks at a time.

At eighteen he was riding shotgun for gold shipments. Outlaws tried twice to take the shipment. Four more men were planted in unmarked graves.

At nineteen, he began scouting for the Army.

Between the ages of nineteen and twenty-five, the guns of Matt Bodine became legend in the west. His guns as well as his fists were much-feared. Bodine knew Indian wrestling, boxing, and down and dirty, kick and stomp barroom brawling.

Bodine's mother was a school-teacher and she saw to it that the boy was very well educated.

Sam Two Wolves—a half-breed, his mother was from Vermont—did not have the name of a gunfighter, but he was still just as feared as Bodine and better educated, having been schooled at a university back east. His mother's dying wish.

Sam's father was the famed war chief, Medicine Horse, who died on Last Stand Hill during the Custer fight. Medicine Horse rode up to Custer unarmed except for a coup stick, wishing to die rather than live in disgrace.

Matt and Sam had witnessed the Custer fight, from atop a hill overlooking the valley of the Little Bighorn. And they would spend their lives trying to forget the awful sight.

"I wonder who those guys following us are, and what they want?" Matt said, his back to a rock, a cup of coffee in his hand.

"If I had a crystal ball I'd tell you," Sam replied, without opening his eyes. He was stretched out flat on his back, in the shade of a boulder.

It was the fall of the year, and it was hot. Not the blistering heat of full summer, but still hot enough to kill a man if he wasn't careful.

A bullet whined wickedly off a rock and went howling off in another direction.

Without opening his eyes or getting up from his prone position, Sam said, "Well, now we know what they want—us!"

"Yeah. But why?" Matt had taken his rifle and moved to a guarded position where he could look out over the land below them.

"I'm certain your sordid reputation has something to do with it. What would my poor mother think? Me keeping company with a notorious gunfighter?" Sam choked back laughter and rolled to his knees, picking up his rifle.

"Very funny." But Matt could not conceal his grin. "I can see it now."

"See what?"

"The inscription on our single tombstone: Here lies the Injun and the white guy!"

"Single tombstone! Ye Gods! You think I'm going to be buried with *you?*"

Matt chuckled. "If we go out together, we probably won't have much to say about it, right?"

"What a dismal thought. Brother? What are we going to do about this slight problem facing us?"

"How about us finding out what they want?"

"What are you going to do—invite them up for coffee?"

Matt ignored that. "Hey!" he shouted. "What's the matter with you guys? What's the idea of shootin' at us?"

A bullet was his reply.

Matt tried again. "I think you people got the wrong guys. We haven't done anything to you."

"Give us the gold and you can ride on!" the voice bounced around the rocks.

"Gold?" Sam said. "What gold?"

"We don't have any gold!" Matt shouted. "I told you, you got the wrong people!"

"You a damn liar. We been trailin' you two all the way from Green River. You thought you'd throwed us off when you left the fork of the Walker just inside the Territory. But I want that poke you mined out. And we'll take that woman with you, too, mister. Then you can ride on. We know she's nothin' but a stray. She ain't worth dyin' over."

Sam sat straight up, his back against the boulder. "Woman?"

"I told you to cut your hair," Matt said, grinning at him.

"Idiot! My hair is no longer than yours."

"What woman?" Matt yelled. "There's nobody up here but Sam and me."

"Have Sam sing out!"

"What do you want, you nitwit?" Sam yelled.

Silence for a few moments. "You boys show yourselves," the man yelled. "If you ain't Wellman and the girl, you can ride on out."

"You believe that, Matt?"

"'Bout as much as I believe in fairy tales. They were going to rob those people, Sam." Raising his voice, he yelled, "Hell with you, mister. I got no reason to take the word of a damn thief."

"Here we go," Sam muttered. "Robin and his Hood strike another blow for the poor and downtrodden."

"We'll starve you out!" the outlaw yelled.

"Not likely," Matt called. "We have plenty of food."

"You'll die of thirst then!"

"No, we won't. The tank was full. But you boys are gonna get mighty thirsty if you hang around long."

Matt and Sam could hear cursing from below them.

"We'll make a deal with you!"

"I don't deal with scum."

"Then die, you bastards!"

The air around Matt and Sam was suddenly and viciously filled with howling, whining lead. Both pulled their saddles over their upper torsos to help against any flattened ricochets and let the outlaws bang away. Their horses were just below them, in a small depression, safe from any stray bullets.

They made no attempt to return the fire. The gunfire stopped and the sounds of galloping horses reached them. Both lifted up to where they could see and looked out. The outlaws were fogging it away from the rocks. Five of them, heading west.

"They must have picked up our trail at the fork, thinking it was the man and the girl," Sam said. "We took the east fork. Now those scum are heading west to pick up the trail."

Matt looked up at the sky. It would be dark in a couple of hours. "No point in taking off after them now. We might ride smack into an ambush. We'll spend the night and pick up their trail in the morning." He met Sam's eyes. "If that's all right with you, that is."

The half-breed smiled. "Oh, I think I'll tag along with you. Somebody has to watch your back trail."

Matt reached down for the blackened coffee pot and began cussing. One of the outlaw's slugs had torn the pot apart.

"Now that irritates me," Sam said. "Anybody who would deprive a man of his coffee is just no damn good!"

Chapter 2

Both men were still griping as they saddled up and rode out the next morning. Western men like their coffee and they like it often. To wake up without a pot of coffee strong enough to dissolve a horseshoe was just a lousy way to start the day.

"I get my hands on those damn thieving bums," Matt said, "I'm gonna make them wish they'd never ridden up to that tank."

"I sure would like a cup of coffee," Sam said wistfully. "Where do you suppose is the nearest town?"

"The way we're heading, there's supposed to be a trading post just built. Some guy named Hubbell built it. But it's a good ninety miles from here. Three days without coffee," he added.

Sam cussed in Cheyenne and then switched to English. He was very graphic in both languages.

They crossed Lukachuka Creek and made camp in Chinle Valley. They did not push their horses or themselves, for this was rugged country and they wanted to spare their horses. The tracks of the outlaws were easy to follow and from the way they were traveling, the thieves were also taking it easy, not wanting to come up with a lame horse and be set afoot in this country.

They reached the trading post during the late afternoon of the third day. A number of horses were tied at the hitchrails in front of the long and low building. The place appeared to be full of customers. Odd for this sparsely populated land.

Matt and Sam reined up in back of the building. Both men slipped the hammer thongs from their guns as soon as their boots touched the ground.

Sam took one look at the hoof-chewed ground around the hitchrails and said, "Those are our people, all right. See the chipped out place on that shoe?"

"Yeah. Come on. I want a drink first and then we'll see about settling up for a new coffee pot."

The adobe and stone post bore the scars of many Indian attacks. The wooden support posts of the porch roof were embedded with arrow heads. Sam Two Wolves looked at the broken shank of one.

"Apache," he said.

"Yeah. They have attacked as far north as the middle of Utah Territory; they back off when they get into Ute country." He stepped up to the porch and grinned. "They might not serve you in here, you know?"

"I hope they try that," his blood brother replied, a dangerous glint in his dark eyes.

The bartender didn't even blink when Matt and Sam ordered whiskey with a beer chaser. But he, along with everyone else in the dark barroom, did notice the tied down twin guns of the strangers.

Two Wolves and Bodine took their drinks to the far end of the bar, where their backs would be facing a wall and they could get a good look at everybody in the place.

It wasn't a pleasant view.

"Did you ever see so many ugly people gathered in one place in all your life?" Sam said, raising his voice so all could hear.

The buzz of conversation stopped abruptly and both men could feel the hot burn of very unfriendly eyes swing toward them.

"For a fact," Matt said. "If a beauty contest was held in this place, nobody would win."

"You got a fat mouth," a voice came from out of the smoky murk of the room.

"Who owns that horse with the Four-V brand?" Matt asked, knowing full well that somebody had used a running iron to make the brand, probably out of a double-W.

"I do," the same voice replied. "If it's any of your damn business. Which it ain't."

"You owe us a coffee pot," Matt told him.

"Huh?" A chair was pushed back and boot heels and jingling spurs moved closer to the bar. "I don't owe you nothin', mister. But I just might decide to give you a skint head if you don't shut your mouth."

"The only thing you're going to give me is a new coffee pot. Now buy it from the man, set it on the bar, shut your big mouth and set your butt back in the chair you just vacated."

The outlaw yelled out a violent oath and lumbered toward the bar, heading straight for Matt, his big hands balled into fists. Sam stepped aside, his hands by his side, so he could watch the crowd and grab iron if anybody tried to interfere.

Matt opened the dance with a short, straight right fist to the man's mouth. The blow knocked the outlaw spinning. He crashed into a table and sent beer mugs and cards and poker chips flying. He bounced to his boots and charged Bodine, screaming filth at him.

Bodine stuck out one boot and tripped the outlaw. He slammed into the bar, belly-high, and knocked the wind out of himself and a plank out of the bar just as Bodine slugged him twice above the kidney, with a left and right, bringing a squall of pain.

The outlaw staggered and turned, his eyes filled with pain and confusion.

Bodine hammered him twice in the face with a left and right combination and then drove his fist into the man's belly. As the burly outlaw slowly sank to his knees, Bodine grabbed him behind the head and brought his knee up, all in one fast, practiced movement. Knee connected with nose and nose got flattened.

Bodine turned his back to the man and faced the bartender as the outlaw fell on the floor, blood pouring from his broken nose. "Fill up the beer mug, friend. I just worked up a thirst."

"You just worked yourself up for a killing, is what you just done," a voice spoke from the murky depths of the barroom. "That there is Ray Porter, the Idaho gunslick, and this room is filled with his men. What do you think about that, hotshot?"

Bodine drained half his beer, set the mug on the bar—when Porter had crashed into it he had knocked it somewhat askew, spilling all the drinks that were there—and looked at the room full of gunslicks.

"Three days ago, me and my buddy here," he jerked a thumb toward Sam, "was ridin' south, just north of the Los Gigantes Buttes, when we decided to camp near a tank. This jerk," he pointed to the unconscious gunhand from Idaho Territory, "and four other jerks started shooting at us. They gave it up after about an hour, but not before they shot up my coffee pot. Now, I'm fixin' to get a couple of dollars out of this hombre's pocket and buy me a new coffee pot. And if anybody feels like they want to stop me, just come on. Now, does anybody want to start this dance?"

"That just plumb breaks my heart," a man said, pushing

his chair back and standing up, his hand close to the butts of his guns. "But I tell you what you should have done, mister. You should have carried two coffee pots. But it don't matter no more. 'Cause you ain't gonna be needin' 'em after today."

He grabbed for his guns and Bodine cleared leather, cocked, and shot him just as the man's hands gripped the butts and he began his lift. The slug took the man directly in the center of the chest, piercing the heart. He was dead as he hit the floor.

"Jesus H. Christ!" a man whispered hoarsely. "He's as fast as Smoke Jensen."

"What's your name, buddy?" another asked.

"Matt Bodine. And this is my brother, Sam Two Wolves."

Someone sighed in the crowd. Another cleared his throat nervously. Another man cussed softly; cussing his bad luck to be in the same room with Matt Bodine and Sam Two Wolves with both of them on the warpath. Still another slowly stood up, his hands in plain sight and walked to the door. "I'm gone," he said, and put his hand on the batwings. Just before he stepped outside, he said, "I'll be takin' me a bath and a shave out back."

Another man stood up, walking carefully. "Tell that boy to fill another tub, Harry. I feel the need for a soak myself. I'll get my extra set of longjohns from the saddlebags and join you in a minute." He walked to the batwings and the both of them were gone.

"A man shouldn't oughta plug another man's coffee pot," a gunhand said. "Hard enough rollin' out on a cold mornin' with coffee waitin.' Plumb discouragin' without it. You hep yourself to some greenbacks from Porter, Matt. He owes you a coffee pot."

"Thank you." Matt knelt down and pulled a wad from Porter's pocket. He took two dollars and handed them to the barkeep. "One coffee pot, please."

"Yes, sir, Mister Bodine. I'll be back in a jiffy. Will there be anything else, sir?"

"Coffee, beans, flour, and bacon. We'll settle up when I leave."

"Yes, sir!"

"And grind the coffee coarse," Sam told him. "We like it stout."

"Yes, sir, Mister Two Wolves."

Matt turned to face the crowd. "One of you tell Porter that we're riding to join up with the man and the girl that Porter wants to rob. Tell him if I see his ugly face again, I'll kill him on the spot, no questions asked."

"My back was getting sort of itchy riding away from that place, brother," Sam said.

"I do know the feeling. And I don't think my words changed any minds back there."

"No. They'll be coming after the man and the girl, whether we're along or not. They smell gold. Some of Porter's men must have linked up with him back at that trading post."

"Yeah. You ever heard of a gunfighter named Porter?"

"No. I think he's probably more thief and outlaw than gunslick. But I did see Don Bradley back there."

"So did I. And I have to wonder about that. He's too good with a gun to be mixed up with a small-timer like Porter. Last I heard, Don was getting top dollar for his skills. Who else did you see? I didn't have much time for eyeballing."

"Bob Doyle is the only other one that I knew. I saw three or four young punks with fancy rigs. I guess they're out to make a reputation."

"What they'll probably get is an unmarked grave. Let's play a hunch, Sam. Let's make a guess that Wellman and the girl deliberately took the west fork of Walker Creek to throw off Porter and his men. You with me?"

"Yes. Then they headed straight south. You know this country, Matt; I don't. Where are they going?"

"I don't know," Bodine admitted. "Green River is a long way from here. They were heading straight south all the way until they took the west fork. Two people, a man and a woman—maybe just a girl—heading straight into Apache country. Why, Sam?"

"And carrying gold. A lot of gold, I would guess." He shrugged his shoulders. "I don't know the why of it. But there's one way to find out."

"Catch up with them and ask."

"That's it."

"You game?"

"That goes without asking."

The two young men turned their horses and headed south. They pointed their horses' noses toward one of the most dangerous places left on the American continent: the great rugged mountains and the inhospitable deserts and the fierce warriors who inhabited that land. It was called Apache country.